*Sister Water*

# Sister Water

*by* NANCY WILLARD

Alfred A. Knopf  New York 1993

THIS IS A BORZOI BOOK
PUBLISHED BY ALFRED A. KNOPF, INC.

This book was completed with the help of a grant from the
National Endowment for the Arts.

Library of Congress Cataloging-in-Publication Data
Willard, Nancy.
Sister water / by Nancy Willard.—1st ed.
p.   cm.
ISBN 0-679-40702-2
I. Title.
PS3573.I444S47   1993
813'.54—dc20   92-54550
CIP

Manufactured in the United States of America

FIRST EDITION

*For Corona*

Praised be my Lord for our sister water.

—Saint Francis of Assisi, *Canticle of the Sun*

I wouldn't joke about the lake. The lake has ears.

—Jean Giraudoux, *Ondine*, Act I

*Sister Water*

# 1

On the twenty-first of June, 1930, in Drowning Bear, Wisconsin, Jessie Nelson saw what she did not wish to meet in this world and did not wish to forget in the next. She was fifteen years old. She wanted her red hair to grow so long she could sit on it, and she wanted to fall in love and travel and have her heart broken. When she got her new glasses, she'd fallen in love with the optometrist. The words on the little chart in his office grew smaller and smaller, as if winding down to a whisper; she'd learned them by heart:

I LEAVE TO CHILDREN EXCLUSIVELY, BUT ONLY FOR THE LIFE OF THEIR CHILDHOOD, THE DANDELIONS OF THE FIELDS AND THE DAISIES THEREOF, WITH THE RIGHT TO PLAY AMONG THEM FREELY, ACCORDING TO THE CUSTOM OF CHILDREN, WARNING THEM AT THE SAME TIME AGAINST THE THISTLES.

Who wrote those words? she wondered. Dr. Gold said he had no idea and asked her what kind of frames she wanted.

The walk back to the old white house where her mother rented rooms filled her with longing for a better time and place —oh, any place but this one. The air hung hot and still. Through the open door of the Baptist church on the corner the organ pumped fragments and false starts of a hymn she could not identify.

She turned the corner and saw her father scrubbing the front steps and heard her mother shouting at him as she plucked the clean sheets from the line stretched between the butternut trees. "A real doctor isn't seen scrubbing his front steps. He sits inside and waits for his patients."

Her father kept pushing the scrub brush in slow, soapy circles. On days when only one or two people came to the office, he hated to sit idle.

Jessie crossed the yard and leaned against her mother and pressed her face into the basket of clean laundry. "Ma," she whispered, "I'm sick."

"Change the shelf papers in the pantry first, then be sick," said her mother.

But when she glanced at her daughter's face, she left the last sheet dragging by a clothespin and hurried to the medicine chest in the bathroom, snatched the thermometer, and popped it into Jessie's mouth. The silver line raced to 103.

Behind the house, the door to the cellar rested flat, like a great book on a lectern. Her mother leaned over, grasped the handle, raised the door, and let it drop with a crash.

They felt their way along the stone steps. Dazzled by the dark, Jessie saw nothing except her father's rollaway cot. When her mother wanted to argue, her father retreated to this place for a nap. Now her mother was tucking Jessie in and drawing the quilt over her.

"You rest, Jessie. You'll feel cooler here. I'll leave the door open. Can I get you anything before I go?"

"Cold water. I want some cold water."

Her mother's bulk in the doorway shut out the light for an instant before she slipped over the rim of the stairs. Jessie lay perfectly still, and little by little the world came back to her: the old kitchen table, with its red oilcloth cover, to which her father had clamped the grinding wheel he used for sharpening knives. In the center of the table gleamed her mother's snow globe. The globe held a white-haired man driving a dogsled. The fine white script running around the base read: THE DOG STAR MAN. SOUVENIR OF DROWNING BEAR, WISCONSIN. When Jessie was small, she had confused the Dog Star Man with Santa Claus. "Oh, he's not as famous as Santa Claus," her mother had said. "The Dog Star Man is only famous in Drowning Bear."

Shaking the globe could bring on a blizzard, which ended in lazy white tides that drifted around the dogs' paws.

A single bulb dangled from the ceiling, waiting for light to infuse it. Behind her stretched the darkness, crammed with sauerkraut tubs, jars of canned tomatoes and cherries, a blue milking stool, the marble top of a parlor table, and a large round mirror.

The rollaway stood at the edge of a pool of light.

Across the open door over her head, a bird darted. Jessie fell asleep to the voices of her mother and her little sister, Ida, calling to each other across the yard, parted by plum and cherry dropping their blossoms, asparagus sending forth its misty wands behind the beehives.

A crash roused her. The wind was roaring, and the cellar door flapped in the wind like a mad wing. Jessie crawled out of bed, terrified. The darkness around her was so great she feared she had gone blind till she saw, in the ashen air overhead, a white turkey and a wooden lawn chair whirl past, and she felt herself tugged toward the upper world.

She clawed at the kitchen table. With a wrenching creak, it shrugged off the grinding wheel and whirled up the stairs and vanished. The wheel landed upright on the floor, as if set there on purpose. Jessie fled further back into the darkness and eased herself into the crawl space between the canned cherries and the sepulchral tabletop.

Then her heart nearly stopped beating.

Behind her, a phosphorescent light woke the jars, the glazed crocks, the dusty shelves. Her father's grinding wheel was spinning and humming to itself. Wrapped in the mossy glow, a tall figure was tossing its head like a horse in a field. By pasture light, by the shimmer of wheat bowing under a hot sky, she caught a glimpse of its face, hawk-beaked and full of news of the earth loved from far off. As it arranged its wings to fit the low space, its huge black eyes stared past her. The light of its vanishing showed her a glass of water beside the globe, on the floor where the table had stood.

In the upper world, the air grew still, the light returned, the full moon gleamed in the exhausted sky. The cellar smelled clean and sweet as a new-mown field. Clutching the globe, Jessie crawled up the cellar steps. A huge limb from one of the butternut trees had fallen into the yard, leaving a crow's nest hidden at the top exposed and empty. Beyond a confusion of small branches and new shoots fluttering their thin leaves, her mother was lighting the cyclone lamps in the dining room; they flickered in the broken light.

Six years later, Jessie was a junior at the University of Michigan living in terror of the science requirement till her roommate gave her some practical advice. "Take Precious Gems. It's a pipe course. You spend the whole semester looking at diamonds and stuff." To Jessie's dismay, Precious Gems was not offered in the second semester, and she had to settle for its sequel, Semiprecious Gems, which her roommate told her wasn't nearly as exciting.

On the first day of class the professor announced that the best private collection of semiprecious gems in their natural state in

Michigan could be found in the private museum on the first floor of the Woolman Scientific Supply Company. It was located, he added, on the Huron River, two miles from the train depot.

Jessie walked the twenty-five blocks from her dormitory to the address her professor had given and was surprised to see an old brick building on which WOOLMAN SCIENTIFIC SUPPLY COMPANY was writ large in white letters. There was nothing to tell her this was a museum. She knocked on the door, and a tall, red-haired man opened it.

"I'm looking for the museum," she explained.

The man introduced himself as Henry Woolman. This was the museum, he said, and she was welcome to look around.

Never in all her life had she seen a room like this one. On the rafters perched stuffed animals: a marten, an otter, two foxes, and an owl carrying a small wheel in its claws. Through the center of the room ran a stream. The museum was built over an underground stream, Henry told her, and he showed her how he'd uncovered it and reinforced the banks on both sides with stones and scattered mica chips in the bright path of the water. The fish were pale, ghostly versions of bluegills and perch that swam out of the dark and hastened back into it.

Beside the stream stood three exhibit cases filled with things he'd collected along the river: pottery shards and fossil coral, copper beads, and a crystal ax head the stream had carried into the museum; he'd thought it was a piece of broken glass till he picked it up. The ax head was cut from a single chunk of smoky quartz. He raised the lid of the case and lifted it out and put it in her hand and showed her the notches where thongs had attached it to the handle of the ax. It was smooth but not clear; wisps of fog spiraled through it like souls caught in the resinous tears of a tree that has long since vanished from the earth.

Tacked to one wall was a map of Ann Arbor, with certain

streets marked in green. These, he explained, were the streets he'd walked.

"I plan to walk them all eventually," he told her. "Nobody else has done it."

As Jessie walked out the door, she realized she'd forgotten to inquire about the semiprecious gems.

"You hurry back," he called after her.

"I will," she called back.

A year and a half later they were married in the museum by the local Congregational minister, a concession to Jessie, who feared the marriage would not be valid if the Unitarian minister performed it. Her mother refused to attend the ceremony; it would have been better, she told Jessie, to marry a local man. To please her, they drove to Muskegon immediately afterwards, crossed Lake Michigan on the *Milwaukee Clipper*, and caught the train north to Drowning Bear. Jessie's mother kept to her room during the visit, but her father offered to show Henry the Pawquacha shell mounds at the eastern edge of the Starr Cheese processing plant. Henry could hardly hide his disappointment; the mounds were small and the water had leveled them away.

After the honeymoon, Jessie and Henry moved into the house behind Woolman Scientific. Henry had been born in it thirty-six years earlier, and living elsewhere never occurred to him.

For their first wedding anniversary, Jessie planned a surprise for Henry. He had walked the last street on the map a month earlier, and she brought it to Frame-All in the Nickels Arcade. Bunnell the framer was not in; his assistant spread it out on the table, weighting the northeast corner with a mug of tea that smelled to Jessie like peppermint.

No, it was not peppermint, the young man assured her, but a species of chamomile found only in Michigan and Wisconsin. "The Indians used it for—"

He waved his hand to show Jessie what they used it for and the mug flipped and rolled over. As the pale green tea flowed across the streets, Jessie thought of the tropical sea that once covered the state of Michigan and of the fossil corals Henry kept in the museum—Petoskey stones, he called them—beside the crystal ax head.

The young assistant was patting the map with a sponge.

I should be furious, thought Jessie. Why am I so calm?

When the map dried, the assistant remarked that it had a rich, hand-colored look, and Jessie agreed. The accident had improved it. The city of Ann Arbor was the luminous green of a luna moth.

Henry loved it.

The map hung over the fireplace in the living room until Martha was born in 1945 and a picture of the infant stretched out on a bear rug replaced it. Henry hung the map in the upstairs hall. Fifteen years later Jessie was astonished to find herself pregnant again. After Ellen was born, Jessie moved the map back into the museum to make room for photographs of the family. As she was dusting the glass, she noticed a network of white lines sparkling under the streets like veins of precious ore. The green tint had darkened. The map looked like an exquisite piece of batik.

She brought it to Henry, who studied the lines and gave a shout.

"Jessie, it's a map of the Great Lakes!"

Henry could easily trace the bold outlines of Lake Michigan and Lake Superior, Lake Huron and Lake Ontario and Lake Erie, as well as the inland bodies of water in Michigan and Wisconsin. But what spidery track joined these known bodies of water to each other like a broken line charting vast underground rivers? Though he couldn't for the life of him tell where it started, he was pleased to see that it ran through both Drowning Bear and

Ann Arbor—along the Huron River past Hopecrest Nursing Home and the train depot.

He carried the map into the front yard and examined it by sunlight. To his horror, the white line faded as he watched. But he had seen it, and he resolved to find that trail. He rented a panoramic camera that could take in 360 degrees at a single shot, and one July morning he and two university maintenance men hauled it up to the windy roof of Burton Tower, fastened it securely, and tripped the shutter. The Farmers' Market had just opened; crowds bustled along Main and Ashley. The next day he sent the film to Kodak, with instructions to handle it with care.

Ten days later a picture arrived which bore not the faintest trace of an image. It was accompanied by a note. Kodak was sorry; the negative was thin as water, and the print, which was nearly too faint to read, had disappeared after it dried.

Henry returned to his tea-green map of Ann Arbor. At the bottom he found the name of the printer: Pawquacha Water-marks. When he called information, the operator told him she had no listing for it.

# 2

---

It was in the dentist's office that Harvey Mack had the great revelation of his life. Dr. McKinley was stroking a needle with a piece of gauze and saying, "Don't worry, Harvey, I'm going to get you so numb you won't feel a thing. Open, please."

Harvey closed his eyes and opened his mouth. He felt a quick stab of pain before the Novocain bubbled its way into his pores, battening them down for the two-hour session, from which he would emerge wearing a crown, carried like a stolen diamond in his mouth.

"I'll be back when your jaw is completely numb. Do you want a magazine?"

"No, thanks," said Harvey.

Free from pain and the fear of it, with not a thing to do but lie back in the chair, Harvey opened his eyes. Just like floating in his pool instead of driving himself to do laps. Just like it. Learning to swim as a kid at Walled Lake, his chunky body floating on his mother's hands, and his dad saying, "He should float like a cork, all that blubber," and Harvey thinking, Blubber—is that good or bad? Floating was good; yet in the silence between the words lurked something that was not good.

Dead man's float. He could do the dead man's float. If he let his head bob under the water, he couldn't hear his mother's praise —"Look how long he can stay under!"—and then her anxious "Harvey? Harvey?" and then his father's voice, "He's only playacting. It's called the dead man's float. Get it? He's playing dead," and his mother snapping, "I know that," just before Harvey, all-powerful puppet master of his mother's anxieties, lifted his head, water streaming off his face like tears.

Under the water he could hear motorboats two miles away, putt-putting at the far end of the lake, which was only an hour outside Pontiac. That was as far away as his mother and dad ever went for a vacation. Got to mind the store, his father said. His father competed with other stores by staying open on Sunday and stocking ten of everything. All around him crouched hardware stores, dime stores, drugstores. Harvey's father sold novelties. If you needed a paintbrush or a colander or a small tin of milk of magnesia on Sunday, you could find it at Mack's Novelties. The store looked as if the merchandise had been dropped into place by a dump truck. That, said Harvey's father, was its charm—the infinite possibilities of the place. Anything might turn up there, not just the milk of magnesia but some odd item you'd lost or longed for, a jackknife or a square of Bazooka bubble gum hard as a domino, wrapped in a tiny comic.

The secret of success, said Harvey's father, was to be on the alert for what people wanted and to be there when they wanted it. You couldn't ever put these matters far from your mind. Shopping is an addiction, said Harvey's father, and selling is a vocation.

On the ceiling of his office, Dr. McKinley had glued a random arrangement of green and gold and silver dots said to be soothing to patients, who forgot their pain as they tried to figure out the pattern. There was no pattern, at least none that Dr. McKinley could ever see. And he wasn't personally responsible for the thin crack that zigzagged across the ceiling among the dots. The office was old; the plaster was cracked but not yet dangerous, and one day he would get around to fixing it. In the blue lava lamp on the windowsill, a shining globule stretched and broke free.

"Open, please," said Dr. McKinley.

Tilted back in the chair, Harvey studied the ceiling. The crack ran like a river—the Huron River, maybe. Now that he'd named it, he was amazed at how easily the dots fell into place. The train station was a green dot, as were the apartment buildings and the Lutheran church. The gold dots corresponded almost perfectly to buildings along the river. Here was Hopecrest Nursing Home, where his father was receiving the best care money could buy. Here, in the empty spaces between the dots, lay Island Park and Nichols Arboretum. And here, on the bluff overlooking the Huron, were Heavenly Rest Cemetery and Barton Hills.

At the foot of the hills, the river widened into Barton Pond, and down by the water, in a cul-de-sac between the road to Heavenly Rest and the old train depot, was the defunct Woolman Scientific Supply Company.

There is something significant in that, thought Harvey, and let his gaze wander into the empty spaces at the edge of the dots.

Dr. McKinley hit an unprotected nerve along the gumline and Harvey jumped.

"Did you feel pain?" demanded Dr. McKinley.

"It's okay," said Harvey. "I can take it."

Dr. McKinley switched off the drill and held it poised and silent over Harvey's jaw.

"I do not work on patients who feel pain. I'm giving you another shot of Novocain."

It was when the needle stabbed his deadened tissue—Harvey saw the point plunging toward him and felt nothing—that he also saw, like a gorgeous mist overlaying Woolman Scientific, the alabaster outlines of a shopping mall, Pawquacha Plaza. The malls he'd constructed in Birmingham and Grosse Pointe, in Pontiac and Farmington, were dross compared with this one. Pawquacha Plaza had a Hudson's, a Jacobson's, a Nordstrom's, a gourmet coffee shop, and two good restaurants, one of them a glassed-in cafe with a view of the river and none of the inconveniences of weather. There were two escalators, a grand staircase, and a glass elevator rising and falling like the bubble in the lava lamp. At ground level there was plenty of parking; the land was paved right down to the water.

Dr. McKinley was handing him a prescription for Advil and a printed list of instructions.

"For the rest of today, take it easy," he said. "No hot liquids. No spicy foods. Don't brush your teeth on the left side for a week. Try to keep the packing on for at least three days. If you need something stronger than Advil—"

"I can take it," said Harvey. "I've got a high pain threshold."

In the front office he asked the receptionist if he could use the phone book. There were only two listings for Woolman: Woolman, H., and Woolman Scientific Supply Company Museum, both on Water Street. Well, that figures, he thought. He would ask Mrs. Trimble, who cooked and cleaned for him, to tell him more about the property. She'd lived in the area so long and knew so many odd corners of its history that Harvey had told her she should give tours—historical tours of Ann Arbor and the vicinity. She shook her head at that one. Said there was no money in tours, and she didn't know any real history, just gossip and what her dad had taught her about the tribes that settled along the river long ago. Nothing you could show tourists.

Harvey crumpled the dentist's instructions and prescription into his shirt pocket, took the elevator to the lobby, headed out to the parking lot, and drove down to the water.

Two kinds of people lived along the river: those who counted for something in the economy and those who didn't. If the lines were drawn more clearly, Harvey told himself, everyone would be better off. The fancy condos and apartments, the new research buildings—those counted. But with the old buildings, it was harder to tell on what side of the ledger they belonged. The New York Central depot, for example. After Amtrak built its own modest station, the depot had counted for nothing till somebody thought of turning it into a high-priced restaurant called the Gandy Dancer. That was a smart move. You had to phone a week ahead for Saturday-night reservations. Harvey had gone once, with his wife, six months before she died. She always wanted to know things other people didn't care about. She'd called the manager over to their table and asked, "What exactly is a gandy dancer?" and listened with exaggerated enthusiasm while the manager explained that a gandy dancer was an itinerant railroad worker who pounded the spikes into the ties. Gandy was the name of the company in Chicago that made the equipment. She'd turned to Harvey with a smile of triumph and said, "See? If you don't ask, you don't learn."

There were long stretches of the river that seemed to belong to no one, except the salvage divers who fished there and built their shanties in thickets of sumac and swampland every summer. Now, in late March, the shanties were clearly visible. Of those people Harvey knew nothing except that they were all relatives of Thomas Bearheart, who ran Pawquacha Hoot 'n Scoot, a bait shop and concession stand at Gallup Park.

But even that land belonged to somebody. Everything in the world belonged to somebody. Behind one of the thickets rose the old three-story brick building on which WOOLMAN SCIENTIFIC SUPPLY COMPANY was emblazoned, in block letters over the third story. There was something about its straightforward usefulness that suggested an earlier time—the Industrial Revolution, mills with children indentured to their looms. Plainly it was no longer a place for selling anything.

Harvey could see, to the east of the building, beds laid out around a sundial, in which grew some low weeds and the thorny skeletons of two rosebushes. The garden ended in a particularly dense thicket. He decided to take the long way and walked around the block until he came to a stone house with a slate mansard roof and dormer windows facing the water at the other end of the property. On either side stood houses, brick and stone, with gardens and big maple trees in the front yards. A little neighborhood, genteel, set apart from the new apartment buildings and the old frame houses where hordes of students found cheap lodgings.

Not a sign of anyone inside or outside the house.

An hour later, he found what he was looking for at the Office of Records in the courthouse. The Woolman Scientific building was owned by the widow of Henry Woolman, who still resided in the stone house.

That afternoon he sat down and composed a letter to Mrs. Henry Woolman. In it he assured her that if she ever wanted to sell the property, he would give her an excellent price.

When Mrs. Trimble saw the envelope on the table in the front hall she exclaimed, "Why, do you know Jessie Woolman?" Her face showed not merely surprise but astonishment.

"We've never formally met," said Harvey.

"I clean for her," said Mrs. Trimble, "on the days I don't clean for you."

She was arranging two floured chicken breasts in a flat Pyrex dish ("one for tonight, and the other for lunch tomorrow") when he suggested, as he often did, that she stay for dinner. He did not like to eat alone, and her company was pleasant and unobtrusive. He'd just bought the Video Aquarium; would she like to watch it with him?

They ate in the den that looked over Barton Pond, and Harvey switched on the TV and the VCR and popped the video in. Mrs. Trimble gazed out the window. The woods across the river from Barton Hills covered the slope in brown confusion; only the willows showed signs of excitement as their drooping branches lightened to gold, their ashy bark waking into amber wands. Sailboats lurked unseen in the boathouses along the shore; in a month they would be bobbing and rocking on the water around the Barton Hills marina. Though the river flowed into the pond at one end and out of it at the other, few sailboats would venture so far. Closer to west Ann Arbor, where the river flowed past the old Pontiac Trail, the Argo canoe livery had not yet opened its doors.

"It's starting," said Harvey. "The color is supposed to be gorgeous."

From the darkness on the screen there welled up an aquamarine sunrise. Over the pearly floor of the glassed-in sea, marvelous fish were passing one another like parcels ribboned in light. He had never imagined such creatures existed. Masked lemons, amber arrowheads, an onion packed with jewels—they darted, glided, nosed, flitted, and gleamed. He knew none of them by name, and he felt a great longing to swim in such company.

There were places in the world where you could do that, he told himself. Those islands—what were they called? The Cayman Islands? He'd seen photographs of people scuba-diving on the coral reefs. You could take lessons in things like that. You could learn to breathe through a mask and swim alongside these brilliant creatures as long as your air supply held out.

Suddenly a dark shape bobbed and drifted across the screen. It took him several minutes to realize that he was looking not at a fish but at a woman's head. Her long black hair floated across her cheeks and parted, like curtains rising on the white stage of her face. She opened her mouth and the water bubbled and hummed in her throat; she opened her eyes and Harvey spied his own face in their blackness.

Speechless, he turned to Mrs. Trimble. She was watching the screen with a slightly bored expression.

"How does it look to you?" he asked cautiously.

"The fish are very pretty," she said.

"Well, I've seen enough," said Harvey. He leaned forward, switched off the set, and instantly felt calmer. No doubt the Video Aquarium had been recorded on used tape, which had retained this stray image. He would return the video tomorrow and demand a full refund.

By an act of will he pushed from his mind the face with its black hair floating. "Tell me about Mrs. Woolman. How long has she lived in that house?"

"Fifty-five years, she told me."

"Alone? Does she live alone?"

Mrs. Trimble nodded. "Her daughters look in on her, though. Martha's married to a broker, Ellen's husband is a teacher. Ellen is the recreation director at Hopecrest. Haven't you met her?"

"Not formally," replied Harvey.

A hawk was hanging fire high over the water, riding the updraft.

"He's seen something," said Mrs. Trimble. "A mouse or a shrew. In a minute he's going to dive for it."

"No living thing can see that far," said Harvey. For the first time since he'd left the dentist's office, he was aware of the ache in his mouth, the gums raw as shucked corn. A current of weakness rippled through him, leaving him drenched in his own sweat.

"I've watched 'em drop from a hundred feet in the air. That hawk knows we're sitting in here. You can't do anything in this world without somebody seeing you," said Mrs. Trimble, as the bird swooped into the strip of woods between road and river and disappeared.

# 3

---

The party in the dayroom was ready, and now Toth had vanished.

"I saw him in the corridor a few minutes ago," said Ellen.

Mrs. Pickering, the head nurse, clapped her hands to her hips. "He couldn't have gotten far!" she exclaimed. "The exit to the stairs is locked."

Under the dark TV mounted high on the wall, a circle of wheelchairs faced a card table set with a package of ice cream and paper plates, like covered wagons around a fire: six men and one woman, Mrs. Kraft, who had been brought in two days before.

The guest of honor, Richard Mack, sat fastened to his chair with a muslin restraint. He kept his eyes closed. Two years ago he'd closed his eyes to rest them after an afternoon of watching TV and forgotten how to open them. Each new stroke had wiped away another skill until now he responded to no one. His son, Harvey, had visited him six times in two years. Today was the seventh time.

"The ice cream is melting," said Harvey. "It's Ben & Jerry's Cherry Garcia." Sweat gleamed on his bald head. He pushed his glasses back on his nose and peered into the shopping bag he'd brought, checking the contents.

Ellen wove her way among the wheelchairs, headed out the

door, passed Dr. Davidson's office, and felt herself drawn to the window at the end of the corridor.

Toth: there he was, in the army fatigues and khaki jacket he wore over his regulation hospital gown, stepping carefully among the pines toward the river, swinging his empty sleeve. Playful but no longer young, he was not much taller than her son Stevie; Ellen could hardly believe that six months ago he'd had a job installing TV antennas.

Oh, how had he escaped? She pushed the button for the elevator and heard its faint creak far overhead. In spite of the flowered wallpaper and Renoir prints in the corridors, the squat brick building depressed her. After three years, she'd never stopped seeing the faces that shadowed the heavy windowscreens.

Her first week as recreation director at Hopecrest, a man with his leg in traction had waved a cigarette at her and asked her for a light. She held the lighter for him, turned to go, and smelled burning cloth; he'd set his bed on fire. That was the first and last time she thought she'd lost a patient.

Until now.

She yanked a key from the ring on her belt, unlocked the door to the stairs, ran down the three flights, burst into the lobby, and nearly collided with the receptionist, who was coming out of the ladies' room.

"Toth," panted Ellen. "He got out again."

The receptionist shrugged. "There's another one of Bearheart's people in ward 6, and they have the same problem with her. Sedatives don't work. She can get through anything. Neat hat."

"What?"

"Your fish hat. I like the way the fish looks like it's swimming through your head."

"Mike loaned it to me," said Ellen. "I'm wearing it for the party."

A warm breeze startled her: the thrill of real weather, the first day of April. Before she reached the pines, she saw Jim O'Brien, one of the security men, stride forward and take Toth's arm, firmly but gently, as one might take the arm of a friend during a walk.

"Toth says he wants to bring a guest to the party," said O'Brien.

"My sister," said Toth. He freed his arm and opened his hand. On his palm gleamed a toad, all mottled russet and green save for its glossy black eyes.

"The stuff that goes on in this place," said O'Brien, staring at Ellen's hat. "I could write a book. My wife tells me I should write a book."

"Toth, it's a beautiful toad," said Ellen. She stroked the top of its head to show him how beautiful she thought it was. "Now let's put it back in the grass."

Toth didn't move; his refusal was palpable.

"I have a nine-year-old son who just loves toads," said Ellen. "He's very good with them."

"The full moon makes them crazy," said O'Brien. "I've seen 'em come and I've seen 'em go."

Ellen kept walking and stroking the small green head.

"My husband is a biology teacher. We could take very good care of your toa—your sister. We have an aquarium."

Toth made a face.

"Toads do not live in aquariums," he observed.

"Okay, Toth. But promise me you'll keep the toad in your pocket."

"You ain't gonna let him bring that toad inside!" exclaimed O'Brien.

They were almost at the front door.

"I don't think he'll come in without it," said Ellen.

"Her," said Toth.

"What?" asked Ellen.

"You said 'it.' She's a lady toad. She's my sister."

She kept her hand on his arm and they rode the elevator together. He looked diminutive next to her; the top of his head reached only to her shoulder. One by one, the numbers lit up, and Toth watched them, as if he were infusing the elevator with power, cradling the toad in his palm. Ellen marveled at how little she knew about the patients, really. Nothing in Toth's chart said how he'd lost his arm, as if the loss were temporary, and like a starfish he would soon grow another. When the doors opened, Toth walked so fast toward the dayroom that Ellen could hardly keep up with him.

"We started without you," said Mrs. Pickering. "The ice cream was melting."

Dirty paper plates and plastic spoons filled the wastebasket. Mrs. Kraft, who would be ninety-nine next month, was licking ice cream off her wrist, like a cat. Ellen glanced at the guest of honor's clean face and turned to Harvey Mack.

"Did your father get any?" she asked.

"My father?" said Harvey. "I don't think he even knows there's a party."

Ellen picked up the container. Empty. How could Harvey Mack have imagined a quart would serve eight people?

"Mr. Mack, we have no idea what he knows. He may be aware of everything we're saying. He's entitled to his ice cream."

She scraped the last traces of ice cream into a plastic spoon and touched it to the old man's lips. They parted slightly, but his teeth stayed clenched, and ice cream dribbled a jagged path down his chin. She pulled a Kleenex from her pocket and wiped it.

Harvey Mack glanced at his watch. Ellen touched the spoon

to his father's lips once more, but they did not open at all, and she put it down on the table.

"Did you sing to him?" she asked.

"You mean 'Happy Birthday'?" inquired Harvey.

"What else?" said Ellen, and though she could hardly carry a tune, she sang in a loud clear voice:

> *Happy birthday to you,*
> *Happy birthday to you,*
> *Happy birthday, dear Richard—*

Harvey Mack chimed in on the last line—"Happy birthday to you!"

"He has a wish," said Toth. "I made it for him. I know what he wants."

His fingers were still curled over the toad. To Ellen's relief, it hadn't moved.

"I brought presents for everyone," said Harvey. "When I do a party, I do it right."

And he picked up the shopping bag and turned it upside down on the table. Out dropped eight small parcels, all square and wrapped in pink tissue.

"What's in them? We like to clear the contents of—"

"They're harmless," interrupted Harvey. "They're just something to open."

Slowly, secretly, Mrs. Kraft was rocking, tipping and bobbing, and now Richard Mack was bowing ever so slightly, and like wind in a meadow the impulse spread and gathered the old bodies in a single wave.

Mrs. Pickering leaned forward. "I think she likes your hat, Ellen."

Ellen smiled. "Richard should get the first gift. Mr. Mack, do you want to open it for him?"

"I'll open it," said Mrs. Pickering.

She picked up a package, and the rocking stopped, and the room grew quiet as she tore off the tissue paper and held up a small paperbound book.

"Isn't this nice," she observed. "Books are always appreciated."

"I hope it's a detective story," said Ellen.

Mrs. Pickering put on her glasses. "It's called *How to Survive on Land and Sea.*"

"You never know when something like that will come in handy," said Ellen.

Mrs. Pickering put the book on Richard's lap and wrapped his fingers around it while Ellen handed the second parcel to Mrs. Kraft.

"Open it, open it!" cried Toth.

Mrs. Kraft began to tear the wrapping paper with her teeth.

"Don't let her chew it!" exclaimed Ellen. "Here—we'll put the paper in the basket, Mrs. Kraft."

In her left hand Mrs. Kraft clutched the pink tissue; in her right, a copy of *How to Survive on Land and Sea.*

"It's the very same book," said Mrs. Pickering in puzzled tones.

"I got the whole bag for a dime at the army surplus."

"Toth, here's your present," said Ellen, offering him a parcel. "Surprise, surprise."

"Hold my sister," said Toth, and handed her the toad.

Its cold thin toes brushed Ellen's palm, and she shivered, though she was no stranger to toads and frogs, turtles and snakes. Before she could hand Toth his book, the toad leapt to the floor and landed at Harvey's feet. Harvey's leg shot out and he stamped on it. The long wail that filled the room sounded like an alarm for an emergency Ellen had never been taught to prepare for; she didn't connect the sound with Toth till he sank to his knees, weeping.

"For Lord's sake!" shouted Harvey. "Toads carry germs."

"Mr. Mack, this has been an unusual day," Mrs. Pickering shouted back. "We all appreciate your visit, but our patients tire easily, and any change in their routine upsets them."

Crumpled on the floor, Toth was sobbing uncontrollably.

"Look here—toads are a dime a dozen," said Harvey. "I'll send him a bushel of toads bigger than that one."

He withdrew his foot and revealed what might have been a broken balloon. As Ellen leaned over and gathered it into a Kleenex, she heard the airy wheeze of the bus beyond the open window.

"Oh, Christ, I've missed my bus. And Stevie doesn't have a key."

"My car is out in front," said Harvey Mack. "If you're going back into town, you can ride with me."

Mrs. Pickering held out the wastebasket, but Ellen shook her head. "I think Toth should be allowed to bury it," she said. As she knelt beside him, his body stopped rocking and she saw his left hand unclench itself. Into it she placed the dead frog, wrapped in its shroud of tissue. The noise of a throat being cleared made her look up. Mrs. Pickering was signaling her: follow me into the corridor.

"Mr. Mack owns this place. I presume you know that."

"He thinks he owns the patients, too, doesn't he?" said Ellen and brushed past her to the door. Crossing the grounds toward the parking lot, she had the feeling that Toth was watching her, though she knew he couldn't even reach the sill without a chair.

Harvey's black Lincoln was the only car in the visitors' parking lot. Ellen didn't know much about cars. Mike always bought old ones and nursed the last drop of life out of them.

When Harvey opened the door for her, she caught a whiff of his cologne, like the piney candles Mike burned at picnics to keep off mosquitoes.

She took off Mike's hat with the fish on it and slid into the front seat and found herself petting the upholstery. It was navy plush; Stevie would love it.

"You can adjust the seat with that knob," said Harvey.

She turned the knob cautiously, and as the seat yawned into repose she realized she was still holding Toth's book.

"I'll have to run back. He'll be heartbroken."

"Mrs. Pickering will give him another one," said Harvey, and started the car.

Once they were on Packard Street, he turned to her and smiled.

"My cleaning woman tells me you're Henry Woolman's daughter. Mrs. Trimble said she cleans for your mother, too."

"Did you know my father?" asked Ellen.

"No. But of course I know the property."

"What property?"

"Woolman Scientific Supply Company."

"Oh." She had never thought of it as a property before, just as her father's business and the museum he maintained on the first floor. On the second floor he and two assistants had handled the orders for the lab equipment, which was stored on the third floor.

"What's happened to the company?"

"Nothing," said Ellen. "We got rid of everything except the museum."

"I didn't know there was a museum," said Harvey.

"It's nothing fancy—just two big rooms on the ground floor. Sometimes Mike opens it on weekends. He keeps trying to interest the city in making the whole building a hands-on museum for kids."

"Mike?"

"That's my husband."

"Ah," said Harvey.

Since he did not ask her to describe the contents, she did not tell him about the stream running through the front room. An underground stream that came up for air, her father called it, and treated it as an honored guest. All through high school Ellen had gone there to do her homework. She loved the shock of glancing up from her geometry book to see a carp paddling quietly past her toward deeper waters. In summer her father laid a screen over the stream, to keep the mosquitoes at bay, though by July the water had nearly disappeared. He and his two assistants would sit on its banks and eat their lunch before climbing the stairs to the rooms of beakers, blenders, lab aprons, balances, and large white boxes whose contents she could not imagine.

Harvey turned on the air conditioning, and Ellen felt as if she'd just inhaled Pentothal; she heard herself talking nonstop, telling Harvey that she and Stevie were going to spend the night with her mother because Mike was off fishing at Sylvan Lake and her brother-in-law, John, was off at another Merrill Lynch seminar but that was okay because her sister, Martha, hated to be alone too and always stopped by their mother's house for a visit and sometimes Martha's daughter, Allison, stopped by with her fiancé though you couldn't count on that because Allison worked at Great Lakes Savings and Loan, and when the bank closed at six on Friday she felt more like heading back to her apartment and putting her feet up than sitting around with the family, though the family was close and always had been.

Harvey appeared to be listening with great interest.

"Are there any plans to sell the property?" he asked.

"What?"

"Woolman Scientific."

"I don't think so," said Ellen, ashamed of herself for having let go so completely in front of a man she hardly knew.

As they drew up in front of Huron Apartments, she was alarmed to hear him say, "Let me walk you to your door. To make sure you get in."

"Oh, there's no need for that," said Ellen. "Thanks so much for the ride." And she jumped out of the car.

After the air-conditioned Lincoln, the apartment was hot and stuffy. A total mess. Mike had been sorting his back issues of *Audubon* before he moved them to the museum library, which didn't exist yet, though Mike talked about it as though the shelves were already built and the books in place.

Ellen opened the icebox and scanned the freezer. The package of low-cal Fudgsicles was half hidden behind the bodies of two birds wrapped in freezer paper—mourning doves, from the look of the tails sticking out.

Mike should get a big freezer and keep it in the museum, she thought, for all the stuff he saves to show his students at Pioneer High. And a worktable for her craft projects wouldn't hurt; she always tested them at home before she took them to the patients. She tried to make the projects useful. The fly-swatters they made out of an old rubber sheet, for example: everybody at Hopecrest had remarked how handy they were during the summer.

Maybe we could move into the museum, she thought, and just leave our stuff here. Mike threw nothing away, and he hated to buy anything new. That green afghan he loved to put over himself when he watched TV: she'd told him it wouldn't stand up under another washing, and now he didn't let her wash it at all.

"I only use it when I'm watching TV," he argued. "How dirty can it get just lying on a sofa?"

She pushed last night's dishes into the sink and saw Toth's face in the dishwater. Everyone had warned her about her job, told her she couldn't take other people's sorrows home at night or she'd burn out.

How dark the apartment was. She was glad for an excuse to leave it immediately. Though Stevie was old enough to take care of himself after school, she liked to meet the school bus. She ripped the pink tissue paper off *How to Survive on Land and Sea* and stuffed the little book into the pocket of her pea jacket.

Standing at the end of the block so as not to embarrass him, she watched the other kids fling themselves out of the bus till she saw a thin boy with ragged black hair who didn't care what he wore as long as it had holes in it; Stevie was always the last one off. Now he ran toward her, swinging his lunch box. He was the smallest kid on the bus.

"Can we go to the mall? Dad said he'd buy me the Visible Man for show-and-tell."

"He won't be home till tomorrow morning," Ellen reminded him. "You can go to the mall tomorrow. We had a party at work," she added. "I brought you a present."

Stevie took the book and flipped through it.

"What's it about?"

"Survival," answered Ellen. "It's written by the United States Navy for—well, for goodness' sake, look at the date on it. Nineteen forty-four."

"Wow," said Stevie. "Is it worth a lot?"

"I don't know what it's worth," said Ellen. "But I know Mike will want to read it."

At five o'clock they walked across campus to the Wolverine Den and slid into an empty booth. Except for the boy studying in the booth across the aisle, they had the place to themselves. The waitress appeared with pencil and pad in her hand. She'd worked here since Ellen was in college, and the thought of what this woman's life must be like depressed her.

"Do you want menus?"

"I don't think so," said Ellen. "Stevie, what do you want?"

"A hamburger," said Stevie.

"With or without fries?" asked the waitress.

"With," muttered Stevie, lost in his book.

"Perch fingers for me," said Ellen.

"Jessie always orders perch fingers, too," observed the waitress. "Like mother, like daughter."

"Do perch have fingers?" asked Stevie.

The waitress smiled.

"Of course not," said Ellen. "Read me something from your book."

Stevie turned to the first page.

" 'Read this book. It may save your life. Keep it in your pocket when you are in a part of the world where you may need it. The greatest obstacle that will confront you in the wilderness or at sea is fear of the unknown.' "

He flipped ahead to the middle. " 'It may not be pleasant to con-tem-plate—' "

" 'Contemplate,' " said Ellen. "That means to think about."

" '—to contemplate, but in an emergency you will find that many un-con—' "

Ellen leaned over to see the page. " 'Unconventional,' " she said. "You know, different from other people. I bet you knew that word already."

"Yeah," said Stevie. " '—in an emergency—' " He was brushing each word with his finger, as if testing it for counterfeit. " '—you will find that many unconventional creatures are edible. Large grasshoppers and cicadas with the legs and wings removed may be toasted on the end of a stick.' "

The waitress set a huge platter of breaded perch before Ellen.

" 'If and when you have caught more fish than you can eat, chew out the juice from the flesh. To do this, put a piece of fish in your mouth. Chew it small. Suck out the juice and swallow it, and then spit out the pulp that is left. Keep it up as long as you are thirsty and have fish.' "

"Stevie," Ellen interrupted, "quit it."

"I can read anything," said Stevie, and folded his hands over the page.

His hamburger arrived and Stevie surrendered himself to it. Why did I order fish? thought Ellen. Mike will come home with a whole basketful.

After dinner, the bus let them off two blocks from Jessie's house. The door was unlocked. In the front hall they met Allison, a tall girl with pale skin and blond hair braided on top of her head.

"I smell popcorn," said Stevie.

"Grandma forgot where she put the lid to the popper," said Allison. "We've been eating it off the floor."

Martha and her mother were sitting at the kitchen table. They looked as if they'd been unpacked for some special occasion, the packing pellets scattered around them. A real novelty item: four women in a dirty kitchen and nobody lifting a finger.

"Where were you?" asked Jessie.

"We went to the Wolverine for supper."

Allison wrinkled her nose.

"Mother says she got an offer from Harvey Mack," said Martha. "He wants to buy the museum and build a shopping mall."

"Harvey Mack?" exclaimed Ellen. "Why, he gave me a ride home from work tonight."

"He wants to buy it for three hundred thousand dollars," said Allison.

"Let's see the letter," said Ellen.

Allison shook her head. "You can't. Grandma lost it."

"I've been looking for hours," added Martha. "It'll just have to turn up. If you see Mr. Mack, tell him we're interested."

"We are?" said Ellen. "Mother, do you want to sell the museum?"

"No indeed," said Jessie.

"Tell him we're interested in exploring the matter," said Martha. "We don't want to sell now but we might someday. Tell him not to forget about us."

"Can I watch TV?" asked Stevie. *"Mummies from the Deep* is on."

"You know your dad doesn't like you watching that stuff," said Ellen.

"This is Liberty Hall," said Jessie. "In my house you can watch anything you want."

"Go watch," said Ellen wearily.

"Where *is* Mike?" asked Jessie.

"Fishing at Sylvan Lake, Mother. I told you."

"I'm surprised you didn't go along," said Martha.

"He asked and I said no. That's where we spent our honeymoon."

"Did you have a wedding?" asked Jessie. "I don't remember it."

Ellen laughed. "Oh, Mother, don't you remember how I called you from the house of the justice of the peace in Harbor Springs and said, 'I'm married,' and you said, 'Who to?' "

"I said that?" exclaimed Jessie.

"And Mike wanted to spend our wedding night in a birch grove, on a bed of moss. I should have known what I was getting into."

"How romantic," said Martha.

"Huh," snorted Ellen. "It was too dark to see the poison ivy."

"Did you ever not love each other?" asked Allison. "Did you ever wish you were married to somebody else?"

33

"No," said Ellen.

"I never gave the question much thought," said Martha.

"There was only one man for me," said Jessie. "There never was a man as good as my Henry."

"But did you ever fall in love with someone else?" persisted Allison.

Martha shot her a sharp look.

"Everybody has that feeling—you know, the last fling. A month before I married your father, I fell in love with the grocery boy. The next day I fell in love with the guy who came to fix the washing machine. He got talking to me about male and female parts of the machine, and I wanted to throw myself on him. That's natural. And then you settle in. Frankly, it was a relief to be done with all that courting and dating."

"The grocery boy!" exclaimed Ellen. "Martha, you never told me that."

"Of course not. You were only six years old," said Martha. "The funny part is, everyone I fell in love with was the exact opposite of John. The *exact* opposite. And after the wedding I thought, Thank God I didn't follow my heart."

"Where's Mike?" asked Jessie.

Ellen and Martha exchanged looks.

"He's gone fishing at Sylvan Lake," said Ellen.

"We told you, Mother," said Martha.

"Does Dad know you fell in love with all these people?" demanded Allison.

"We never spoke of it. He knows I'm true blue. Maybe he was going through the same thing."

"I've read it happens again when you hit forty," said Ellen. "Guess I have ten good years ahead of me."

"Now, where did I put that globe?" murmured Jessie.

"What globe?" asked Martha.

"The one with the Dog Star Man in it," answered Jessie.

"Do we still have it?" asked Ellen.

"I think I saw it in the cellar," said Martha, and left the table.

"Excuse me," said Ellen, "while I see what Stevie is watching."

In the sunroom, Stevie's bare feet rose over the arm of the reclining chair. He had fallen asleep; the light from the TV flickered across his face. Very quietly Ellen turned off the set, picked him up, and carried him into the kitchen; and with her son half awake on her lap, she took her place at the table opposite her mother.

When the telephone rang, she heard Allison answer it and call, "It's for you, Ellen."

There was a pushing back of chairs, and Ellen heard herself say, "So late? I hope Mike hasn't had an accident," as the minutes before the news of Mike's death crystallized into a scene out of time, and the glass globe of memory held two women and a child sitting at a kitchen table. Shake them and they don't fall. The water covers but doesn't drown them, the stars rise and set over them, the sun gleams and glares and passes on, and they keep their places, forever and always, telling their stories on the last day they were all together and happy.

# 4

Just as the tide was flowing,' " sang Jessie in the living room and played the last chord fortissimo on the grand piano. Henry had taught her that song; she would never forget it.

Martha said, "We have to pick out a casket at Schmidt's" and Ellen said yes let's go, and John said, "The paper needs the obituary by Friday" and Ellen said yes let's write it what shall we say? and Martha bought twenty-five copies of the paper when it came out and sent one to Aunt Ida in the nursing home in Denver and Ellen said good, and Mike's mother said, "I'll keep an eye on Stevie" and Ellen said thank you, and Dr. Whittaker next door sent a casserole nobody could identify and Ellen ate some for lunch but it had no taste nothing did anymore, and Mike's mother said she hoped it would be a closed casket and Ellen said yes and thought of how Mike must have looked when they pried him out of his car but all she could see was the toad flattened on the floor of the dayroom and she hoped Mike didn't look like that, and one of Mike's students called to say they'd gathered a bouquet of flowers that grew along the river and where should they send it and Ellen said they could send it to Schmidt's Funeral Home thank you, and Mrs. Trimble offered to watch the house during the funeral and Ellen said thank you, and somebody from

Hopecrest delivered a bouquet of daffodils and pussywillows and Ellen said how lovely thank you, and a platter of cold cuts arrived from the faculty at Pioneer High and Ellen said thank you thank you thank you.

Mr. Schmidt was all sympathy, just the way he was when Henry died and he'd shown Jessie and Ellen and Martha the catalogue of designs for brass plaques, roses for women and pine cones for men, because Heavenly Rest allowed no headstones, only plaques that lay flat on the ground. And Jessie said, "Henry loved pecans. Could you do a border of pecans?" and Mr. Schmidt shook his head and said the company didn't do special jobs but if she ordered her own plaque now she could get in on the special rate. And Jessie said no no no no no she didn't want her own plaque, she wanted her name right next to Henry's. "There never was a man as good as my Henry."

Upstairs in the showroom, Ellen and Martha drifted among the open caskets, giant oysters pearled with creamy satin, gathered, turned, and tucked.

"If it was me, I'd take the walnut," said Mr. Schmidt.

But it isn't you, thought Ellen. The ruched lining of the caskets nauseated her. Nothing in the manmade universe could make life right again.

"I don't like the lining. Mike hated fussy things."

"Mrs. Hanson, our top-of-the-line caskets all come with satin lining."

"Mike's won't," said Ellen.

Fascinated, she watched her own hands claw the lining of the rosewood casket loose, yanking it and tearing it till yards and yards of bridal satin foamed and frothed on the floor.

"Mrs. Hanson! Mrs. Hanson!"

How strange their voices sounded in this still place. When she caught her breath she faced Mr. Schmidt, who had turned pale as satin himself.

"I'll be bringing my own lining this afternoon," said Ellen. "Goodbye."

With the tyranny of the bereaved, she ordered Martha to go with her to the apartment, so she could pick up Mike's old green afghan and deliver it to the funeral parlor. Also his Levi's and red flannel shirt and sneakers, though Mr. Schmidt had told her not to bother with shoes. Stevie offered to give his father *How to Survive on Land and Sea* and Martha assured him that Mike would want him to keep a book he was so fond of, especially since Grandma Hanson was putting her rosary in the casket to protect Mike even though he'd left the church years ago.

When they entered the apartment, Martha felt the weight of its silence. It looked like a sty, but this was not the time to judge. Dirty dishes, old magazines, birds' nests, boxes of bones, a guitar.

Stevie said, "I forgot to feed the fish," and scurried into his bedroom.

Mike's death hasn't hit him yet, thought Martha.

The afghan was balled up at the foot of the sofa, and when Ellen saw it she burst into tears.

"What we both need is a cup of tea," said Martha, and marched into the kitchen. The icebox was almost empty except for three dead birds in the freezer, and the cupboard seemed to hold nothing but cornflakes and brewer's yeast. The two mugs in the sink looked clean; she set them on the counter and put a saucepan of water on the stove to boil and poked around till she found a box of tea bags. Some herbal thing: it smelled like sawdust, but the Chinese sage on the front looked trustworthy. Ellen was still sobbing in the next room, and Martha didn't wait for the water to boil before she poured it.

Tea is what you make when this happens, she told herself as

she carried the mugs into the living room. Like boiling water when a baby is born.

Suddenly Stevie shot past her. "Mom! Mom! Dad sent me a message!"

He was waving a postcard. Peering at it over Ellen's shoulder, Martha recognized it at once. Five years ago Mike had gone on a fishing trip near Mackinac Island. He'd sent everybody the same card, which showed a man loading a huge fish on the saddle of his pony under the words "Great Northern Pickerel."

Ellen turned the card over and read the message.

"Love to Stevie. Here's the one that got away."

"It flew through the air," exclaimed Stevie, "and landed right in my hand!"

"I'm not staying alone in this apartment tonight," cried Ellen.

"Of course not," said Martha. "You can stay at Mother's as long as you like. She'll be glad to have you. She gets so lonely. She even offered to help Allison and Elmer address wedding invitations. Told Elmer she got an A in handwriting—the Palmer method."

"What's the Palmer method?" Ellen sniffled.

"I haven't a clue," said Martha.


At dinner nobody sat down. Even Allison was eating cold turkey with her fingers and urging Elmer to try it. "The green is broccoli sauce. Elmer, you need to expand your palate." Grandma Hanson wanted to know why the fire was lit in the living room, since it was seventy degrees outside, and John said, "Jessie always keeps the fire burning, summer and winter."

Ellen was walking around the table waving a tablespoon. She dipped it into a big bowl of Jell-O and ate a bite; she dipped it into the pureed squash and ate a bite.

Stevie was glad when Grandma Hanson leaned over him and said, "I fixed you a plate. Let's you and me find a nice quiet corner. We have to keep our strength up."

Stevie followed her out to the back porch, where she sat down on the glider and Stevie wiggled in beside her. She was as neat and handsome as a ship, and he enjoyed looking at her, slim in her black suit with her short white hair combed in crisp waves across her scalp. Except for Elmer they had the place to themselves. Was Elmer crying? His face was flushed and his nose was running.

"I'm Allison's fiancé," he said, and he shook Grandma Hanson's hand, though she hadn't offered it. "I'm on my way to Kroger's. We've run out of toilet paper."

Allison wandered after him, licking her fingers. The shade cast by the honeysuckles on the screened porch deepened, and Stevie smelled rain coming a long way off.

When Ellen announced they were all going to the funeral parlor, Allison glanced at Stevie and said, "Are you going to let him go like that?" and Ellen said, "Those jeans are brand-new." Stevie wanted to ride with his mother, but she seemed surrounded by an invisible wall that kept him out.

"Stevie can ride with me," said Grandma Hanson, and John asked if she wanted him to drive, and she shook her head; since she'd driven herself here from Grosse Pointe she could probably make it to the funeral parlor, if he would be so kind as to give Stevie directions.

"Stevie?"

"He's my navigator."

Stevie took pains to read her all the signs so that she would not get lost, and when she said, "I believe that's the place up ahead," he was dismayed to find the funeral parlor was nothing but a big old house; he'd imagined a motel, very new, with lots of rooms. The parking area behind Schmidt's was nearly empty, and Grandma Hanson said, "We got here ahead of them all. We'll park in the shade." Her car had a stick that came out of the floor, and he liked to watch her pull it back and forth while she positioned the car in the space under the maples.

As they entered the foyer, he took the hand she offered him. Never in his life had he stepped into such a profound silence. No radiators clanked; no TV muttered unseen in another part of the house; no women's voices rose and fell in the kitchen. Their footfalls, their whispers, their very breath sank into oblivion.

Grandma Hanson stopped at a large room on the left and let go of his hand.

The room looked like a church. Dozens of chairs faced a fountain of flowers; they cascaded from white vases and white baskets in sprays and bunches and wheels, heaped into a brilliant hill of blossoms that did not smell at all like flowers outside. His grandmother walked down the aisle and knelt on a little step beside the casket and crossed herself, and Stevie hurried after her and knelt also.

"The real Mike is with his father now," she said.

Stevie felt as cold as he had the time last winter he'd fallen through the ice into the river. The ache of tears coming took him by surprise; he tipped his head and rested his ear on the polished lid and heard his father not moving, not breathing, just lying there all alone in the dark.

When Martha saw Stevie curled at the foot of the stairs, leaning against the umbrella stand, she said, "You'll be sleeping with your Grandma Hanson in your mother's room, Stevie. You can go to bed any time you feel like it."

Grandma Hanson was laying out his pajamas on the rocking chair. "Can you put yourself to bed?" she asked.

"Oh, yes."

"I'll leave the hall light on. Ellen is in the guest room."

At the door, she hesitated. "Do you want a story?"

He shook his head no, though he wanted one very much, and he waited while her footsteps whittled away to nothing before he pulled off his jeans and polo shirt, stepped into his pajama bottoms, and ran his tongue over his teeth to clean them.

His mother's ponderous chest of drawers and vanity table comforted him; they were so steady and kind. But her brass bed was high and chilly. Scrunching against the wall, he tried to bring back his father's voice, for he did not want to lose a thing so precious.

*Michael, row the boat ashore,* sang his father's voice, *Hallelujah!*

Already he sensed that he was hearing not exactly his father's voice but an imperfect memory of it. Like the voice of the mynah bird a friend of his dad's had brought to the museum. Not just anyone could speak to Wampus; you had to know his owner. Wampus had started visiting when Stevie was five, and the bird kept all their voices inside him—his dad's, his mom's (even from when she had laryngitis), and his own, high and lisping at five, lower and more confident at nine. It was queer to hear their lost voices coming from a bird. You couldn't ask him for the voice you wanted to hear. No, you had to wait till he gave it to you. And he might not give you the one you wanted for years and years. But Wampus would remember them all till the day he died.

Suddenly the overhead light flashed on, and he closed his eyes. Grandma Hanson's breath smelled of wintergreen as she bent over him, listening, checking his sleep, before she turned off the light.

In the dark he opened his eyes again and was startled to see her in silhouette, pulling her slip over her head. He had never thought about his grandmother taking off her clothes, but of course people took off their clothes at night. Even a kindergarten baby knew that.

He watched her shake her white cotton nightgown over her head.

Last of all she raised both hands and took off her hair. It came away all in one piece, and he was so astonished he forgot to breathe. Under the wig, with its neat waves, two white braids fell down from their hiding place; she was turning into a child, skinny, alert, with dark eyes like a bird's that missed nothing.

A draft brushed him as she drew back the covers and climbed in beside him. He tried to keep a ribbon of space between them, but her trim bulk left him pinned against the wall.

"Stevie, are you asleep?"

He heard her turning over to look at him, and when he did not answer, she pulled the sheet over her head and cried very quietly for a long, long time.


Jessie could not say exactly when the fear first nagged her that she'd lost something important. A face, a name, a reason. She was sure someone had told her whom the service was for, but she'd forgotten and didn't want to ask again. She'd just be glad to get everyone out of the funeral parlor alive. She'd heard stories of how the dead love to take the living with them. You had to keep a sharp watch and take count. The dead never took anybody who'd been counted.

John, Martha, Ellen, who looked the same yet different, as if she'd turned into a poor copy of herself. Stevie, Allison, Elmer. Who was missing?

Ida. Ida was missing.

But she hadn't been missing long. If I count again, thought Jessie, if the dead hear me counting, they might give Ida back.

The mass of flowers made her throat itch; she groped for the package of cough drops at the bottom of her purse. Worth their weight in gold.

John, Martha, Ellen. Next to Ellen and Stevie sat a woman who looked familiar. Was she a relative? Not knowing whom to save was terrible.

Reverend Peele was giving the benediction. The same one he gave for Henry. He'd helped her pick the hymns for that service. " 'Time like an ever rolling stream bears all her sons away.' I know Henry loved that one, Mrs. Woolman. And 'The Old Rugged Cross.' "

Today there were no hymns at all. A young lady played the violin, and three or four young men stood up front and talked about how much they'd learned from their teacher, which made Jessie lose count, no matter how hard she tried not to listen.

Ellen, Stevie, Allison, John, Elmer.

As if summoned by her counting, John and Elmer stepped forward and, joined by four young people Jessie did not know, picked up the casket and carried it down the aisle, out of the room into the sunlight.

There was a flurry of car doors opening and closing, and Mr. Schmidt took her arm and urged her into one of them. She was relieved to find herself next to Allison. Someone she knew. Elmer sat in front beside the driver. Through the darkened windows they watched Mr. Schmidt's assistants stow the wreaths in the hearse.

"I wonder who sent that huge basket of yellow lilies," said Elmer.

"Harvey Mack," said Allison. "I saw the card."

"Who is Harvey Mack?" asked Jessie.

"You got a letter from him," said Allison. "He wants to buy Woolman Scientific."

"What an absurd idea!" exclaimed Jessie. "What would he do with it?"

"Turn it into a shopping mall," said Allison.

Well, he's not one of us, thought Jessie. That's one person I don't have to worry about.

A light rain was falling. Where were they? Peering through the darkened glass, she scarcely recognized anything; they were driving along the river past open fields that stretched along the road that led out of Drowning Bear. She saw herself and Henry waiting in her uncle's black dinghy on the empty floodplain of Lake Michigan, Henry in the rower's seat, the oars poised over the mud, herself in the stern, shading her eyes, waiting for the tide to find them.

From far off, they watched its shining lip advance.

The car turned left at two granite pillars, over which stretched the familiar sign: HEAVENLY REST—A NEW CONCEPT IN CEMETERIES. Jessie wondered if she should speak to the driver, tell him the trouble with Henry's grave was finding it, since the japonica bush she'd used as a landmark had disappeared.

Under an awning, on a carpet of bright green chenille tucked around the open grave, stood the casket and a dozen folding chairs.

Elmer helped Jessie out of the car. All along the dirt road, doors opened, motors fell silent. As sun broke into the midst of the rain, Jessie searched the sky for a rainbow. The science books always promised one. It's been just years since I've seen a rainbow, she thought. Wonder if they still make them anymore.

She nudged Elmer and whispered, "Where's Mike?"

"Right there," he answered, and pointed straight ahead.

Ah, they had tricked her. How could she have forgotten that Ida was still alive? Under her very nose the dead had taken Mike, while her attention was snagged by the dinghy rippling the dark skin of the water and Henry sinking one black oar into the ooze before he pushed off, just as the tide was flowing.

# 5

_____

If you stand for hours by the window in the dayroom at Hopecrest, you can stare at the parking lot and grounds that stretch half a mile west to Drummond Avenue. But if you walk down the corridor of second floor east, past Dr. Davidson's closed door till you reach the window at the very end, you can see the Huron River. The choice is yours.

If you have a hawk's eyes, you can travel upriver to Delhi and Dexter. The fishing is good there, and if you go in the fall you can refresh yourself at the Dexter cider mill. Summer and spring, canoes glide under the viaducts, about half a mile south of Barton Pond.

Paddle slowly across Barton Pond toward the dam and you'll see blue herons reading the water for sunfish, red-winged blackbirds glinting in the cattail marshes, and carp lolling like fat little islands, their fins rising above pickerel weed in the shallows. You can stop here all day, watching for muskrats, turtles, and dragonflies. You'll miss the grand houses of Barton Hills, the country club where the small boats dock, and the golf course. The choice is yours.

Or you can let the current carry you past Riverside Park toward Fuller Park. If you trust the river, it will carry you all the way to Lake Erie.

But maybe you don't want to travel that far. You say, Fuller Park is far enough. You can stop at Pawquacha Hoot 'n Scoot, operated by Thomas Bearheart, who sells bait to the fishermen and cold drinks to the swimmers and picnickers. For fifteen cents you can buy a postcard showing the great horned owl of Michigan in 3-D. There is a bait store out back, famous for its copper fishhooks hand-forged by Thomas Bearheart's cousin in Drowning Bear, Wisconsin.

But mainly people come to read the notices tacked on the walls inside. Rumor has it that the people who put them there are all relatives of Thomas Bearheart, and they have been here, in one guise or another, almost as long as the river; generations of Pawquachas have lived and died on it. Fishermen, scavengers, divers, dowsers. Water is their occupation. The people who specialize in pool and fountain installations are as skillful as beavers at making structures that water must pass over or through. Some notices promise to find "the well that's right for you." Others advertise "Lost articles found" or "Expert divers available" or "Salvage for sale cheap." Those who dive at night are so sensitive to the light that their skin darkens at sunrise and pales when the sun goes down.

Others, nimble as squirrels, will shingle your roof or fix your TV antenna.

Only one phone number is given: Thomas Bearheart's. If you call Thomas Bearheart and state your problem, he will dispatch someone to do the job. There are those who say that Thomas Bearheart's relatives don't fix things, they only exchange old problems for new ones. A woman on Devonshire, for whom a river man installed a new drain, complained it was badly clogged with moccasin flowers and water hyacinths. A plunger couldn't begin to unclog it; the roots were endless. A man on Spring Valley Road had his television set repaired by one of the river women, and shortly thereafter a strange shadow swam across the screen and blocked out half the picture. It looked like a little-mouth bass, and in spite of the expensive efforts of the Sears, Roebuck service department, it stayed for a month.

Folks who wouldn't dream of answering one of the notices on the walls of Pawquacha Hoot 'n Scoot will not hesitate to buy crab apple jam from Thomas Bearheart's relatives on Saturday morning at the Farmers' Market. Or black cherry jam or rosehip jelly, or hickory nut bread, or their special sumac relish, which they call shandygaff. A few passengers on the Lake Shore Limited rushing toward Chicago claim to have seen marvelous gardens in the wildest stretches of the river at twilight. Once a man came to the market with nothing to sell but three small black masks. He claimed he'd traded a dozen ears of sweet corn for them, and the masks were good and fearless; he knew the raccoons personally. No one had the courage to buy them. It is known that the Pawquachas live by secret tides in their blood, as distinctive for each of them as the whorl of their fingerprints, and under certain conditions a deep instinct turns them into animals of the river. When they meet danger, they will almost certainly change, as a chameleon changes, if they see it in time. They will also change when the moon unsettles the delicate balance in their blood. By means of this simple defense, they have survived the loss of their land, their religion, their government—everything except the river, which has kept them alive.

What sells fastest is their wild rice, and Thomas Bearheart's relatives will not tell where it grows or who harvests it. If you are seized with a desire to find the source, change yourself into a trout and take the long way, following one of the underground streams into Lake Michigan. If you cross the lake and keep a northerly course, you will find yourself knocking at the Door Peninsula. "Door" is short for Door of the Dead—Porte des Morts, as the French sailors called it. The ships that sank here may be rolling across the floor of Lake Huron by this time. Everything is connected, and the water people know this.


Or you can take the shortcut and paddle to one of the passages in the Huron River, which reflects this world so clearly you can see into the next one. When wild flags blossom along the river's edge in this world, snow whitens the banks in that one. And when trout and sunfish sleep under a skin of ice here, the swamps there hum with bees and cicadas, kingbirds and vireos and warblers. Walk against the current. Follow one of the streams that spill into the river till you find the spring at the bottom. You have found a doorway into the spirit world. Be careful. It is not safe to pass through that doorway without a guide.

But maybe you don't want to travel that far. You say, Ann Arbor is far enough. Stand still in the stream. Listen. Thomas Bearheart's cousin picks up her hammer. Can you hear it ringing as she forges copper fishhooks in Drowning Bear, Wisconsin? Put your ear to the water as if it were a train track and listen for travelers rushing toward you, invisible as the dead and noisy as a pack of dogs.


Ellen could see that everyone was trying to help her. Allison dropped by and filled Jessie's icebox freezer with frozen dinners, wedging them side by side like the matched volumes of an encyclopedia. Elmer offered to advise her on "tying things up," as he put it, though estates were not his area of expertise.

"Mike didn't own anything valuable," Ellen confessed. "He always meant to."

Jessie, who did not drive, said of course Ellen should use Henry's car instead of taking the bus. The old blue Buick rarely left the garage, since Mrs. Trimble took her own car for the shopping and errands. It needed a few repairs; the defroster belched black smoke. You had to drive with the windows open.

When Ellen told Stevie he wasn't going back to school till the following Monday, he looked scared.

"What about my homework?"

"Your aunt Martha is going to pick it up."

"Mom, we haven't fed the fish for three days."

Ellen knelt down and hugged him hard and felt his wiry little body go rigid; he did not hug her in return.

"Don't worry," she said. "We'll go right over to the apartment and get them."

Trying to park the Buick in front of the building, Ellen felt as if she were navigating a huge shark. How could her father have chosen this car, she thought, with its foolish fins and chrome stripes?

"Mail's here," she said. "I can see the box is full."

Stevie watched her flip through the letters. His silence was frightening. Appeals, junk, the bill from Schmidt's. She opened that one, and her knees turned to water as she saw the stages of her grief counted and charged. Coffin. Flowers. Hearse. Four thousand dollars. She had never owed anyone that much money in her life. Maybe they would let her make time payments.

She unlocked the door.

"Come on, honey. Let's go inside."

At the top of the stairs he whispered, "Are we going to stay at Grandma's forever?"

"Of course not. Just till—just for a while."

Oh, how could she explain to Stevie that she didn't have the energy to cope with Mike's stuff? God forbid she should throw any of it away, but in a four-room apartment, where could she store it? His books on birds, his boxes of clippings, his shirts, his knapsack, his back issues of *Audubon* and *Smithsonian* and *Natural History* already crammed the floor of the closet they'd shared for ten years.

And what should she do with the oriole's nest hanging from the molding over their bed—his answer, he'd told her, to the universal worship of technology? And the jars of old keys on his bureau, and boxes of duplicate library cards, feathers, seedpods, snapshots, and notes from his students at Pioneer High? And the bureau itself, still stuffed with his underwear and socks and T-shirts? She never could close those drawers when she brought up the laundry, and she couldn't bring herself to open them now that his laundry was finished for good.

Hearing the bubble of the aquarium, Ellen dreaded going into Stevie's room. What if the fish were dead? She couldn't bear any more losses. The water glowed a murky green.

"They're real hungry, Mom," said Stevie.

Behind the glass glimmered two angelfish and a moon platy, their mouths biting at the surface of the water.

"We'll need something to hold the fish while we move them."

"Dad said they needed special water," said Stevie. "Not the water that comes out of the faucet."

"It won't hurt them for such a short trip. We can buy distilled water at Kroger's. I think the old fishbowl is in the study."

Cautiously Ellen opened the door. The silence that met them was so profound it seemed to have gathered in this spot from the four corners of the earth.

"It feels like Dad is in here," said Stevie.

Filled with rocks, the fishbowl sat on top of a filing cabinet. Ellen turned the bowl upside down on the desk and the rocks clattered across the desk blotter.

"Mom, look!"

"What is it?"

He pointed to the blotter; on it Mike had scrawled words he had trouble spelling.

"Look, Mom. 'Delicious.' He couldn't spell 'delicious.' I could spell that when I was in second grade."

Mike's reading glasses were resting beside "delicious," as if he'd just set them down. He'd gotten them six months before, on his fortieth birthday, and he was always losing them. Ellen tucked them into her purse; she could almost hear him calling her, asking her where she'd seen them last.

Outside, stars fell and birds flew north. In another month, the maples would send pale green wings spinning onto the sidewalks and lawns, with instructions to take root.

The following Monday Ellen was crossing the parking lot when she spied Mrs. Pickering running to meet her.

"Ellen, I'm so sorry. You could have taken more time off. You didn't have to come in so soon after the funeral."

"I'm trying to keep busy," said Ellen. "The flowers you sent were really beautiful."

"Toth picked them before he disappeared."

"Toth disappeared?" All around her people were slipping out of sight, like swimmers out of reach.

"With Bearheart's people it's the same story every year. They check themselves in for the winter. When the warm weather hits, they're off. Seems like they manage somehow on the outside."

"Have you any idea where he went?"

"To the river. They all go to the river." Mrs. Pickering opened the door and held it for Ellen. "If you want to go home early . . ."

"No," said Ellen. "Working keeps my mind off everything else."

As she debated going to pick up Stevie at school so he wouldn't have to ride the bus his first day back, she could almost hear Mike saying, *Let him come home the regular way. Keep things normal.* Probably Stevie would be embarrassed if she came for him. Better to meet him at his old stop, near the apartment.

She watched from the driveway as the yellow bus lumbered into sight and braked with a screeking of gears across the street. A gang of children tumbled out, and for an instant she couldn't find Stevie; he seemed to have vanished as completely as if he had slipped through a crack in the universe. Fear unlocked all the hiding places in her heart.

Then he separated himself from the others and walked slowly toward her and she rushed forward to meet him.

"How was school?"

"It felt funny," he said. "They studied China and I missed it."

By the time they got home, Stevie had a headache. Ellen laid her hand on his forehead; it was burning.

She helped him into his pajamas and pulled the shades against the late afternoon light and saw herself in that room, in that bed, six years old, sick with measles, and her own mother pulling the shades so she wouldn't lose her sight.

Downstairs, Jessie had fallen asleep on the living room sofa in front of the fireplace. The flames burned low, but sometimes an ember hopped as far as the rug. Got to check on her, Ellen reminded herself.

"I'm freezing," said Stevie, and shivered.

Aspirin, thermometer—where did her mother keep these things? The medicine cabinet over the sink was crammed with old prescriptions, shoe polish, Chap Sticks, hand lotion, two empty thermometer cases. No aspirin. A fine skin of grease anointed everything.

"Somebody's at the door," called Jessie from the living room.

To Ellen's surprise, for she had heard no knock, Mrs. Trimble was standing on the doorstep, touching her new permanent.

"Thought I'd drop by to see if you need anything." She smoothed an invisible wrinkle out of her baby-blue polyester pants suit.

"Aspirin," said Ellen. "Stevie has a fever."

"It's behind the encyclopedia. I have yet to see a childproof top your mom can't crack." She rummaged in her purse for several minutes, pulled out a check, and handed it to Ellen. "I hate to mention this, but your mother paid me twice last week."

"Her memory's not terribly sharp these days," admitted Ellen. She wished Mrs. Trimble would go away; she could not bear to think that her mother was growing old.

"The electric bill came and she lost it," said Mrs. Trimble. "If you don't pay your electric bill, they shut off the lights."

"What happened to that nice file Martha crocheted for the bills?"

"Jessie unraveled it." Mrs. Trimble hesitated, then blurted out, "I guess you've met Mr. Mack's father in Hopecrest."

"I've seen him," said Ellen. "We had a birthday party for him."

"You'd think Mr. Mack would hire a nurse and keep his father at home," she said. "He can afford it. You ever seen his house?"

"How would I see his house?!" exclaimed Ellen. "I hardly know him."

"It used to be the old Campbell estate. I have my own apartment over the carriage house at the end of the property. After I've cooked his supper, sometimes he asks me to sit down and eat it with him."

"I don't know how you find the time to come and help Mother," said Ellen.

"Well, of course he keeps most of the rooms in the house shut off. And he's very tidy; there's the laundry to do, but not much heavy cleaning. It was his wife's house till she died three years ago. Tripped over a blind man's cane and fractured her skull. I never met her."

"That's bizarre," said Ellen. "Really bizarre."

Mrs. Trimble frowned. "I think she'd had one too many. Believe me, I know the signs. I was married for ten years to a man who couldn't quit. That was a long time ago, thank God."

As Mrs. Trimble started down the walk, Ellen headed for the living room. The sofa was empty.

"Mother?"

No answer.

She peeked into the kitchen, the dining room, the back porch. "Mother?"

She's hiding, thought Ellen. I won't go looking for her. I won't.

Even when Ellen was a child, her mother loved to hide. Sometimes she'd hide in the cellar. Sometimes she'd simply slip behind the coat rack or into a bedroom closet and listen to Ellen shouting her name in tones of increasing desperation, waiting till she heard the roar of her daughter's weeping before she made her appearance.

The thought that her mother might be watching and snickering at this very moment made Ellen so angry she decided to show no concern. She walked around the TV room, turned on the lights, glanced behind chairs, shook out the curtains.

Nothing.

Taking a flashlight from the telephone stand in the hall, she crouched under the grand piano, darting the beam this way and that, and, finding nothing, headed for the dining room, where she peered under the buffet. One leg was broken, propped into place but not glued.

The beam of her light under the china cabinet caught a stack of chipped plates Jessie had stopped using but could not bear to throw away.

Lord! As if her mother could hide behind a stack of plates.

Ellen picked up the newspaper on the coffee table, kicked off
her shoes, and sat in the wing chair and pretended to read it, all
the while listening for a footfall behind the curtain, a crash of
hangers in the front hall. The chair wobbled. The arm was loose.

The longer she listened to the deepening silence, the more she
became convinced that her mother was not in the house. She
stood up, dropped the paper, and called, "Mo-*ther!*"

Terrified now, she fled through the silent rooms, shouting,
"*Mother!* MOTHER!" The faintest shuffling in the cellar answered her and sent her stumbling down the cellar steps. At the
the foot, she stubbed her toe on the old movie projector.

I'll never find her, she thought. Like that time she'd lost Stevie
in Jacobson's. He was two, and she'd let go of his hand for an
instant to pick up the price tag on a sale dress. How easy it was
to lose someone; how easy it was for a star to fall through the
fingers of light into eternal darkness.

The glow from a single bulb traced bags of Christmas orna-
ments and school papers, racks of old clothes, a box of silverware,
a set of dishes, broken bridge tables, mason jars crammed with
pears aged to a brown pulp. And all those cans of Dinty Moore
beef stew stored in the "fallout shelter."

She brushed past Aunt Ida's dresses, the paper sheaths from
the dry cleaner still guarding them ten years after she'd gone
into the nursing home.

On a hook under the stairs hung her old figure skates, dan-
gling over Martha's wedding bouquet, so dry and fragile it might
have belonged to a mummy. She could scarcely believe how
many of her things and Martha's had ended up in the cellar,
brought here for safekeeping because no matter how often she
and Martha might move from town to town and from house to
house, their mother's house stayed the same forever.

"Mother!"

She rushed upstairs, flung open the closet doors in all the bedrooms, and headed for the third floor. The attic was locked; her mother could not possibly be in there. The bathroom—she looked under the tub. The spare room opposite the attic was cold, the bed stripped to the mattress, the desk bare. The door of the empty closet swung open. Beyond the closed window lay Dr. Whittaker's garden. After Henry died, Dr. Whittaker, long widowed, had laid a brick path linking his garden to the Woolman yard. Jessie would never use it.

Ellen clattered down the stairs to the telephone in her mother's bedroom. The bed, made this morning, had not been disturbed. Her fingers shook as she dialed Martha's number. Suddenly she caught sight of Stevie in the doorway, staring at her.

"Is Grandma dead?" he demanded.

"No, of course she's not dead—Martha?"

"Hello?"

"It's me, Ellen. Mother's gone."

"What do you mean she's gone?"

"I've looked all over the house, and I can't find her. She was sleeping on the sofa when Mrs. Trimble came by, and when I looked for her, she'd disappeared."

"She's probably hiding. Pay no attention to her and she'll—"

"Martha, this is an emergency."

"I'll be over."

Stevie was tugging at her blouse. "Mom, is Grandma lost?"

"Grandma is playing a joke," said Ellen. "And not a very funny one."

"Can I stay up and watch for her?"

He looked so frightened that Ellen hadn't the heart to send him back to bed alone. Together they carried his pillow and blanket downstairs and she made up his bed on the sofa and tucked him in. To her relief, his forehead felt cool.

"My head doesn't hurt anymore," he said.

"That's good," said Ellen, and kissed him. "You know, you don't have to stay awake for Grandma. If she sees you on the sofa, she'll know she's home."

As Martha's car crunched up the driveway, Ellen flew barefoot across the lawn to meet her.

"I'm sure she's not in the house. I'm just sure of it."

They decided to cover different territory. Ellen would stay in the house with Stevie, and Martha would poke around the neighborhood. If she found no clues, they would call the police. Neither said what both of them feared: Jessie had hidden herself somewhere and died of a heart attack.

As Martha opened the front door, the garage door gave a drawn-out groan. Ellen froze.

"Who is it?" called Martha.

And now they both heard it, a thin, cheerful voice singing:

> *What a friend we have in Jesus,*
> *All our sins and griefs to bear.*
> *What a privilege to carry*
> *Everything to God in prayer!*

Their mother walked toward them, her arms laden with clothes as if she'd just taken the wash off the line. Ellen didn't know whether to laugh or cry.

"Ellen, I found a whole box of Henry's pajamas. Maybe Mike can use them."

"Oh, Mother," groaned Martha.

"The bottoms are like new," said Jessie. She was headed toward the house. "The first year we were married, Henry wore both tops and bottoms, but pretty soon he gave up wearing bottoms. Told me one night he'd never wear bottoms again. I bought him a bathrobe, but he didn't like that either. Believe me, you can get used to anything."

"Martha," said Ellen, "we have to talk."

Stevie had curled up on the floor in front of the fire and fallen asleep, and now Jessie said, "I believe I'll finish my nap," and lay down on the sofa. Her labored breathing both disturbed and comforted them.

Martha said, "Oh, she shouldn't sleep through supper."

"Let her sleep," said Ellen. "I'm not hungry."

The sisters sat by the fireplace in the wing chairs, their feet propped up on the old wooden coffee table. Martha moved the morning paper, still folded, away from the flames as Ellen reached down and turned the key on the hearth and said, "Thank heaven for natural gas," and Martha said, "Oh, yes, thank heaven."

"I don't know where to start," said Ellen. "There's all this stuff I never had to think about before. The bill from Schmidt's is four thousand dollars, and I haven't the faintest idea where Mike kept our insurance policies. The man at the funeral parlor asked me how many death certificates I wanted. I don't even know who to ask for help."

"John will help you. And Elmer."

"I've already spoken to Elmer. He asked me for a copy of Mike's will, and when I told him Mike never made one, he threw up his hands and said, 'Everybody should make a will. Have you made yours yet?'"

"Maybe you could quit your job and live here, and Mother could pay you for staying on with her," suggested Martha.

Ellen shook her head.

"There's something immoral about getting *paid* for taking care of your own mother. She didn't get paid for taking care of us."

The flame danced between them in silence.

"Besides, I'd go nuts. It's better to have someone who's not family."

They decided to advertise in the paper. Discreetly. They would use a box number and ask for references.

Martha drew a pen and notebook from her purse. "What do we want to say?"

"I don't know," said Ellen. "Let's find an ad we can copy."

Martha unfolded the newspaper carefully, the way she opened presents wrapped in paper she wished to save, and pulled out the want-ad section.

"Here's one. 'Wanted: Nurse's aide, live-in companion for elderly woman. Private room and bath. Must be reliable and have own car. References required.'"

"That's great," said Ellen. "That's perfect."

"But we can't just copy it," said Martha. "We have to change something. What about Mother's car?"

"I'm using that one," said Ellen.

They changed "have own car" to "have own transportation."

"I don't know when I'll be moving back to the apartment," added Ellen. "Right now I can't even think about moving back."

"Don't worry," said Martha. "You just stay in the guest room as long as you need to. And Stevie can keep your old room. I think we should say, 'Respond in writing.' That will eliminate anyone who's beyond the pale."

"I wish we could say something about red hair," said Ellen. "I mean having it. Mother loves people with red hair."

"You can't say anything about color anymore," Martha reminded her. "You just have to take what comes. What about the salary?"

"What about it?"

"We have to pay the person a decent wage. John says a thousand dollars a month is the going rate."

"A thousand dollars!"

"That's nothing compared to what it could be. If Mother breaks her hip and needs twenty-four-hour nursing care, it'll run us eighty thousand a year."

"You know Mother doesn't have that much money," said Ellen.

"If it comes to the worst, we could sell the museum," said Martha. "Harvey Mack is still interested."

Ellen jerked forward. "Have you been talking to Harvey behind my back?"

"He called Mother while I was over here, and we had a long talk," admitted Martha. "He wants to put in a big science store for kids. You know, like the one out at Briarwood."

"There's nothing real in that store," cried Ellen. "Nothing alive—"

A loud snore startled them.

"We'll never get her upstairs now," said Martha. "She won't wake early, believe me. You need a good night's sleep yourself."

At the doorway she turned and said, "I didn't mean to upset you, Ellen. We don't have to sell—not yet, anyhow."

Ellen gathered Stevie into her arms and carried him upstairs and tucked him into her old bed. A pale glow from the aquarium lit him; he was turning into a pearl.

The bed in the guest room was strewn with papers, but she was too tired to care, and she pushed them aside, drew the comforter over her. Suddenly she remembered Mike's glasses and reached for her purse hanging on the bedpost and fumbled through it till she found them. At night he'd tucked them under his pillow. Now she tucked them under hers.

*Michael, row the boat ashore.*

In her dream she stood on the shore and watched him rowing hard over the ruffled water, and didn't he have plenty of work crossing the river that wanted to keep him?

> *Michael, row the boat ashore,*
> *Hallelujah!*

His face shone; he was so close his eyes gleamed blue-black like the bottom of a well and they looked straight at her, as lonely and fierce as if she had left him instead of him leaving her, and Ellen's heart thumped with love and fear.

> *River Jordan is chilly and cold,*
> *Hallelujah!*
> *Chills the body but not the soul—*

Joy was dawning in his face; he was very near her now, and she saw the trembling of his hands on the oars because they both knew that if he rowed hard enough, if he hurried, if he jumped in and waded toward her, his knees pushing aside the heavy fabric of the water, if he pulled the boat ashore before the morning broke, if she kept her own eyes closed and stayed asleep long enough for him to make it ashore, she could save him.

And waking, knew she would never again meet him in this world.

# 6

---

At lunch Stevie dropped his spoon.

"A man is coming," said Jessie.

"He dropped his spoon, Mother, not his knife," said Ellen. "The spoon means a child is coming."

"A man is coming," said Jessie, "to see the museum. He called and said he'd be right over."

"Who?" exclaimed Ellen.

"He wants to buy it," said Jessie. "Isn't that the silliest thing you ever heard?"

"Harvey is coming here?" cried Ellen. "When did he call?"

"I don't know," answered Jessie. "He didn't tell me."

Ellen pushed back her chair and jumped to her feet.

"I'll go out and watch for him."

She grabbed the key from its hook in the kitchen and took the shortcut through the thicket across the garden; the woody stems on the rosebushes were waking into green. Harvey was standing on the doorstep, ringing the bell. The sun gleamed on his bald head as if he'd lacquered it. He wore white shoes and a yellow sports jacket, and Ellen could not help thinking of the yellow jackets that hovered around the pears when her mother ate lunch in the backyard during the summer.

"The bell hasn't worked for years," said Ellen. "I have the key."

"Ah," said Harvey.

A strong scent of artificial pine surrounded him. Just like he's come courting, thought Ellen, and felt flattered, though he was hardly her type. And she hated perfume on men.

The door opened at her touch, and they stepped into the moist darkness of the museum. Almost immediately the sounds of the street fell away. Ellen had noticed that it always took time for her ears to catch the faint gurgling of the stream, just as it took time for her eyes to pick out the exhibit cases in the twilight of that place, lit now by sunlight falling from a great distance into the water. Harvey, rooted to the floor, stared wildly about him.

"Do you want the tour?" asked Ellen. "I heard my father give it so often I know it by heart."

"Nobody told me there was a water problem in the building," said Harvey.

"The stream isn't a problem," said Ellen. "It hardly ever overflows."

"I wonder if it could be channeled into a fountain."

Ellen frowned. "I don't think the fish would like it. How would they visit their cousins in Ypsilanti?"

"Ypsilanti?"

"Or their friends in Dexter? If the fish ran into a fountain— well, it would feel like the Berlin Wall."

"An underground stream could easily be filled in without disturbing the course of the river."

"My mother would never agree to filling in the stream," said Ellen angrily. "Do you want to see the museum or not?"

Harvey was standing by the stream, peering into it and trembling, as if the air in the room had chilled him. It was a mistake letting him in, thought Ellen; he had no interest in the museum at all. He did not admire it; he was busy counting the pennies in the streambed. Shiny once, brown now. When she was little, she loved to toss a penny into the water and make a wish. Martha had told her there was a fifty-fifty chance the stream would grant it.

"Let's go out," said Ellen, and she took Harvey's arm.

Harvey pulled back from her. "That face at the bottom of the stream," said Harvey. "Who put it there?"

Ellen leaned over the water. "I don't see a face."

"You don't see a woman with long black hair?"

"No." Not wishing to hurt his feelings, she added, "But that doesn't mean she's not there."


The notice ran in the *Ann Arbor News* from Monday till Friday, and during that time the post office box Martha had rented till Memorial Day stayed empty.

On Saturday, as Ellen and Martha and John and Stevie and Jessie were sitting in the dining room eating lunch, they heard the clatter of a dozen catalogues being pushed through the mail slot.

"Mail's here—I'll get it!" exclaimed Martha, and sprang from her chair.

Shuffling through the bills and circulars, she found to her surprise two letters marked, "P.O. Box 83. Please forward." These she stuck down the front of her blouse. Fanning herself with the gas bill, she handed the rest of the mail to her mother.

"It's so hot in the house," she said. "I think I'll go sit on the back porch."

Through the French doors the others could see her, tearing a letter open with her teeth.

"I think I'll go sit on the back porch too," said Ellen.

"Everyone is leaving me," said Jessie.

"I'm not leaving you," said John. "Stevie's not leaving you. Are you, Stevie?"

"No," said Stevie.

"Looks like Martha and Ellen are going to be gone for a while," observed John. He pulled his briefcase from under his chair, opened it, and pulled out yesterday's *Wall Street Journal,* into which he disappeared.

Jessie gave her grandson a puzzled smile. "Where'd you get that black hair?" she asked. "Nobody in our family has black hair."

"My daddy did."

The sisters sat down on the glider, out of their mother's sight.

"This one is sealed with packing tape," said Martha. "The kind with threads in it."

"Just rip the envelope," said Ellen.

The note Martha read aloud was badly crumpled and written in pencil:

> *Dear Sir or Madam,*
>
> *Though I have no experience caring for the elderly, I am a good cook. I will do light housekeeping. I have four-year-old twin boys.*
>
> *Sincerely,*
> *Bettylou Sebby*

"Twins," said Martha. "Out of the question. You read the other one. Maybe you'll have better luck."

Ellen opened it, or rather it opened itself where Martha had bitten the top flap open, and into her hand fell a sheet of notebook paper, on which was printed:

> *Gentle Reader:*
>
> *I am twenty-five and was born in Drowning Bear, Wisconsin. I am a graduate of the University of Wisconsin–Madison, where I had a double major in biology*

*and religion. I took one year of post-graduate work in the
college of veterinary medicine and have worked at a variety
of related jobs. At the age of thirteen I cared for a dozen
sled dogs left to my father by an old friend. In college I
worked at Calling All Strays Small Animal Clinic. I had
responsibility for birds and amphibians under two pounds. I
am presently caring for a wounded cat whose paw was
crushed in a trap and who was brought in to be "put
down." The veterinarian from whose lethal injection I saved
her says she is probably twelve years old. In cat years that
amounts to 72 years. So I've had some experience in caring
for the elderly.*

*As Black Elk says, This life is holy and good to tell, and
the two-leggeds share it with the four-leggeds and the wings
of the air and all green things. I believe my experience
caring for these creatures qualifies me for the job you are
offering.*

*I am presently employed as a waiter at the Buddha
Uproar Cafe on Liberty Street. The phone number is
668-8989, and you may call for references.*

*I hope someday to start my own clinic for healing both
four-leggeds and two-leggeds. But more of this later.*

*Ever sincerely yours,*
*Sam Theopolis*

Ellen looked up from the letter. "Drowning Bear, Wisconsin,"
she said. "You hardly ever meet anybody from Drowning Bear.
That's a good omen."

"This has got to be a joke," said Martha.

"Maybe not," said Ellen. "We can't be fussy."

"Let's go inside," said Martha, "and I'll make the call. You get
on the upstairs extension in case I need help."

Stevie had pushed his chair away from the table and was

showing his grandmother his new pack of baseball cards. Keeping one ear cocked for the low babble of their voices, Martha pulled up the chair by the telephone table in the front hall, dialed very carefully, and waited. One, two, three, four, five rings.

A faint sawing and chugging alarmed her. "Operator?"

"It's me," said Ellen. "I'm brushing my teeth."

"Who is this?" demanded a man's voice. It was barely audible over the clatter of dishes and the roar of voices.

"Hello," said Ellen.

"Hello," said Martha. "I'm calling in regard to a Sam Theopolis."

"There's a waiter here named Sam Theopolis."

"Could I speak to him?"

"Now? Are you crazy? Lady, we have a full house and ten waiting for places."

"Well, could you have him call me, please? I'll leave you my number. Do you have something to write with?"

She pronounced each number with exaggerated distinctness, and the man growled something into the receiver and hung up.

Ellen was still on the line.

"I hope he gets my message," said Martha. "Somebody's probably wiping the counter with it. If we haven't heard from him by five o'clock, we'd better phone Best Care for Seniors and see what they charge an hour. God, I hate to do it. I've heard that their people steal you blind."

What puzzled Jessie was how the dead had managed to steal the house without anyone noticing it except herself. Though Jessie wasn't fooled by the exchange, she had to admire how meticulously they'd reproduced it, right down to the broken reading light over her bed and the missing stopper on the cut-glass perfume bottle that gleamed on her dressing table. They'd managed to reproduce the drawer of tangled necklaces with their broken clasps and the cracks in the flowered porcelain brooch Henry had bought her in Switzerland on their honeymoon. They'd duplicated her hats, which sat on the top shelf of the closet above Henry's overcoats, and they hadn't forgotten the ten dollars hidden behind Henry's picture over her bed.

Odd how they liked old things best—used things, broken things with a story to them. Things permeated with human lives, things with a soul they could suck out, leaving the carcass behind.

She hoped the dead wouldn't go to the trouble of finding an Oriental rug identical to the one in her living room. They could not counterfeit that, she felt sure, a genuine Sarouk. But when she discovered they'd duplicated the dust on the old *Book of Knowledge* behind the TV and the white rings on the coffee table left by cups of hot chocolate set down without coasters, a deep terror lodged in her. What power could one woman have against those engaged in so vast a scheme? All she could hope to do was keep her eye out for what was real among the fakes.

But what if they managed to replace all her furniture, even the Sarouk? Would they start taking members of her family? She could not rid herself of a nagging fear that someone she loved was missing, though after dinner when they sat around watching television in the sunroom, she counted heads and told herself that everyone was accounted for.

Martha and John.

Ellen and Stevie.

Allison.

Allison's friend, Elmer. Of course he was not as real as her own flesh and blood. Not much to look at, either—bad complexion, hair the color of a grocery bag. Allison said he was terrific in court, though. He'd stopped by to return the punch bowl, though Jessie was sure she'd never loaned it to him. She sat upright in the reclining chair, watching the weather channel, attuned to the minutest changes in the room that might show her a real chair lapsing into a fake one, captive under the beguiling surface of the replacement. Stevie was curled up on the love seat. She marveled at his knees showing through the holes in his jeans. He'd kicked off his sneakers, and his bare toes were pink and new as a possum's snout. Ellen, wearing a scarf wrapped around her head, was massaging them.

My old purple scarf, thought Jessie. I wore it after I left the henna on too long. Why did Ellen's head look so lumpy? Were her daughters in on the plot? Surely not—and yet sometimes they talked about her as if she had no more hearing than a table.

"Are those my curlers?" she asked.

"Why, yes," said Ellen. "I didn't think you'd mind."

"You might have asked me first. I have a hard enough time keeping track of things in this house without people borrowing them."

"I think you should switch to the news," said Elmer. "It's more challenging for her."

His nose was running, his pale grey eyes were watering: a robot whose inner workings had sprung a leak. Jessie stared at him, fascinated.

"No news," said Ellen. "I was up with her till two last night, calming her down. Whatever she watches, she thinks it's happening in Ann Arbor. Shootings in Colombia, bombings in Iraq— she thinks they're happening right down the street."

"Elmer," said Jessie, "do you have a cold?"

"Allergies," said Elmer. "I was on my way to pick up a prescription."

"Are you certain it's not a leak?"

"I beg your pardon?"

"You did say 'allergies,' " she persisted, "did you not?"

He looked so perplexed that she decided to believe him, and at that instant she knew who was missing.

"Mike," she said. "Ellen, where's Mike? I haven't seen him all day."

"Oh, Mother, he's dead," cried Ellen.

"Now, you know that, Mother," said Martha.

"Dead!" exclaimed Jessie. "And so young!"


Late in the afternoon the phone rang, and Stevie answered it and ran into the living room. "It's a man named Sam, and he says he's on his way over."

"Let me talk to him," said Ellen, and headed for the hall.

"He already hung up."

"He's coming over now?" exclaimed Martha. "Lord, where's the vacuum cleaner?"

"Who's coming over?" asked Jessie.

"The man who wants the third-floor room," said Ellen.

"This is my house!" snapped Jessie. "I do not want a strange man in my third-floor room."

"Oh, I'm sure he's not strange," said Ellen. "And he'll mow the grass for you, Mother."

"I have Mr. Ross to mow the grass," said Jessie.

"Not anymore," Martha said. "Not since his heart attack."

She plugged in the old Hoover. It puffed up its chest and roared.

"I wish you could just push a button when you want to die," said Jessie. "I've lived long enough."

"I can't hear you," shouted Martha.

"She said she wants to die," Ellen shouted back.

Martha snapped off the vacuum cleaner. "Nobody has these heavy clunkers anymore," she panted. "Nobody."

Ellen turned to her mother.

"Dr. Whittaker has someone living in *his* house," she observed. "Ever since Mrs. Whittaker died, he's had students."

"Who does he have now?" asked Jessie.

"Gregory," answered Ellen.

"What happened to that nice girl he was so fond of?"

"She left," said Martha.

"She'll be back," said Jessie, and watched her daughter shove the Hoover behind the coat rack.

"There's dust everywhere," said Martha.

Jessie smiled. "We'll turn the lights low."

"I suppose he'll be coming any minute now," said Ellen.

"Who?" asked Jessie.

"The man who wants the third-floor room, Mother," replied Martha. "We already told you."

"This is my house and I do not want—"

The phone rang and they all jumped, and Ellen ran and caught it.

"He's *where?* Well, of course we'll be right over. But don't you think you should call a locksmith?"

"Who is it?" demanded Martha.

Ellen leaned into the living room with her hand over the mouthpiece of the receiver. "He went to the wrong house. He's at Dr. Whittaker's."

"Who? Who?" cried Jessie.

"The man who wants the third-floor room," said Ellen.

"A man wants the third-floor room?!" exclaimed Jessie. "You never told me."

"Why can't he come over here?" asked Stevie.

"He's in the bathroom," said Ellen, "and something's gone funny with the lock."

Ellen led the way across the muddy yard to Dr. Whittaker's door, which was never latched in warm weather, and they stepped without knocking into the deep darkness of the front hall. All that walnut wainscoting and heavy dark furniture. She wondered how anyone could stand so much darkness. Only the dining room admitted much light, through French doors opening onto the garden.

Dr. Whittaker and Gregory were seated at opposite ends of the table, eating chocolate pudding and creamed corn out of pots and pans. No one had ever seen Gregory wearing any shirt but his old black Lou Reed with the torn sleeve. Dr. Whittaker was ninety-four and so thin he seemed transparent. Unannounced visitors always found him wearing a tie.

"This is an occasion!" he exclaimed. "I hope you'll stay for tea. The water is on—won't take but a minute to reheat it."

"Nothing for me," said Jessie. "I'm full as a tick."

Gregory stopped scraping the pudding from the bottom of the pot and pointed his spoon toward the closed door of the bathroom. "He's in there."

"You might knock," suggested Dr. Whittaker, "and let him know you've come."

Ellen put her mouth close to the door. "Mr. Theopolis?"

A pleasant voice from the opposite side answered her. "To whom have I the pleasure of speaking?"

"I'm Ellen Hanson."

"Ellen," repeated the voice. "That's a fine old name."

"And this is my sister, Martha Murray."

"Delighted to meet you."

"And my son, Stevie, and my mother, Jessie Woolman."

"Stevie, Mrs. Woolman, it's my pleasure."

"Mr. Theopolis," said Martha, "would you—"

"Please call me Sam," murmured the voice.

"Sam, would you like us to call a locksmith?"

"If he had a screwdriver, he could take the door down," said Gregory.

"Take the door down!" exclaimed Dr. Whittaker.

"Is there a screwdriver handy and convenient?" inquired the voice. "If someone would be so kind as to step outside and pass it through the window . . ."

Gregory rose from the pudding pot, wiped his mouth on the bottom of his shirt, and said, "Where's the screwdriver, Doc?"

"Look in the tool drawer."

From the kitchen came a great clatter as Gregory pawed through the knives and forks. Presently he appeared in the garden, dragging a stepladder, and soon those assembled in the dining room heard the crunch and splintering of wood.

"One gone!" the voice sang out. "You're a great help, Stevie."

"Stevie?!" exclaimed Ellen.

"I'm here with Sam," said Stevie. "Gregory pushed me through the window."

"One what?" asked Jessie.

"One screw," answered Sam. "Oh, this will be easy."

Something chimed against the floor, and the bottom half of the door shifted ever so slightly. In the kitchen, the teakettle shrieked and died.

"That's Gregory," said Dr. Whittaker. "He's making tea."

"How much longer will this take?" asked Martha.

"Ask him about his references," whispered Ellen.

"We need references," said Martha. "Have you got any?"

A soft laugh rippled through the door. "Unfortunately, my cat can't give me a reference—at least not the usual kind. Anyone at the Buddha Uproar will vouch for my good character."

"We don't need a waiter," said Martha. "We need a care-giver."

"But that's what I do," said the voice. "I'm the comforter. I calm the customers when Fred insults them. Do you know Fred?"

Ellen shook her head and realized Sam couldn't see her, though he went on speaking as if he had.

"He's the owner and manager. He makes the chili. If he doesn't like your necktie, he'll cut it off."

"Terrible," whispered Dr. Whittaker.

"Where did you work before?" asked Martha.

"In a variety of places. For a month I worked on the maternity floor at St. Joseph's, snapping pictures of the newborns."

"That sounds fun," said Ellen.

"It wasn't. My flash set the whole nursery roaring. Then I took a job at a museum cleaning the skulls of birds. I had under my supervision a colony of carnivorous ants. They could clean two skulls in an hour."

"Your letter says you were studying to be a veterinarian," said Martha. "Why did you quit?"

A long silence followed.

"I had an accident."

Ellen and Martha exchanged glances. It seemed indelicate to question him about an accident with the door between them.

Gregory entered and set the teakettle on the table but did not pour any tea. He was staring at the door. The top gave a little heave.

"Have you ever eaten at the Buddha Uproar?" inquired the voice. To Ellen's relief, it sounded cheerful again. "Fred's five-alarm chili is without equal. And the garlic in it is positively addictive—I mean, if you like garlic."

"I don't care for garlic," said Jessie.

"Oh, you'd love Fred's chili. He lived for two years in an ashram and he prays over all the food. He knows this very soothing mantra. I'll sing it to you," proposed the voice, but got no further. With a wrenching and ripping of hinges, the door plunged toward them. Gregory leaped forward and caught it.

Dust and sunlight haloed the space around Stevie and a young man wearing jeans and carrying a white button-down shirt over his arm. His red hair was pulled back into a ponytail. As he took the child's hand and led him over the threshold, Ellen read the confession on his T-shirt with astonishment: I AM A MOTHER WHO LOVES TOO WELL. I HAVE FIFTEEN CHILDREN.

Jessie's face brightened.

# 7

---

They would go to the Barton Hills Country Club, Harvey decided. That would impress her. Only members and their guests were allowed. When he called Ellen and invited her to lunch, however, he was surprised to hear her hesitate.

"The Barton Hills Country Club has a wonderful smorgasbord," he said. "The Memorial Day special."

Ellen was so quiet he wondered if she'd hung up without his noticing.

"We could go someplace smaller," he added. "The Campus Inn. Or the Tuscany Villa."

"How about the Buddha Uproar?" she suggested.

He did not tell her he could not imagine going to the Buddha Uproar, deterred by the throngs of students and the greasy list of "specials" taped to the front window.

"If you like Indian food," he said, "I know a very good Indian restaurant in Briarwood."

"The man we've just hired to take care of Mother works at the Buddha Uproar," said Ellen. "He promised me a wonderful meal on the house if I came during his shift. Tomorrow is his last day."

"You hired a man from the Buddha Uproar to take care of your mother?"

"Not to take care of her, exactly," said Ellen. "Just to be in the house. Take her shopping, drive her to the doctor's. He has his own car. It's hard to find people willing to live in with someone they don't know."

"He's a live-in?" Harvey was incredulous.

"We gave him the third-floor room. It has a private bath." It took him less than an hour to move in, Ellen explained, because he had nothing to move except two boxes of books and a small leather valise. "And he can hardly wait to see the museum. Mother and he have great plans for it."

Harvey tried to sound calm. "You should never rush into things, Ellen. People prey on the elderly. Get them to sign over all their property. Oh, I've heard stories. What do you really know about this man? He might be hiding a terrible past."

"I don't think he was hiding anything except the cat," said Ellen. "He didn't tell us he was bringing the cat."

"That's very important, a cat. He should have told you."

"Her name is The Everpresent Fullness," added Ellen.

"Nothing smells up the icebox like an open can of cat food."

"The Everpresent Fullness eats rice."

At noon the next day, Ellen and Harvey drew themselves up to the last free table at the Buddha Uproar. Harvey marveled at the crush of customers in so small a place. Why, it was hardly worth opening a restaurant that served no more than ten tables. Posters layered the walls, and business cards for every service under heaven: rent-a-clown, calligraphy, healing with crystals, shamanism for the beginner.

The kitchen was tiny and open to view. At the grill, two cooks were arguing over a deep well of smoking oil, where chunks of broccoli hissed in wire baskets with long handles.

Three tables away sat Jack Chu, the district attorney, who nodded at him. Harvey nodded back. Well, of course he'd come here, Harvey told himself. This was the kind of food the guy grew up on. Chu always wore a suit and tie, and he had a habit of jingling the change in his pockets so that his smallest gestures seemed to be accompanied by tinkling bells.

The rest of the customers appeared to be students.

Ellen tapped him on the arm. "That's him," she said. "That's Sam."

A rangy young man, his hair pulled into a ponytail, was weaving his way among the tables. On his bare arms he balanced platters of rice like pieces of peculiar armor. He recognized Ellen and his face broke into a smile.

"Does his mother have fifteen children?" asked Harvey.

"No. His mother and father died in a fire. He told me he found the shirt in the laundromat. It was all tangled up with the stuff in the dryer. He figured somebody wanted to get rid of it."

Harvey touched his ear; the chatter of voices was so loud he could scarcely hear her. He loosened his collar. "There should be air conditioning in this place."

The heat weighed on Harvey's chest like a great soft stone. He could not take his eyes off the two cooks in the kitchen. The older man, heavyset and bald, might have been working under an invisible waterfall. Sweat poured down his face. He wiped his forehead with his apron; he shrieked to the other cook, "If you don't like it hot, get out!"

The other man, thin and dark-haired, didn't sweat at all. Dry and cool as a reptile, he chopped the scallions with swift strokes, as if he were executing them.

Sam was wiping their table with a wet dishcloth. "The curd patties with rice soup are good today," he said, "if you don't mind waiting for the patties."

Harvey found himself gazing up into Sam's face. He unfolded his handkerchief and wiped his forehead. To draw a breath in this room seemed more than any mortal should be asked to do.

"I'd like a dry martini."

"I'm sorry, sir, but we don't have a liquor license," said Sam. "You could get a very fine martini at any of our local bars—the Paradise, the Oasis, the Flamingo, the Purple Avocado—"

Harvey interrupted him with a wave of his hand. "Never mind. What'll you have, Ellen?"

"I'll have the rice soup," said Ellen.

"What's in the patties?" asked Harvey.

"Milk, coriander, and ghee."

What was ghee? He glanced around to see if anyone else was having a curd patty and observed, at the next table, something resembling an albino hamburger. "I'd like to see the menu," he said.

"You *are* seeing it, sir," said Sam. He pointed to the blackboard over the cash register, on which Harvey's gaze was resting.

"That's the menu?" asked Harvey. "That blackboard?" Though he stared and squinted, he could not turn the spidery scribbles into words. "What do you recommend?" he asked.

"Upma is good, sir. If you like brussels sprouts."

Until that moment, Harvey had never given brussels sprouts much thought.

"I'll have the upma," he said.

"There isn't any more," said Sam. "Jack Chu ate the last piece."

"You just told me it was good," said Harvey.

"It *was*," agreed Sam. "You asked me what I would recommend. Upma is one of Fred's specialties."

"Could you recommend something else?" asked Ellen.

"The tofu quiche is very good, if you like ginger." Pause. "It comes with a watercress and ginger salad."

"I've no objections to ginger," said Harvey.

"Are you enthusiastic about it?" asked Sam.

"Look," said Harvey, "can't you just take my order?"

Sam nodded and glided into the kitchen. He returned bearing a single bowl of golden broth, which he set before Ellen. A few grains of rice lay clumped together at the bottom.

"I'm sorry, sir, but we're out of tofu quiche. Jack Chu just ate the last piece."

Involuntarily, the three of them glanced over at Jack Chu. As if waiting for their attention, he lifted the metal cover from a footed dish and forked a golden wedge into his mouth.

"Well, I'm not having much luck, am I?" said Harvey. He was famished. It required a great effort to be polite. "Perhaps I'd better read the menu for myself."

He rose and made his way among the tables and planted himself directly in front of the blackboard. Sam, who had followed him, raised his dishcloth and swabbed away the words "upma" and "tofu quiche."

"There's only one thing left besides the tomato chutney," Harvey informed Ellen as he took his seat again. "I hope to God they have it. I loathe chutney."

Sam appeared at his side, pencil poised over his pad. "What'll it be, sir?"

"Prasadam. Whatever it is, I'll take it."

"You want to order prasadam?" inquired Sam, with a look of surprise.

"Yes. Don't tell me Jack Chu just ate the last piece."

"Oh, you can have prasadam," said Sam, "but not alone."

"What does it come with?"

"Tomato chutney."

"Chutney!"

"Or curd patties. You could have it with curd patties."

"Make it one order of soup and patties for me," said Harvey. "And two orders of prasadam. One for me and one for her."

"She already has it, sir."

"Where?" demanded Harvey.

"It's in the soup. It's in her mouth as she eats the soup. 'Prasadam' is Sanskrit for 'the mercy of God.' "

Ellen put down her spoon. "That's wonderful."

"To eat prasadam is to know the joy of tasting food that's been offered to Lord Krishna, sir. Krishna's lips have tasted this food and given it a soul. Fred prays over all the dishes."

What else does he do to them? Harvey wondered. And did praying affect the taste?

"I'll have the rice soup and patties, with or without prasadam," said Harvey.

Sam nodded and disappeared into the kitchen.

"Have some of mine while you're waiting," said Ellen. "I feel awful eating when you haven't even been served yet."

She handed him her spoon. Harvey dipped it into the soup, tasted it, and smacked his lips.

"Not bad. Quite good, really."

"Have some more."

"No, thanks. I can wait."

Presently Sam arrived with a second bowl of soup and set it before Harvey. It was murky as swamp water; something withered and black, like a mummified finger, floated toward him.

"I thought I was getting what she got," said Harvey, pointing to Ellen's bowl.

"You are," Sam assured him. "Yours came from a different part of the pot. Is there anything else I can get for you?"

"Before you go," said Harvey, "would you mind telling me what this is?" He nudged the mummified finger with his spoon.

"That's a tree ear, sir," said Sam.

"Isn't that a kind of mushroom?" asked Ellen. "I've seen them for sale at Foodtown."

Harvey wanted to ask, "Will it hurt me?" Instead, he ate

ravenously. Six pale patties arrived. He speared them on his fork and gobbled them up in a single bite.

"How are they?" asked Ellen. "Good?"

"They taste like wet blotting paper," replied Harvey. "No taste at all."

The words had scarcely left his lips when he bit down on a seed, and his tongue simmered and throbbed with a pain so exquisite that even as he reached for Ellen's water—Sam had not brought him any—he knew nothing would quench the fire. His tongue was destroyed; he would never speak again. His head ached. His stomach pursued a course of its own; it churned, it wambled, it heaved. Posters, announcements, business cards for calligraphy and catering, the two cooks fighting in the kitchen, even Jack Chu, merged like bees balled into an angry swarm.

I've been poisoned, thought Harvey.

"Are you all right?" asked Ellen.

"I'm fine. Don't I look fine?"

"You're gripping the edge of the table."

By a great effort, he managed to make his voice sound normal. "I think you should do a reference check on Sam."

"Mother wants him in the house to scare away burglars."

"He might be a burglar himself," said Harvey, "for all you know."

"He doesn't act like one."

"You never know how they're going to act," Harvey warned her. "You should watch this guy carefully. Appearances are deceiving."

Ellen laughed. "If appearances are deceiving, what's the use of watching him?"

By late afternoon the clouds over Ann Arbor shimmered a pale yellow, darkening quickly like bruised fruit. The air held its breath; parking lots all over the city glistened as if they were melting.

The third-floor room was stifling. Stevie thought he'd never seen a place so wonderful and so empty. Three plain brass bowls on the desk, one large, one medium, one small, held nothing at all. Sam's one-eyed tabby snoozed beside a notebook called "Ledger" and a slim paperback called *Invisibility: Mastering the Art of Vanishing*. Stevie fingered the book and Sam went right on mending the hole in his sock.

"Can you make me invisible?" asked Stevie.

"That book is disappointing," said Sam. "It doesn't tell you how to become invisible, just how to make people think you're invisible."

"Neat," said Stevie.

"But dangerous," said Sam. "I knew a guy in Drowning Bear who made himself invisible and nobody ever saw him again. What's *your* book about?"

"Surviving," said Stevie, and held it out to Sam, who took it and flipped through it slowly. It was then Stevie noticed the whistle Sam wore on a leather strip around his neck—not much bigger than a police whistle, but all patched together from different kinds of wood.

"That's a funny-looking whistle," he said, hoping Sam would invite him to blow it.

"I got it from the Dog Star Man, the guy I was just telling you about. It calls up spirits. Of course you can only see them if you have skinned eyes."

Stevie was appalled. How terrible to have your eyes skinned! Did Sam have an eye skinner? Probably it was a kind of potato peeler. He stared at Sam's eyes; they were green and clear, not raw. They didn't look different from his mother's or his own.

"Did you have your eyes skinned?" he asked.

Sam gave a whoop.

"Sweet Jesus, I didn't mean the skin actually comes off! Skinned eyes means you see what most people can't."

Outside the window, the world grew dark, as if a lid had been set over their lives.

"Bad storm coming," said Sam.

Thunder clapped Stevie on the back, and he jumped as he heard it rip the sky from its moorings. The gooseneck lamp on Sam's desk flickered and died.

"There was a tornado watch on TV," called Ellen from the second floor. "Head for the cellar. Mother is already there."

Ellen kept her hand on the banister and crept downstairs toward the windowed vestibule, past the photographs of Martha and herself as children, past her father and mother on their wedding day, all of them wide-eyed behind glass and touched with the faintest filament of light as the thunder struck again and lightning crazed the pear trees beyond the front door.

Behind her, Sam's voice had never sounded calmer. "Stevie, this is nothing compared to the thunder I've heard up around Thunder Bay. If you go to Thunder Bay, you can watch the Thunderbird throwing fireballs at the Water Tiger. And when the Water Tiger switches his tail—watch out!"

Ought to have flashlights, Ellen told herself. Trying to hurry, she bumped into the telephone table and groped her way to the kitchen and the basement door.

"Mother, we're coming."

"Clump, clump, clump," sang Stevie as he and Sam marched down the cellar stairs. "Look, Mom, I brought my survival book." By the ashen light sifting through the windows from the world above he opened the book and read, " 'Your greatest obstacle is fear of the unknown. Remember that many men, and women too, have faced the unknown and come through. What they did, you too can do.' "

"Dinner's all ready," Jessie said cheerfully. "We're having Spam."

"Spam?!" exclaimed Ellen, and almost bumped into the card table, set with plates and forks that had lost their luster thirty years ago, and four kitchen chairs Martha had twice tried to throw away; Jessie always found them and hauled them back. A wedge of Spam squatted cold and lonely on the broken platter.

"It smells divine," said Sam. "We should do this more often."

"Mother, how old is this meat?"

"It's perfectly safe," she said. "I just opened it today."

"But how long has it been in the cellar? You haven't eaten Spam since the Second World War."

And now the rain clattered hard against the glass, battering but not breaking it.

"I can't see a thing," said Jessie. "If only we had Henry's map."

"Sit down, Mother."

"Here's Henry's barometer and my father's stethoscope," said Jessie, "and a nice picture of John in Vietnam."

"You have wonderful night vision, Mrs. Woolman," said Sam.

"I can tell by the frame. It's got a flag carved on it."

"Maybe you can see what just fell on the house," said Sam.

"Can I have the stethoscope?" asked Stevie.

"You can borrow it," said Jessie, "for as long as you need it."

"And here's my father's little grindstone," said Jessie. "Henry used to sharpen our knives on it."

At that moment something crashed against the window, throwing the cellar into total darkness. Ah, it was the old elm, the rotten one Mike had warned Jessie about. *You've either got to get it braced or take it down.*

Ellen started; his voice in her head sounded as clear as if he were in the room. Behind her, something was sucking in all traces of human warmth around her, tucking her into a small icy pocket.

Oh, how had she never noticed the dangerous undertow pulling her toward him and his bed under the earth? Molecule by molecule she was drifting to meet him, like an old barn caving in on itself.

She opened her mouth to cry out, but her voice had gone on without her and no cry came.

"Mom?" whispered Stevie, edging closer to Sam. "Mom?"

Sam's arm reached out, circled her shoulders, and drew Stevie and Ellen toward him, and she found herself clutching his shirt and hanging on for dear life.

At eleven o'clock Martha set the laundry spinning and climbed into bed beside John, who was already asleep, his arm thrown over his head as if protecting it from the storm.

Thank God we didn't lose power, she thought.

She tried willing herself to sleep, but questions bombarded her. Which is better, confetti or rose petals? Did the Episcopal church have kneeling cushions? She'd never set foot in the Episcopal church. Elmer wanted kneelers in the pews and a long aisle; he'd measured the aisles in four different churches. When Allison pointed out that her family was Congregational and his was Methodist, Elmer assured her it didn't matter. On Saturdays the church was used by a congregation of reformed Jews who had lost their temple in a fire. The star of David, hinged to the cross over the altar, was flipped down on Friday night and flipped up on Sunday morning. Reverend Peele had designed it himself and was applying for a patent.

It was funny how many things Elmer and Allison couldn't agree on, Martha thought—like that fight they'd had over the wedding dress. With their apartments right across the street from each other, you'd think they could talk their problems out.

Closing her eyes, she saw simplified versions of John and herself, Allison and Elmer, Ellen and Stevie, Jessie and Sam, lined up on the coffee table like chess pieces. She picked up Ellen and Stevie and moved them into Jessie's house. Into Ellen's apartment she dropped several blank pieces labeled "Extra Guests."

A voice in her mind went on writing and rewriting the story for the *Ann Arbor News:*

> *Allison Murray, the daughter of Mr. and Mrs. John Murray of Ann Arbor, was married on Saturday, July 20, in an afternoon ceremony at St. James Episcopal Church to Elmer Schautz, the son of Emma Schautz of Kalamazoo and the late Peter Schautz.*
> *The bride, 21, is a graduate of Eastern Michigan University. She is employed at Great Lakes Savings and Loan. The bride-groom—*

She wondered if the paper would let her mention that big lawsuit Elmer won against Kmart. Probably not. But she would include it, just in case.

> *The bridegroom, 32, graduated from Boston University and received his law degree from the University of Michigan. He is with the firm of Beebee, Link, and Stein—*

Martha climbed out of bed, careful not to wake John, and groped her way to the telephone in search of a pen. As if it were lying in wait for her, the telephone rang. She snatched the receiver off the hook.

"Hello?"

"Martha? There's a strange man on the third floor, and he's running the bathwater."

"It's all right, Mother. That's Sam. He's supposed to be there."

"He has wings," whispered her mother.

"Mother, I'm sure he doesn't have wings."

The stillness on the line was so sudden that Martha feared the phone had gone dead, and she was about to hang up when Ellen's voice broke through.

"Hello?"

"Ellen, is Sam taking a bath?"

"For heaven's sake, did you call just to ask me that?"

"I didn't call you. Mother called me."

"She's been awfully upset. A tree blew down in the yard and we lost power for two hours. Did you and Allison—"

"We postponed it till tomorrow. Because of the storm," said Martha. "I'll call the tree people in the morning."

Two blocks from her mother's house on the following afternoon, Martha could hear the whine of the saws.

Lord, but the yard was a mess! Sawdust heaped in blond piles on the grass, the broken trunk and chunked branches looking like parts of a torso branded with rings around a rotten core.

No use even saying good morning to the two men working the saws. They couldn't hear a thing.

All at once the sawing stopped and in the silence that followed she heard the tinkle of the piano and Sam's strong voice floating over it:

*Well, the first days are the hardest days.*
*Don't you worry anymore.*

*When life looks like Easy Street,*
*There is danger at your door.*

Alarmed, Martha pounded on the front door.

"It's open," called Sam. "Come on in."

Sam and Jessie were sitting together on the piano bench as if they were playing a duet.

*Like the morning sun you come,*
*And like the wind you go.*
*Ain't got no time to hate.*
*Barely time to wait.*
*Where does the time go?*

Jessie caught sight of Martha and waved at her.

"Sam plays all his music by ear," she said. "I told him, 'If it's not in the hymnal or the *Michigan Song Book,* we don't have it.' "

"You have a marvelous ear yourself, Mrs. Woolman."

"And Sam is writing us all down. He's filled up a whole notebook already."

"What kinds of things do you write?" asked Martha. The discovery did not please her.

"I'm not exactly a writer," Sam corrected her. "I'm a listener. I'm listening for clues about day-to-day life on the planet."

"But you do write things down?" asked Jessie.

"Of course," said Sam.

"Are you writing a book?" demanded Martha.

"No," said Sam. "I'm saving stories. So a hundred years from now people will know how it was with us. What a stroke of luck that we're on this planet at all—a small change in time or temperature, and we might never have made it."

.    .    .

From the fitting rooms of the bridal salon rose a bustle and hum. Martha noted with satisfaction that almost nothing had changed since her own wedding twenty-four years earlier. The white satin dais in front of the three-way mirror, the lace slipper, the white satin pillow and prayer book on the glass coffee table; the desk with its album of photographs, showing perfect weddings in which no detail had been overlooked. As Allison fingered the veil on the head of the mannequin, Martha felt a twinge of hope: maybe they would get through the fitting without a crisis. But kindly Mrs. Plum, the bridal consultant whom Martha remembered, had been replaced by a sleek young woman in a tweed suit who rose from her desk when she saw Martha approaching.

"I'm Mrs. Nollman. How can I help you?"

"We'd like to look at this dress," said Martha, and uncrumpled the page from her purse.

Mrs. Nollman glanced at it and nodded. "We have it. But the fitting rooms are full."

"We'll wait," said Martha.

A mother and daughter emerged from behind the curtain that hid the rooms.

"Let's get a cup of coffee and think about it," said the girl.

The mother gave a low cluck, like a grieving hen. "Marie, if you could only lose ten pounds."

"The last room is free," said Mrs. Nollman, nudging Allison forward. "Why don't you just pop in, honey, and I'll bring you the dress. What are you—about a twelve?"

Martha sat down on the wicker settee and waited for her daughter to emerge. Here comes the bride, she thought. Thank heaven. I ought to look through that rack of bridesmaid's dresses, but I'm just too tired.

A shrill voice assaulted her from one of the fitting rooms. "And while they were on their honeymoon, the septic tank exploded! Believe me, I'd have gone to the wedding with my dress wrong side out. I mean, with her luck, why take a chance?"

"Can I use your phone to make a local call?" asked Martha.

"Dial nine first," said Mrs. Nollman. She pointed to a gold phone on the wall nearest the cash register, and disappeared behind the curtains, shepherding Allison before her. Martha took Elmer's number from her purse and dialed.

"And to top it off, he's bald," the shrill voice continued.

"I happen to like bald men," said a softer voice. "It takes some people a couple of husbands to find the right one."

"Beebee, Link, and Stein," said the receiver.

"Can I speak to Elmer Schautz?"

"He's away from his desk for a few—"

"I'm here," Elmer broke in. "How's it going?"

"Allison is in the fitting room."

"I wonder if she'd mind my coming over now," said Elmer wistfully. "I'd love to see how she looks."

"Of course she wouldn't. Come right away."

"Is it the dress on page 163?" asked Elmer.

"That's what the clerk said."

"The one on page 305 was also nice."

"Elmer, this is a one-dress day. It's a real mob down here," said Martha. "We were lucky to get any service at all."

What is taking Allison so long? she wondered. Mrs. Nollman was directing a brisk traffic between the fitting rooms and the dais in front of the mirror. "Which booth did my daughter go into?" Martha inquired.

"The one on the end," said Mrs. Nollman.

They hovered outside the pink chintz curtains, listening to the chatter of mothers and daughters all around them.

"The buttons go in back, honey," called Mrs. Nollman.

No answer. In the next booth, a thin, dark woman wearing a blue silk cocktail dress pushed the curtain aside and stepped out for inspection. The tags twinkled at her wrist like cheap jewelry.

"Elsie wants to get married in all fifty states," she announced. "They'll hit California in November, New Mexico in January, Arizona in March, Kentucky in April—"

"That's wonderful," said Mrs. Nollman. She was eying Allison's booth.

"She just graduated from Washtenaw Community last month. She wanted to major in the Bible, but I told her, 'Why pay money to read the Bible? You can read the Bible in a motel.' "

"Blue silk looks great on video," said Mrs. Nollman.

The thin woman went out into the store to study herself in the mirror. A short, plump woman emerged from another booth, wearing the same dress. "Videos are the ultimate," she sighed. "I wish I'd had one when Tom and I got married."

"Did you ever watch Fergie's wedding on video? The kiss goes on forever," said Mrs. Nollman.

"It's so much easier for kids to kiss these days," said the plump woman. "Whenever Tom came to my house, my mother watched him like a hawk. We used to go to the airport and kiss by the gates."

What on earth is taking Allison so long? thought Martha. She drew near the closed curtains and hissed, "Allison, you've been in there for hours."

"No, I haven't." Her voice was damp and tragic.

Oh, God, was she crying? Martha was about to push the chintz aside when Mrs. Nollman said, "Someone's here to see your daughter."

"Who is it?" demanded Allison.

"Elmer," said Martha. "He wants to see you in your dress."

"Mother, I *hate* this dress. I want the one on page 42."

"Honey, give the dress a chance. It's so important to Elmer."

"You think it's not important to me?"

"A lot of men don't care about details like this. Elmer is one in a million."

Elmer was waiting on the wicker settee, and he jumped up when Martha appeared.

"She'll be here in a second," said Martha. Out of the corner of her eye she spied Allison in the mirror, leaning on Mrs. Nollman's arm.

"We'd hate to get anything on that gown," said Mrs. Nollman, handing her a Kleenex. "Mascara is so hard to get off."

Allison, who was not wearing any makeup at all, accepted the Kleenex and blew her nose, and allowed Mrs. Nollman to help her ascend the dais. Martha and Elmer stepped back to admire her. Elmer was holding the store copy of *Modern Bride* with his finger at page 163.

"This is the prettier gown," said Elmer. "No question about it."

"The seed pearls on the bodice simply make this gown!" exclaimed Mrs. Nollman, as if she'd never laid eyes on it before in her life. "And we have a shorter version in yellow for the maid of honor."

"Has she asked anyone yet?" said Elmer, turning to Martha.

"No, I haven't," said Allison.

"Oh, good," said Elmer. "I thought we might ask my sister."

"Elmer, I've never met your sister."

"I mean, if you have no one else in mind. My sister is very calm and responsible."

"Does it have to be a maid?" asked Allison.

"You mean, you want a man for your maid of honor?!" exclaimed Mrs. Nollman.

Martha said, "You two can settle this without me. I've got lots to do at home."

As Allison stepped off the dais, Martha caught sight of them all in the three-way mirror, a chain of mothers and daughters and bridegrooms marching to eternity, growing smaller and smaller as they moved down that lonesome road to love.

# 8

---

Ten days before Stevie's school term ended, Ellen got a call from Mr. Gould, the counselor, urging her to come in at once. Stevie, he said, was having problems.

Ellen hurried down the quiet corridor, tapestried with small painted animals taped to the walls under the words SAVE THE EARTH! SAVE THE AIR! SAVE THE WATER! Through the window in each door, she saw children, heads bent to their tasks. When she stepped into the counselor's office, crammed with file cabinets and coffee mugs, she felt as if she'd failed something—she could no longer remember what, so completely had she sloughed it off like an old skin—and now she would have to defend herself.

"I'm Mr. Gould." He stood up to meet her and offered her a chair. He was a short man, nearly bald except for a russet tuft in front that made Ellen think of a titmouse.

Ellen nodded and sat down.

"It's perfectly normal for a child to do badly in school after an emotional trauma," said Mr. Gould, gazing out of the window as if he were speaking of someone else's child who happened to be walking by. "Especially when the trauma is a sudden death. Your husband died in a car accident, didn't he?"

"Yes," said Ellen.

"According to Mrs. Scott's report, your son is having trouble with numbers. He thinks they have personalities."

"Personalities?"

"He told her that two and four can't stand each other. So when the answer to a problem is twenty-four, Stevie changes it."

"To what?" asked Ellen, baffled.

"Thirty-four. Or twenty-five. Or twenty-three."

"You mean he deliberately gives the wrong answer?"

"He changes the answer," said Mr. Gould, "to two numbers that like each other."

"Stevie has never said a word to me about numbers liking each other," said Ellen. She tried not to sound as if she were accusing Mr. Gould of lying. "Or not liking each other."

"Mrs. Hanson, we'll do everything we can to help Stevie through this period. In the fall we'll re-evaluate him. I'm sure your talking to him will help—"

A bell rang in the corridor and Mr. Gould stood up, and Ellen understood that the interview was over.


When she returned to the house, she found Martha, barefoot, wearing her green silk dress and mowing the lawn.

"The ChemLawn people didn't show up," she panted as she pushed the mower uphill. "The front yard looks like a field, and the electric mower is broken—Sam took it in for repairs. You got a call from Harvey Mack. He wants you and Stevie to join him for dinner."

"Did he really say to bring Stevie?!" exclaimed Ellen.

"He did," said Martha. She stopped mowing and leaned on the handle. "He said he thought Stevie might like to use his pitching machine."

"I thought only health clubs had pitching machines."

"Didn't you tell me he lives in Barton Hills?" said Martha. "All the houses up there are huge."

When he came home from school Stevie saw his long pants laid out on his bed and asked his mother if they were going to church.

"Who said anything about church? We're going to dinner at Harvey Mack's house. He wants to show you his pitching machine."

"A real pitching machine?" squealed Stevie.

"That's what he says."

As he ran for the car, his mother called out, "We're not leaving till five. He's invited us to dinner."

Stevie was surprised. He knew that certain parts of his mother's life did not include him, and he did not hold it against her, since these events unfolded when he was in school or asleep, and he was sure they lacked the brilliance and permanence his attention would have given them.

Now he sat in the front seat of the Buick, trying not to wrinkle his shirt. The sleeves were too short, and he tugged at them.

His mother drove down Main Street, climbing along the river into Barton Hills. Suddenly the houses grew shy and went into hiding behind shaped hedges and stone walls, though now and then a chimney or a weather vane over the trees gave one away.

Ellen turned into a broad circular drive; the gravel crunched under the wheels.

The house at the top of the drive was enormous. With its white pillars and neatly clipped shrubbery, it looked to Stevie like the public library, only grander; an expanse of lawn stretched to the left toward a tennis court and sloped to the right into a rolling hill that ended at the water. Dwarf trees gazed out of the picture windows at the freeborn maples, sycamores, and oaks.

Spotlights hidden in the shrubbery were trained on the house, though Stevie could not imagine anyone needing a light to find it: darkness would not arrive for hours.

Was his mother a little frightened too? he wondered, as she took his hand and led him up the steps to the front porch. Over the doorbell gleamed a brass plaque: HOUSE OF MACK. ESTABLISHED DECEMBER 12, 1972. The doorbell glowed. It could be radioactive, thought Stevie.

"Press the button," said his mother.

He rested his finger on the button but did not push it. "Is Harvey rich?" he asked.

"Yes," said Ellen. "But it's not polite to talk about money."

"Are we poor?"

"Certainly not! Go on, ring."

He pushed the button, and two loud tones sang out: *ding* DONG.

Instantly, as if he had been watching them through the keyhole, Harvey opened the door. He leaned over—oh, the terrible blue of his eyes behind his spectacles!—and seized Stevie's hand in his cold, dry palm.

"I'm so glad to see you, Stevie."

The moment he stepped indoors, Stevie felt he was in danger of becoming extinct. A thick blue carpet flowed from the hall into the living room; he could no longer hear the sound of his own footsteps. A ponderous urn of lilies leaning out of a niche in the foyer brushed him. Stevie touched one. Fake.

In the living room, two black leather armchairs were facing off. Against the silver flowered wallpaper rose three floor lamps, crowned with milky bowls of light. There was an ebony coffee table and a black leather sofa in front of the fireplace, and a grand piano with its top raised, giving it the risen bulk of a beached whale, and an enormous globe of the world on a thin wooden tripod. Stevie wanted very much to run over and spin it. Instead, he tiptoed to the piano and brushed the keys.

Harvey stole up behind him. Stevie smelled him coming: a strong spicy scent that made his nose prickle.

"This was my wife's piano," said Harvey. "I've always regretted that I can't play."

But you can, thought Stevie. You can come into this room and play it any time you want to.

Ellen sat down on the sofa; the cushions hissed at her like well-bred serpents. Stevie nudged as close to her as he could. The fireplace was very clean. A brass fan gleamed where the fire should be.

"Something smells good," said Ellen. "What is it?"

"My famous lemon chicken," replied Harvey. "Make yourselves at home. I have to check my traps."

"What are you trapping?" asked Ellen.

"I've had a perfect invasion of toads in the kitchen, and I can't imagine how they're getting in. This house is built on a bluff. I've sprinkled poison pellets in every corner. Excuse me."

They listened to the rattle of pots in the kitchen.

"Mom, let's go home."

"We just got here," said Ellen. "We can't get up and leave before dinner."

"I don't want to see his pitching machine," said Stevie. "He poisons toads."

Before Ellen could answer, they heard footsteps and Harvey returned carrying a plate. "Help yourselves," he said, and knelt to offer it. Some of the crackers were smeared with—was it cheese? What Stevie saw on the others appalled him.

Ellen reached for a cheese one.

"What about you, Stevie?" asked Harvey.

"No, thank you."

"In my house, children try a little of everything," said Harvey. "Take one, Stevie."

"I don't like minnows," said Stevie.

Harvey burst out laughing. Stevie had not imagined his laughter would sound so clattery and hollow, as if something deep inside were laughing for him.

"Those are anchovies, Stevie," said Harvey. "Not minnows. Maybe you'd rather have the Brie?"

The cheese, soft and pale, smelled like vomit. Stevie was dismayed to see his mother eating hers as if she really enjoyed it.

"I'm waiting, Stevie," said Harvey.

Stevie plucked an anchovy cracker from the plate and held it in his hand.

"I'm dying of thirst," said Ellen.

"Let's have something to drink," said Harvey. As he turned to set the plate on the coffee table, Stevie stuffed the cracker into his back pocket and rubbed his polluted hand on his trousers.

"Stevie, my little man," said Harvey, "you can help me. Keep your eye on that wall." And he pointed to the wall behind the quarrelsome chairs.

Why Harvey should want him to keep an eye on the wall Stevie could not imagine, but he fixed his gaze obediently on the silver flowers and noticed an area in which the flowers flared more brightly, as if a picture had once hung on that space, protecting it. Behind their petals, something rumbled and whirred.

Alarmed, Stevie leaned forward. What was happening to the wall that had looked so ingenuous, so free of mystery? Between jerks and creaks, a secret drawer was thrusting itself toward them, bearing a dozen cans of Pepsi, Vernors, and Dr Pepper huddled together, clinking and clanking, obviously taken by surprise.

"Wow!"

Stevie reached for a Dr Pepper, and Harvey's large hand closed over his own small one. "Not so fast, Stevie."

From deep in the hidden heart of the wall tinkled a tune.

"It's 'Raindrops Keep Falling on My Head,' " observed Ellen. They listened respectfully to the end.

"Ever seen anything like that, Stevie?" asked Harvey. Stevie shook his head, and Harvey smiled at him. "I'll bet you haven't. Take a Dr Pepper."

"No, thanks," said Stevie.

"Why, Stevie," exclaimed Ellen, "you love Dr Pepper!"

"I don't want any," said Stevie.

Harvey touched a spot on the rug with his heel. With great dignity, the beverages retreated, and the wall sealed itself up as before. Though Stevie stared at the site of their disappearance, he could not tell where they had gone.

"He says he doesn't want any, Ellen. I'm not going to offer it to him again. You and I can have something stronger if Stevie would be kind enough to open that globe. Let's see if he can figure out how it works."

Stevie examined the globe. It was much larger than the globe of the world at school, whose countries he could recognize at a glance. Harvey's world stood on the four legs of a beast. You could not tell what kind of beast it was, only that it had claws. A wooden ledge ran all around the equator. The oceans were the color of pancake batter, and the nations had lost their familiar cities, houses, and boundaries. He could not find Africa or South America. He could not even find his own country.

"Well, Stevie?"

The boy saw neither latch nor handle. The globe remained as shut and secretive as an egg.

"Does the top lift?" asked Ellen. "Try lifting the top."

He grasped the brass rim and pushed. To his delight, the upper hemisphere, deep blue and sown with stars, rose on a single hinge. "Oh," he breathed. "Oh, wow!"

Four crystal decanters and six goblets nestled in the deep bowl of the earth. He peered into heaven and recognized his old friends—the ram, the fish, the eagle, and the swan. His dad had often shown him their bright bodies in the summer sky.

"What'll you have, Ellen? Gin? Vodka?"

"I'll have a Dr Pepper," said Ellen.

"Dr Pepper? Whatever you want, Ellen."

Harvey spun around and stamped his foot at the small lump in the carpet. Deep inside the wall, the creaking and groaning of gears started up again. And then came a new sound: a gnashing and grinding of teeth.

Harvey jumped to his feet. "It's jammed. Nobody touch it."

Nobody was. An ominous silence followed.

"I think Stevie would love to see your pitching machine," said Ellen.

She took Stevie's hand and they followed Harvey, who touched the light switches as they passed through his house, waking room after room, immaculate, unused, until they stopped in front of a door at the end of the hall. "This is where I keep my toys," announced Harvey, and he opened it.

The room was large and looked so empty that Stevie was surprised at the number of machines kept in it. There was a rowing machine and an exercise bicycle with headphones attached and several machines whose use he could not fathom. Behind the bicycle stood the pitching machine, in its caged corridor. Stevie plucked a baseball from the basket by the machine.

His mother was studying a large drawing on the wall. It

showed several dozen buildings on different levels connected by winding stairs, built around an empty circle on which was written "Pool and Memorial Fountain."

"What is this?" asked Ellen.

"Plans for the Pawquacha Plaza," answered Harvey. "My new shopping mall," he added.

"Where's the museum?" said Ellen. "I don't see the museum."

"The museum would be about here," said Harvey, and he made a sweeping gesture across the bottom half of the drawing. "It would require extensive remodeling, of course."

"Mother will never agree to remodeling," said Ellen. "And Sam loathes shopping malls."

"What does Sam have to do with it?"

"He's going to open the museum again."

"That's not a museum. It's a storehouse full of junk. Nothing is catalogued. Nothing is for sale."

"Why should there be anything for sale?"

"Museums sell things, Ellen. They have gift shops. Museums are big business."

"Not this one," said Ellen. "Sam and I will run it the same way Mike did."

"You're planning to run it with Sam?" exclaimed Harvey.

"I couldn't possibly run it with anyone else," said Ellen.

Suddenly Harvey drew back. "Stevie, did you scribble this face on my plans?"

His voice was so severe that Stevie dropped the baseball. "What face?" he whispered.

"Right in the middle of the fountain." Harvey laid his finger on the space in the center of the pool. For several minutes the three of them stared at it.

"I don't see a face," said Ellen. "And Stevie would never scribble on someone else's walls."

"It's gone now," said Harvey. "Must have been a shadow. My apologies, Stevie."

Better not to look at the drawing if it was going to behave that way, Stevie decided, though he couldn't imagine how their looking at it could possibly have changed the drawing itself.

To the left of the pitching machine stood a full-sized silver tricycle. The intricate radiance of its spokes and the cunning workmanship of its gears almost took his breath away. As Stevie darted forward, a hand clutched the back of his collar.

"It is polite to ask permission, Stevie, before using other people's things."

Stevie stood rubbing the back of his neck.

"You can play with my tricycle," said Harvey. "I give you my permission, Stevie."

"No, thanks," said Stevie.

"Changed your mind?" asked Harvey.

Stevie nodded.

"If there's anything you want that you don't see, just ask for it," said Harvey.

"The Visible Man," said Stevie. "Do you have the Visible Man?"

"Who is the Visible Man?!" exclaimed Harvey.

"Harvey didn't mean anything you *want*," said Ellen. "Just— anything he happens to have."

"He said 'anything,'" muttered Stevie.

"Who is the Visible Man?" demanded Harvey.

"He comes in a kit," said Stevie. "You have to put him together. You start with his bones—"

"Something's burning!" cried Ellen.

Harvey turned and fled down the long hallway toward the kitchen.

"I think he could use some help," said Ellen, and followed him.

Stevie sat on the rowing machine and listened to their voices and averted his gaze from the plans for Pawquacha Plaza.

What was in the other rooms? He tiptoed down the carpeted hall. A light shone under the first door to his right, and he pushed it open. Everything, from the toilet to the sink to the scales, gleamed a fierce antiseptic white. A marble goddess held the toilet paper aloft for his inspection. The marble bowl at her feet held an enviable collection of matchbooks: the Four Seasons, the Continental, the Hilton.

Four steps led down into the sunken bathtub, pearly-white and six-sided, like a jewel box for a giant. And beside the bathtub —he could hardly believe it: a telephone.

He touched the goddess.

He touched the sink, perfect and creamy as an ostrich egg.

He touched the towel rack over the tub and found it pleasingly warm.

He touched the medicine cabinet over the sink, and its mirrored door swung open. Medicine bottles crammed the shelves —not the drugstore kind, he noticed, but the small brown canisters with typed labels you got from the doctor. Harvey must be very sick to have so many. Maybe he would die soon.

Cheered by this discovery, Stevie stepped on the scales. To his astonishment, a voice said, "You have lost one hundred and forty pounds. Have a nice day."

Ah, this was better than the silver tricycle! He lugged the goddess to the scales, and the voice informed him he had gained fifteen pounds.

He shoved the goddess off and stood on the scales himself, and again the voice made its rapid calculations without complaint.

He pushed the goddess back on board and climbed on behind her. "My battery is getting low," the voice warned him.

Stevie gave a little jump. "Overload," said the scales severely. "Goodbye."

Fright gripped him. He tried to remember exactly where the goddess had stood; Harvey would surely notice she'd been moved. But maybe not until after he and his mother were safe at home.

As he sat in the rowing machine waiting for her, a smothering weariness came over him. He did not remember falling asleep, only waking up. His mother was shaking him.

"We'll stop at the Wolverine on the way home," she said. "You slept right through dinner. I couldn't wake you up at all." And to his surprise, she picked him up, just the way she used to when he was much younger.

Harvey said, "He's much too old to be carried."

But now Stevie and his mother were outside, and she was lifting him into the front seat beside her and buckling his safety belt, and Harvey's voice sounded fainter and fainter, powerless to follow them between the grass and the stars through the clear winding space that led home.

# 9

---

He came back. He kept coming back. Not as a ghost or a spirit or a voice; not in a spooky way. But he came back because he was always there, at the edge of her consciousness, and the slightest fragrance or trick of the light would unmask him.

Before Ellen climbed out of bed, before she even opened her eyes, she saw Mike in his coffin drifting over the place of his own darkness, not turning to silver or quartz or garnet but sinking into the vast bed of the spinning earth, the only place they would ever again sleep together.

I've got to break free of this, she told herself as she stumbled to the bathroom. The alarm clock on the dresser said five. Five in the morning. Nobody else would be up for hours.

Stevie's door was open, and she made a quick check on him. He'd wrapped a corner of his sheet around his thumb and he was sucking it. In the green light from the aquarium, his face seemed that of a drowned man. At his feet curled The Everpresent Fullness, who peered at Ellen through her slitty eye.

Feeling her shadow across their landscape, the fish woke up and nosed the surface of the water for food, and she admired the glint of their bodies, splinters and chips of light.

Was it harmful for a kid to sleep by water light and listen to water talk, she wondered, night after night?

Across the top of the aquarium lay the old stethoscope. A loan from her mother to Stevie; when he showed no interest in it, Jessie would carry it back to the cellar or maybe the museum. Ellen picked it up, plugged the ends into her ears, and pressed the little amplifier against the glass. The hum of the motor and the bubbling from the filter disappointed her. Two angelfish drifted past her like coins dropped into a well by wish makers.

Mike buying the angels, bringing them home in a paper carton. Nose pressed to the glass, Stevie on his lap, the two of them watching.

She tiptoed out of the room, sat down at the top of the stairs, and broke into sobs.

Suddenly the front door opened, and she froze. There at the foot of the stairs stood Sam, in denim shorts and T-shirt, his hair lank with sweat. He was holding a small scythe.

"I'm sorry," he stammered. "Mrs. Woolman's yard needed mowing, and both the lawn mowers are broken."

"Both of them?" said Ellen. The steadiness of her own voice surprised her. "That's funny."

Sam was staring at her. "How about you and me going to the Wolverine for breakfast?" he said. "It's open twenty-four hours."

She hesitated.

"Your mom won't be up before eleven. And Stevie didn't fall asleep till two."

"Two? I said good night to him at nine."

Sam shrugged. "That was before he came upstairs to visit me. I'm teaching him to play my singing bowls."

"Singing bowls?"

"If you strike them, they hum in harmony. Stevie got interested in them when I showed him how to write the intervals as a series of numbers. He said he was very glad to know that the numbers were getting along so well and now he wouldn't have to worry about them."

"He's had trouble in school with numbers," said Ellen. "Look, I don't want him bothering you."

"He's not bothering me. He knows I like to write at night."

"What are you writing?"

"A journal on the present, stories from the past. Get dressed and leave him a note telling him where we've gone. I'll wait for you downstairs."

She splashed cold water on her face, gathered her hair into a barrette, slipped into her jeans and work shirt, and met him at the foot of the walk in front of his car.

"You look beautiful," he said. "Do you feel like walking twenty blocks? My car is in delicate health. And you know it never runs on Saturdays."

No wonder, thought Ellen. It wasn't a car; it was a blue pastiche—a Dodge Dart overlaid with a Ford fender and a Chrysler door and an Oldsmobile bumper. He'd bought it from a girl who was getting her doctorate in Jewish studies. On the Sabbath, the car rested.

They set out along the quiet streets into a day not yet cluttered with tasks and appointments. Not talking much. Glad for the blessing of sunlight.

Suddenly Sam said, "I know a man whose girlfriend died not long after he'd graduated from college. She died but she hung around too. She'd show up in his dreams and lay these tasks on him. One night she said to him, 'I want you to sponsor a baseball team in my memory. I want nine men to wear my name on their uniforms.'

"The man told his girlfriend that such an undertaking would be awfully expensive, and the girlfriend said she'd settle for a

Little League team, as long as she got her name on the uniforms. It pained the man to tell her that baseball season had already started. If she wanted a team, she'd have to wait till next year.

"The girlfriend stayed away for a couple of weeks, and then one night she showed up again. 'I want you to win the Boston Marathon in my honor,' she told him. The man explained that he couldn't possibly win the Boston Marathon—he wasn't a long-distance runner, and no amount of training would turn him into one. 'You were on the track team in high school,' she told him. 'You must have been pretty good.' 'Not *that* good,' said the man.

" 'How about building a bridge over the English Channel and naming it after me?'

" 'Molly, what's gotten into you?' the man said. 'You were never this competitive when you were alive.'

" 'When I was alive, I could make things happen. Now I'm nobody. I'm forgotten.' "

Sam paused, as if waiting for Ellen's permission to finish the story.

"So what happened?" asked Ellen.

"Every night the girl showed up in his dreams, saying, 'Along State Street my name is no longer spoken. After you're gone, who will care that a girl named Molly Flannagan lived and died in this town? So long as you're alive, I'll come back.' "

" 'Enough is enough,' said the man.

"First he went to a priest, though he wasn't Catholic. The priest said, 'Since you can't change your girlfriend, change yourself. Don't let these visits bother you. Welcome her spirit as you would a distant relative. You'll get used to her. You can sleep through an earthquake if you're tired enough.'

"The man thanked the priest and went to a rabbi, though he wasn't Jewish. When the rabbi had listened to the whole story he said, 'What kind of flowers did this girl like best?' 'Daisies,' said the man.

" 'When this girl was alive, what places did she love to visit?' 'The Farmers' Market and Pasqual's Mexican restaurant. Sunday morning she loved to read the paper on the terrace at the student union, where she could look out across the lake.'

" 'And what places did you visit together?'

"The man was silent. He had already forgotten.

" 'I want you to run, at your own pace, to all the places this girl loved. I want you to stop at each one and leave daisies. Not just at the market and the lake, but the places you loved together. You won't know those places until you start running.' "

"And did the girl ever come back again?" asked Ellen.

"Only once," answered Sam. "On Thanksgiving. Somebody who'd read about the mysterious appearance of daisies all over the city made up a song about it. It was called 'Who Left the Daisies and Who Stole the Rain?' and all the local stations were playing it. The girlfriend wanted to hear it for herself, loud and clear. She said where she'd just come from the reception was terrible."

They had arrived at the Wolverine Den, and Sam held the door open for Ellen. The restaurant was empty save for the cook, visible through a window in the kitchen door.

"Do you want a booth or a table? We have the place to ourselves."

"Oh, a booth," said Ellen.

They slid into a booth, and Sam pulled out two menus, sandwiched between the catsup and the ashtray, and handed one to Ellen.

"Is that a true story?" she asked.

"It's true," said Sam, "the way stories are true."

"Why did you tell it to me?"

"I thought you could use it."

"I'm not a runner," said Ellen, "and Mike doesn't show up with instructions. He just shows up."

"When did you visit him last?"

"You mean his grave?"

Sam nodded.

"I haven't been out to his grave since the funeral."

The appearance of the cook interrupted them. A sleepy-eyed, tousle-haired kid, he leaned over them with foul breath. Though Ellen came here often, she didn't recognize him.

"Nothing is ready," he said. "I overslept."

"Can you make us some tea and toast?" suggested Sam. "That doesn't take much fuss."

"Sure," said the kid. He looked relieved. "Been on the road long?"

"Oh, not too long," said Ellen.

"Nothing beats an early start," he said. "How far you going?"

"Niagara Falls," said Sam.

"Congratulations," said the kid. "I should've known. The tea and toast is on me."

He vanished into the kitchen, from which they soon heard the energetic clatter of pots and pans.

"Ellen, you have to visit Mike. Tell him how things are."

"Talk to a dead man? My God, what could I possibly say that would make any difference?"

"Tell him a joke. It'll take his mind off oblivion."

It seemed to Ellen she'd never felt so confused. "I don't know any jokes. I always forget the punch lines."

"What did the Buddhist say to the hot-dog vendor?"

"I don't know. What?"

" 'Make me one with everything.' That's a short joke. A two-liner. A riddle. You can remember that one. But don't give Mike the answer. Just give him the question. Let him find the answer for himself. Maybe he'll come up with a better one."

The kid brought them two mugs of tea and a plate of burned

toast. By Ellen's place he put a plastic engagement ring set with a lemon sour ball. "This should keep you going as far as Toledo," he said.

Sam reached over and slipped the ring on Ellen's finger. "I take thee, sour Ellen—"

In spite of herself, she started to laugh.

"Ellen, do you trust me?"

"I trust you," she said. And felt she'd just uttered the punch line—and forgotten the joke.

"When I open my clinic, I'm counting on you to tell stories."

"You're opening a clinic?"

"Right next to the University Hospital. That's my dream. There will be people healing animals and animals healing people. And there will be stories. We aren't made of atoms, Ellen. We're made of stories."

Not till much later in the day did she discover three brass bowls nested on her bureau, the first no larger than an ashtray, the second the size of a candy dish, the third as big as a mixing bowl. In the bottom of the small one was a note: "Make me one with everything."

# 10

SUNDAY   June 9

The room she's given me on the third floor holds everything I need: a desk and a bed and a reading lamp, a chair and a bureau. The window looks down on Dr. Whittaker's garden. The john is around the corner. The bathtub has legs, a feature in tubs I have always admired. When I step out of my room, I see the door to the attic, which Mrs. Woolman keeps closed, and I hear her playing the piano and singing,

> *Just a song at twilight*
> *When the lights are low,*
> *And the flick'ring shadows*
> *Softly come and go.*

She likes her fireplace. Even on warm days she turns the key and brings up the gas flame and sits staring into the fire, making the flame short or tall, as it pleases her. On the hearth curls The Everpresent Fullness, her paws tucked in, making herself a neat bundle, offensive to nobody. Her crushed paw has nearly healed.

I gather dead branches in Mrs. Woolman's yard and chop them into kindling, and I build her a fire that crackles and fills the room with fragrance.

She fetches water from the kitchen and pours it on the kindling. Then she turns the golden key till the gas flames swoop out and singe the hem of her dress.

"Mrs. Woolman," I say, "you should sit farther back."

"This is my house," she says, "and I can do what I want in my own house. Who are you?"

"I am Sam."

"I forgot," she says. "Whose cat is that?"

"My cat," I say. "The Everpresent Fullness. She is neat in her habits and has a good heart."

"I do not remember seeing that cat before," says Mrs. Woolman. "Why does she only have one eye?"

"She was that way when she found me," I tell her.

I arrange two pillows and the afghan of crocheted butterflies on the sofa to tempt Mrs. Woolman away from the flames. One of the back legs of the sofa is cracked, and two volumes of *The Book of Knowledge* are wedged in, to hold it up.

"Mrs. Woolman," I say, "your sofa needs fixing. Where do you keep your tools?"

"This is my house," she answers, "and I do not want anyone changing it. That rug you are standing on is a genuine Sarouk."

I wonder if I should stand somewhere else.

"Henry bought it for a song during the Depression," she adds. "If a burglar broke in here, he'd go straight for that rug."

"He'd have to move all the furniture first," I remind her, "and that would exhaust him."

"Burglars have accomplices. Two men could roll that rug up and carry it out the door."

While we are talking I notice that the rungs on her rocking chair are also broken and the leg on the buffet is just leaning in place against the wall. I make no remark but at night I get up and fix the sofa, the buffet, and the rocking chair. There are no tools in the basement or anywhere else, as far as I can see. Just some carpenter's glue and a roll of masking tape. The tape is brittle and all stuck together, but it does the job.

After a while Mrs. Woolman does not ask me who I am when I come downstairs in the morning, and Mrs. Hanson tells me to call her Ellen. Mrs. Woolman does not tell me to call her Jessie.

I notice the lamps on her bedroom wall do not work, and when I try to change the bulbs I find twenty-dollar bills rolled up in rubber bands where the bulbs should be. I disconnect the switches on these fixtures. I do not want Mrs. Woolman to reach in and electrocute herself. I bring down the reading lamp from my room and hang it over her bed.

She says, "Where did this old lamp come from?"

I say, "I found it in the closet of the third-floor room."

"I get so tired of people moving in and borrowing things," she says. "I have an out-of-town guest arriving tonight. I will need your room."

In the afternoon Ellen's sister calls. I use the phone downstairs in the front hall; the upstairs phone is in Mrs. Woolman's bedroom.

"Just checking to see if things are all right," she says.

"Oh, yes," I tell her. "Things are fine."

"Is Mother eating well?"

"I made her a chicken curry for lunch but she said she wasn't hungry."

Mrs. Murray sighs. "She pieces. You have to watch her. I know it's not easy."

"We'll be fine, Mrs. Murray. Don't worry."

"You might try putting her food on those souvenir plates in the china cabinet. I notice she eats best on Niagara Falls."

"Sure, Mrs. Murray."

"If Mother tries to fire you, pay no attention. Are you getting her out much?"

"She's not exactly an enthusiastic traveler, Mrs. Murray."

That evening I say to Ellen, "Your mother mentioned a guest coming tonight."

"There's no guest coming," Ellen says. "You and Stevie and I are the only guests."

When I return to my room, I see the desk is bare and the bureau empty. My clothes and my books and my three Tibetan singing bowls have been thrown into my valise. I unpack my books and the singing bowls and put them back on the desk. I put my clothes back in the bureau—but where are my sandals? I hear a shuffling on the landing in front of my door.

"Mrs. Woolman," I say, "is that you?"

I open the door. She is eating chocolate ice cream with a bent spoon out of a half-gallon package.

"I need this room," she says, "for those guests I told you about."

"Mrs. Woolman," I say, "where are my shoes?"

"You're wearing them," she says, and she points to my sneakers.

"My sandals are missing, Mrs. Woolman."

"Did you look in the cellar?" she asks.

"If you've taken my shoes to the cellar," I say, "I would be very pleased to have them back."

"Let's go down and look for them," she says.

She leads, I follow.

The cellar looks as if the tide had just gone out and left in its wake a wash of baskets, books, boxes of papers, cans of paint, crocks, plates, Christmas lights, a punch bowl, a thermos jug. Mrs. Woolman stoops and opens a suitcase papered in brown tweed and out tumble a dozen old movie reels. As she picks one up it begins to unwind. The film breaks off; she holds the broken end to the light.

"Look at all those children," she exclaims.

I look. In celluloid squares like a coil of black and white stamps, children are parading across the front yard.

"I always gave Ellen and Martha the most wonderful birthday parties. I used my best silver and my black Fostoria plates. Never those awful paper things."

"Mrs. Woolman, we could watch some of these movies. Didn't you tell me you have a projector?"

"The projector hasn't run since Henry died. It's turned into a fake. I'm not accusing Henry. He knows how I love watching our old movies. I think the people he's with have taken the real one."

She has an answer for everything.

"What people? I thought you told me he's dead."

"The people in the place—where—he—is. They're always coming back for souvenirs."

The idea of the dead coming back for souvenirs is very disturbing when you're standing in a basement so crammed it looks like a model of human memory.

She touches the little grinding wheel clamped to a low shelf. It makes a contented sound—whirr, whirr—like an enormous invisible cat.

"Henry used to sharpen my knives on this wheel."

She silences the grinding wheel with one finger. I think of the knives in her kitchen, how dull they are.

"A grinding wheel is a very useful thing," I say.

"Oh, yes," she says. "Of course I don't come near it when it runs by itself."

"This wheel runs by itself?"

"At night. Because of that winged person I told you about."

I don't want her to know I haven't the faintest memory of being told about a winged person in the cellar.

"An angel is nothing to worry about, Mrs. Woolman. When did you see it last?"

"I saw it the day the cyclone blew the shingles off our roof. I was fifteen. And what I want to know is, did it come to take me or to take care of me?"

"Don't worry, Mrs. Woolman. When you see the Angel of Death before your time is up, he's bound to grant you one wish the next time you meet him."

"One wish? I never heard that."

"Oh, it's a well-known fact, Mrs. Woolman. Believe me, you have nothing to worry about."

She looks as if she has plenty to worry about.

"Do you think it was the Angel of Death?"

"Mrs. Woolman, how can I answer? I wasn't there to see him. Maybe you saw Zachriel," I suggest. "He's the angel of memory."

"There is no angel for memory," says Mrs. Woolman.

"There are angels for everything," I tell her.

"Where in the Bible does it say there is an angel for memory?"

"I didn't read it in the Bible," I tell her.

"I hope no one has taken Henry's map," she says. "I can't rest till I know Henry's map is safe."

"Where is it?"

"In the museum."

She rests her hand on my arm, and together we stroll down the street. No lights shine in the neighboring houses but from the pear trees, lit by the full moon, rises the steady chirping of small creatures that also love the night. Honeysuckle is filling the air with a heavy sweetness.

I wonder what Ellen will think if she wakes up and finds us both gone.

Something brushes my leg: The Everpresent Fullness is keeping watch over us, a task she has recently taken on herself.

The door to Woolman Scientific looks locked but Mrs. Woolman pushes it open easily, and we step into a room that appears to run the entire width of the building and opens into a second room at the back. Even before she touches the light switch, I can hear the bubbling of water.

"Such a comforting sound," says Mrs. Woolman. "I love to come here and listen to the stream. Henry found it, and he always treated it like a guest."

By the single overhead light I see half a dozen old exhibit cases and the stream, like a long sparkling animal gliding through the curved bed it made long before Ann Arbor was even imagined. The banks on either side have been reinforced with stones to keep the stream from forgetting the way home.

The Everpresent Fullness steps forward and peers into it, hoping for a fish. As for me, I can find no words to tell Mrs. Woolman it is love at first sight, except to say that if God were to design himself a miniature golf course, it would have a stream running through it like this one. The full moon floods it with brilliance. The shelf on the far wall holds beakers, Bunsen burners, dozens of large bottles with glass stoppers.

"Those came from upstairs," she says, "in the warehouse."

A stuffed owl carrying a small wheel is peering down at us from the rafters.

"You have a lot of interesting stuff around here," I say.

"Oh, yes," she says. "Oh, yes. Henry could sell you anything you needed. Anything at all. If he couldn't find it in one of his catalogues, he'd make it for you."

She leads me over to what looks like a framed swatch of darkness, caught in a network of green lines.

"Such a way Henry had with maps," she remarks. "They'd do anything for him. Can you read maps?"

"Yes, but it's awfully dark here, Mrs. Woolman. Maybe we could read it tomorrow."

"Pffft!" She walks away from me with an air of impatience, and I know I've failed some test I didn't even know she was giving me.

"Henry was very smart," she says. "Very careful of his health. I never knew anyone who loved shredded wheat as much as Henry."

Half-hidden among the stoppered bottles, a child's snow globe gleams at me. When I pick it up I can scarcely believe my eyes.

"The Dog Star Man! You have the Dog Star Man!"

"I wanted to move him back to the cellar, but he's happier here," says Mrs. Woolman. "How do you know the Dog Star Man?"

"Everybody from Drowning Bear knows about the Dog Star Man."

I am about to suggest to Mrs. Woolman that she and I could be distant cousins, since everyone in Drowning Bear is kin, one way or another, when I happen to notice, on a shelf just out of reach, a pair of black dress shoes and a pair of two-tone oxfords with a mesh panel for ventilation.

"Mrs. Woolman, whose shoes are those on the top shelf?"

"Those shoes belonged to two wonderful men," she tells me, "but I can't remember their names."

"Maybe you can remember where you last saw mine," I say.

"Pffft! Did you look in the piano?" she asks and guides me to the front door and opens it. Miles away from this place, a train passes our sleeping city and whistles.

SUNDAY   June 16

In the middle of the night, when Mrs. Woolman wakes up and can't fall asleep again, she knocks on my door. I get up and follow her downstairs for show-and-tell. We go outside and she shows me the path Dr. Whittaker planted between their houses. It is so overgrown that she can't find it except by the scent of the thyme. Arm in arm, we walk to the museum and check on the stream, to see if it needs anything.

I show her how to tie a St. Alban's knot.

She tells me she kisses Henry's picture every night before she goes to bed and she shows me the postcard he sent her from a conference in Zurich. The Alps on one side, Henry's message on the other: *Oh, for a shredded wheat.*

"There was only one man for me," she says. "There never was a man as good as my Henry."

She asks who among the dead I'd like to see again.

I tell her I'd like to see Molly so I could tell her I'm sorry.

She says she knows a girl in Kalamazoo named Molly and is it the same one?

I say, "It can't be. The Molly I knew lived in Madison."

She tells me she rode in the ambulance with Henry and stayed with him in the emergency room as long as she could.

I tell her about the fight I had with Molly the last time I saw her alive. She wanted to give up a year in England on a Marshall Fellowship and stay in Wisconsin so we could be together, and when I told her not to, she jumped up and tipped over the canoe.

"Whenever you see someone," says Mrs. Woolman, "it might be the last time."

"We fought a lot," I say. "Lord, I can't even remember what we fought about. But we stayed together because of the good times."

"Henry and I never had a cross word," says Mrs. Woolman.

She shows me how to waltz while humming the theme song from "The Lone Ranger."

I show her how to open a car door with a coat hanger.

She shows me how to make a cat's cradle with string and how to wind the cradle into a Jacob's ladder.

I show her how I can wiggle my ears.

She says, "Wiggling your ears runs in families. Not everyone can do it."

I say, "It doesn't run in ours. Molly taught me."

"I could never wiggle my ears," says Mrs. Woolman, "not even if my life depended on it."

She shows me over a hundred places to hide a house key.

I show her how to make a flamingo out of a newspaper.

She shows me how to fold the flamingo into a boat.

I show her how to fold the girl on Land O Lakes butter so that her innocent knees turn into voluptuous breasts.

She shows me how to shake the cans of cat food in the store and listen for the gravy, which is the part cats love.

I tell her how I tried to bring Molly ashore the way I'd once seen a lifeguard do, with my hand under her chin.

"She tried to pull me down with her. I figured if I didn't break free, she'd drown us both."

"Anyone would have done the same," says Mrs. Woolman.

"And after I let her go—how could I find her when the water was so deep I couldn't even see the bottom?"

"No, indeed," says Mrs. Woolman. "No, indeed."

"Especially at night."

She tells me she is afraid of the dark because that's when the dead cross over to visit the living. Just talking about ghosts agitates her.

"Oh, Mrs. Woolman," I say, trying to calm her, "ghosts aren't so bad. You know, I heard of a man in California who runs a ghost adoption bureau."

Mrs. Woolman looks very interested.

"He sends ghosts through the mail?"

"I don't know how he sends them. But a lot of people order them. Mostly single mothers. You know why single mothers want a ghost?"

"No. Why?"

"So their kids won't be alone in the dark."

"I'd have them send Henry," says Mrs. Woolman. "But they're not supposed to come back. It's right there in the Bible. So he'll never come back. He was always a law-abiding man."

I tell her about the pet star I had as a child, to help me be brave at night. "It's the one at the tip of the handle of the Big Dipper. We can share it, Mrs. Woolman."

She asks me if I'm afraid of the dark.

I tell her I'm not afraid of the dark but of a dream the dark shows me just as I'm falling asleep: a dead girl at the bottom of Scroon Lake.

She tells me about the smell of a new-mown field that lingered after the angel disappeared.

I tell her how I went to visit Molly in intensive care. She was brain dead but no one had informed the machine, so it went on breathing for her, sighing in, sighing out, sighing in, sighing out.

"It's a great life if you don't weaken," says Mrs. Woolman. "This is my house, is it not? This is Liberty Hall?"

Between us, The Everpresent Fullness stretches and purrs.

"Yes," I tell her. "The rug we are standing on is a genuine Sarouk. This red flower is you, this blue one is me, this green one is Ellen, this purple one is Stevie."

I teach Mrs. Woolman to remember.

She teaches me to forget.


THURSDAY    July 4

The Everpresent Fullness has started sleeping at the foot of Stevie's bed.

"She's the guardian of sleepers," I told him. "You're in excellent hands."

"Paws," he corrected me.

Is there such a word as feliogony, the belief that God is a cat?

## Monday July 15

When Ellen asked me to haul some boxes from her apartment and stash them in Mrs. Woolman's cellar, I figured it was useless to point out that all the good seats were taken. I said, "Are you moving in?"

"Oh, no. I just need a place to sort through the stuff Mike saved for the museum. I'll stay here with Mother. Do you mind?"

And she handed me the keys to her apartment and to Mrs. Woolman's car.

"Do you mind taking Dad's Buick? It has more space. Don't tell Mother."

"Why not?"

"Mother's a little funny about the car. She doesn't drive, but she takes wonderful care of that car. I think she's doing it for Dad."

"I'm driving the Henry Woolman memorial car?"

"It's not exactly a memorial," Ellen explained. "My father is dead but not gone. Mother is sure he's still hanging around the place."

"I'll be very careful," I said.

"Thanks. You can park in the lot behind the building."

Ellen's apartment looked as if she planned on leaving it for good. I counted twenty-two cartons, half of them taped closed, none of them labeled. The closets and drawers were empty. I made five trips, and the last box I carried burst open when I heaved it into the trunk. Out spilled Ellen's jeans and the embroidered Hungarian blouse she was wearing the day I arrived and locked myself in Dr. Whittaker's bathroom. A woman wearing a garden—what a grand sight to greet the eyes of a man stepping into freedom.

Not until I'd loaded the last box did I discover the front grille of the Buick was lying in three pieces on the pavement. God knows how it got there. Whoever hit the Henry Woolman memorial must have left in a hurry.

When I'm in trouble, I like to find someone who's worse off than I am and offer comfort and solace. It clears the brain. The only hardship case that came to mind at this moment was Mike Hanson. Hardly anybody remembers to talk to the dead, and naturally they're concerned. Every time they call us, they get a busy signal.

So I drove out to Heavenly Rest and stood in front of Mike Hanson's grave. The bare earth was heaped like a newly risen loaf. Ellen still hasn't bought a plaque to mark the grave. She says she can't spare the money. The wreaths had been taken away, though; the custodian doesn't like anything that withers or sheds.

"Mr. Hanson," I said, "we've never formally met. I just want you to know that Ellen is okay. She's doing fine, and when she's feeling up to it, she'll be coming out to visit you. Stevie misses you a lot but he'll be all right, too. I don't want you to worry about them, Mr. Hanson."

Suddenly I forgot what else I wanted to say. Six feet away, on Henry Woolman's grave, a woman was eating a bag of potato chips and fixing her bright black eyes on me. She looked to be in her forties, maybe, slim in her jeans and navy T-shirt. Her long hair covered her shoulders like black wings.

"Nice shirt," she said. "What'll you trade for it?"

I considered her offer. She had nothing to trade that I could see, and I wasn't eager to part with my I AM A MOTHER WHO LOVES TOO WELL T-shirt.

"What I need you can't give me," I told her. "I need a new grille for a '61 Buick. Immediately."

The woman strolled over to the Buick and surveyed the damage.

"I'll ask my brother," she said. "He has grilles, headlights, fenders. Big ones, little ones. All kinds."

"Where's your brother?"

"Down by the water." She started walking toward the river. I ran after her.

"If you want that grille fast," she called over her shoulder, "you better stay put."

Where the manicured lawn of Heavenly Rest ends in an embankment hidden by sumac, the woman disappeared. On the barbed wire fence that wove through the sumac and wild grapes, I noticed a handpainted sign: SALVAGE CHEAP.

I stopped walking and considered the universe.

At the outermost fringe of my sight, a blue heron flapped its wings and crossed the water.

The sky was empty, the air still.

All at once I saw the woman trudging toward me, and the sight of her was enough to take my breath away. The grille she was hauling was a perfect match.

She dropped it at my feet.

I don't question miracles. I pulled my T-shirt over my head and handed it to her and she grabbed it and lit out over the rise.

Thank you, angel of broken grilles. Angel of accidents, thank you.

I put the grille in the backseat and drove to the nearest Mobil station. Under the sign of the winged horse I parked the car and the mechanic on duty—just a kid, about sixteen—came out to appraise it. He stroked a back fin and said, "I'll give you a hundred for it."

"Can't sell what's not mine. Can you put this grille on in a hurry?"

Probably he thought I stole it. He took off his shirt, as if he wanted to keep me company, since I'd lost mine. We screwed on the new grille, grunting and sweating, and we didn't exchange a word; it was as if we'd lost the use of our tongues. By the time we finished and I'd paid him for his labor, you wouldn't have known anything had ever disturbed the peaceful existence of Henry Woolman's car.

# 11

----

When Sam asked Stevie if he would teach him how to swim, Stevie was both pleased and astonished. He'd assumed that all grown-ups knew how to swim, that knowing how to swim happened to you when your voice changed if you hadn't learned it before. People who drowned were either drunk or cramped or scared or knocked unconscious. Those few to whom the knowledge of swimming did not arrive had to learn the art from other grown-ups. In all his life he had never heard of anyone learning anything from a child.

Sam asked Stevie where they should go, and Stevie said, "Fuller Park. They have a beach." He did not tell Sam that he'd chosen Fuller Park because he liked the Cracker Jack at Hoot 'n Scoot. Also, there was a lifeguard. What if Sam stepped out over his head? The sandy bottom dropped away sharply even in the roped-off swimming area.

Early one morning, Sam explained to Ellen that Stevie and he had some important business and would be away for a few hours.

"She thinks I'm taking you swimming," said Sam.

"Aren't you?"

"No. You're taking me."

At nine-thirty, the beach was quiet. The tracks of yesterday's bathers were raked away and the sand, with its pattern of fine stripes, looked as if someone had just finished knitting it. Two young women were lying facedown on towels, and farther off, an elderly man was sitting in the sand under an umbrella, reading a newspaper.

Stevie wore his swimsuit under his clothes, because Sam told him that was the right way to change at the beach. Together, they spread out their giant towel. As if he were throwing off an earlier incarnation, Sam stepped out of his jeans and T-shirt and rolled them into a neat bundle, which he laid on one corner, and Stevie, watching him closely, rolled his and laid it on another.

"We have almost the same clothes," said Sam, and Stevie said, "Almost the same," and a wave of pleasure flooded him.

Side by side, they waded into the water, till it reached Stevie's chest.

"Well," said Sam, "what next?"

"You have to lie on your stomach and kick," said Stevie. He hoped Sam would understand what he meant by this, and he was glad when Sam flipped forward on his stomach, thrashed his legs, and slowly propelled himself around Stevie, like a motorboat protecting him from invisible forces. He would be very careful of Sam. He would not lead Sam into deep water until he was ready.

"Look over there," said Sam. "A turtle."

The turtle was making its way slowly toward the water like a man exercising for his health.

"Oh, let's catch him!"

But Sam made no move to catch the turtle. He kept on paddling in dreamy circles around Stevie. "I wonder if he's carrying a message," he said at last. "He's headed straight for us."

"Let's catch him," said Stevie. "Come on, Sam. Let's catch him."

"If you catch him, he can't do his work."

"His work!" exclaimed Stevie. "What work?"

"Keeping an eye on you. Or maybe me. Didn't you ever hear about the giant sea turtle who saved the life of a woman lost at sea?"

"Is this a true story?"

"Of course. It happened in the Philippine Islands. The woman rode on the turtle's back for two days. If someone had caught him, he couldn't have saved her."

As they watched, the turtle slipped into the water, out of sight, and Stevie gave a little groan of disappointment. Sam stopped paddling and touched bottom.

"I see the Hoot 'n Scoot is open for business," he observed. "Do you want a lemonade?"

Wet and shivering a little in the morning air, they took long steps over the sand. Something winked and gleamed there; Stevie leaned over and picked up a tiny horseshoe. He'd already gotten two of them in boxes of Cracker Jack and lost them. He held this one up to show Sam.

"You could give it to Allison and Elmer for good luck," said Sam. "I'm sorry you aren't going to the wedding. I was hoping we could sit together. Guess you'll have a better time at your Grandma Hanson's, though."

Stevie shrugged and tossed the horseshoe away. He did not tell Sam that he'd never stayed with Grandma Hanson by himself, and though he was looking forward to the visit, he also wished it were over; his mother had told him to eat whatever his grandma served him and to behave himself.

When they returned to the house, Allison and Elmer and Jessie were sitting around the dining room table. Their coffee cups were almost empty. Someone had wheeled in the TV. A man in a lumber jacket and waders was plunging across the screen.

"A big box came for you while you were gone, Stevie," said Allison. "I'll get it."

"I don't know what happened to Ellen," remarked Jessie. "She told me she had an appointment to keep and it was urgent."

"Our scientist has found what he's looking for," said the over-voice. "He has constructed a blind so he can film the nesting behavior of these remarkable birds—"

"That man is stealing," interrupted Jessie. "He's taking eggs from that nest."

"He's studying them," said Elmer.

"He's stealing them," said Jessie.

Allison returned with a box wrapped in gold paper. She set it in front of Stevie.

"Can I open it even if it's not my birthday?" asked Stevie.

"God, yes," said Allison, "so we can find out who sent it."

Stevie tore off the wrapping paper and the note taped to it and stared at the black box. The skeletal figure on the lid gazed back at him.

" 'The Visible Man,' " read Allison. " 'Take Apart Transparent Body. Vital Organs and Skeleton Included.' "

"Who sent this?" asked Sam.

Stevie held up the card. "It says 'For Stevie. From the Desk of Harvey Mack.' " What a funny thing for a grown man to keep on his desk, thought Stevie, as he set the box on the dining room table and ripped off the lid.

"Don't open it," said Elmer. "You can take it to your Grandma Hanson's."

But the pieces of the Visible Man tumbled forth. Though no one had called her, The Everpresent Fullness landed on the table in one glorious leap and laid her paw over the man's little plastic heart.

"For God's sake!" exclaimed Allison. "You guys have to eat here!"

"This is Liberty Hall," said Jessie. "In my house cats can do whatever they want."

Sam sat down beside Stevie and retrieved a printed sheet from the debris. "I'll read the directions, and you do the work," he said. " 'Press round skull button on top end of spine. Press spine and button into skull. Snap jawbone into place, inside cheekbones.' "

"Did you ever see so many bottles of shampoo coming out of each other in your life?" asked Jessie.

"When my TV does that," said Elmer, "I give it a good kick."

Stevie kicked the set and the many became one. A young woman holding a bottle of White Rain mouthed its praises in dumb show.

"There goes the sound," said Elmer. "I hope you have a service contract."

"Some things are better with the sound off," said Allison. "Her hair, for example."

The woman was shaking her head: *No no no.* Her blond hair floated across her face in slow motion.

"One of our clients got a big settlement because she paid a thousand dollars for a scalp treatment and all her hair fell out."

"How awful!" cried Jessie.

"Of course it grew in again," said Elmer. "But she got fifty thousand dollars to compensate her for stress. She put a new addition on her house."

"Where's Ellen?" demanded Jessie.

"She had an appointment," replied Sam. " 'Snap the two halves of the large intestine together. Before closing the ribs, insert the heart.' "

"Look at his heart, Grandma," said Stevie, and he held it up, cunning as a jewel, brick red, laced with thin blue veins that hugged it close.

"It looks like an old purse," said Jessie. "A little old purse."

"Keep an eye on it," cautioned Allison. "Don't let The Everpresent Fullness knock it off the table."

Stevie put it down, and Elmer bent low and examined it. "You have the valves reversed."

"How do you know?" asked Sam.

"I just won a malpractice suit for a girl who had open heart surgery. The doctor left a clamp inside her."

Sam uncapped the glue and Stevie picked up the bean-shaped halves of the spleen and poured a generous amount of glue on them both. "Hold this," said Stevie. "It's drying." And he handed the spleen to Elmer.

"Always glad to oblige," said Elmer, and extended his hand for the spleen. "How long does it take?"

"Five hours," replied Sam.

"Five hours!" exclaimed Allison. "You should use that quick-drying Super Glue."

"We won a settlement for a woman whose eyelids got stuck with Super Glue," remarked Elmer. "She got it on her hands and then she rubbed her eyes."

"Is she blind?" asked Stevie.

"Don't you worry about her," said Elmer. "All she lost was her eyelashes. She took the money and bought a house in Bermuda."


Ellen spotted Mike's grave the moment she drove into Heavenly Rest. She'd made a list in her head of things to tell him. Practical things he'd want to know. That she was giving up the apartment. That she'd moved all his stuff for the museum into the basement of her mother's house. That she'd be buying him a grave marker soon. She didn't mention money. No sense burdening him with her problems.

Maybe when you die you can look into the minds of the living, thought Ellen. Maybe Mike already knows about the money.

But maybe he was already too far away to care.

She folded her hands and stood in front of the mound of bare dirt that marked his resting place. Her heart felt numb and her head felt as empty as the moon. Wherever Mike was, he was not subject to the whims of a universe in which people could simply disappear through a seam in the cosmos. Check themselves out, lose touch.

He'll forget you, her heart whispered. And when you finally catch up with him, he'll be married to earth and air and fire and water.

"Mike, can you hear me?"

He won't recognize you without a sign, a question only you will be able to answer.

"What did the Buddhist say to the hot-dog vendor?"

She turned back to the car. The sense of someone watching her was so strong that she half expected to hear a voice calling her. Not Mike. No. Someone among the living.

# 12

---

$F$riday night, twelve hours before Allison's wedding, Ellen dreamed she had been turned into a three-foot alabaster jar, perfectly plain except for the wings incised on either side. A hawk-headed canopic jar. The ancient Egyptians would have used her to store the organs of their royal dead. Through some mineral instinct she knew the inside of the jar she had become smelled faintly of resin. She missed her hair.

As she considered her emptiness, Toth appeared, swinging his empty sleeve.

Did you pay your respects to the dead?

I did, she answered. I gave Mike a riddle.

Good girl, said Toth. The jar awaits your question. Limit is one to a customer.

What was I made to hold? asked Ellen.

Ashes, muttered her right wing.

A heart, whispered her left.

Slowly the chest of drawers revealed itself in the morning light.

*Rnnnng! Rnnnng!* sang the telephone.

It's Grandma Hanson, she thought. Something's happened to Stevie.

She stumbled downstairs to the front hall and snatched the receiver off the hook. "Hello?"

"It's me," said Martha. "Can you have Mother over here by nine?"

"Sure, but why so early? She and Sam were up prowling half the night."

"The makeup lady is coming. She's going to do all our faces."

"Mother doesn't wear makeup," Ellen said.

"Oh, Mrs. Alexander is wonderful. Allison says all the best brides use her." Sensing Ellen's alarm, Martha added, "You don't have to have yours done. But Mother does. She looks like a spook."

When Ellen and Jessie arrived at Martha's house, they found a sign taped on the screen door: MEET US IN THE GAZEBO. "Martha's Folly," John had called the gazebo when he bought it for her fortieth birthday, because it filled the backyard like a bandstand. But he admitted that it was better than what she'd originally asked for: a lily pond and two black swans.

As they walked around the side of the house, the gazebo with its peaked blue roof and airy sides looked absurd and exquisite, moored among the lilacs and honeysuckle. The voices of women laughing floated out to meet them before Martha caught sight of them and called, "Mother—Ellen—over here!"

Ellen could not stop staring at Martha. Her eyes were ringed with shadows that blended into the suggestion of lavender wings at the laugh lines, as if her very flesh were dreaming of twilight.

"How do you like me?"

"Wow," said Ellen. "You really look made up. I mean, she did a great job."

Jessie said nothing. So it had come to this: the dead had started taking members of her family and substituting counterfeits that were not even plausible. This was not her Martha. If they asked her, she would tell them straight out: you can counterfeit a table or chair, but you can't counterfeit a human being.

"Have you two met Elmer's mother, Emma Schautz?" inquired the counterfeit Martha. "And Mrs. Alexander, our makeup lady?"

In the middle of the gazebo, Mrs. Alexander, a well-preserved woman with fluffy blond hair, was rubbing a foundation cream on Mrs. Schautz, who was swathed in towels, her head tipped up against the back of the wicker chair. Her face was the uniform color of putty; eyebrows and eyelashes had given up the ghost. On the table of makeup, a radio was talking to itself.

Mrs. Alexander stopped rolling up the sleeves of her smock and extended her hand to Ellen, who shook it politely.

"What are you using on me?" said the beige lips of Mrs. Schautz.

"I start with Maybelline Ultra Performance pure foundation," said Mrs. Alexander, rubbing her victim's temples. "Then I use Natural Beige Satin Complexion pressed powder."

"Counterfeit humans do not fool anybody," said Jessie, and sat down on a wicker settee.

"Where is Allison?" asked Ellen.

"Taking a bath. I always do the bride last so her face stays fresh. Girls, how old is your mother?"

"She'll be seventy-five next year," said Martha.

"Seventy-five! Why, that's wonderful. What do you want for your birthday, Mrs. Woolman?"

"A glass of iced tea," said Jessie.

"Maybe she'd like to look at the wedding presents," said Mrs. Alexander.

"I'll bet your mom would be interested in that funny bottle Harvey Mack sent," murmured Mrs. Schautz. "It's there on the table."

"Harvey sent a wedding present?!" exclaimed Ellen.

"And we didn't even send him an invitation," said Martha.

Beside the radio, among the eye shadows and pots of foundation, sparkled a crystal decanter of clear liqueur.

"What's that stuff floating in it?" asked Jessie.

"Flecks of gold," answered Martha. "Pure gold."

"He must be worth a mint," said Mrs. Schautz.

"I went to high school with Harvey Mack in Detroit," said Mrs. Alexander, "and he wasn't worth a mint then. He used his wife's money to get started, but let me tell you, once he got going, she didn't have to work a day in her life."

"I never heard of eating gold," said Jessie. "But I'll gladly eat gold for you, Martha," she added.

"Heavens, Mother, nobody is asking you to eat anything," said Martha.

"I won't eat for people I don't like. Only for you and Ellen and Sam."

"On to the shadows," said Mrs. Alexander.

"What shadows?" asked Jessie.

"I'm blending Blooming Colors eye shadow. I'll use the suedes on you, Mrs. Schautz."

"Money can't buy everything," said Mrs. Schautz. "I saw a movie about a gangster who wanted to buy eternal life. He thought he could find the secret if he looked into the eyes of people who were dying."

"And did he find it?" asked Ellen.

"No, he died just like the rest of them."

"Turn up the radio," said Mrs. Alexander. "See if they found out any more about the body."

"What body?" asked Ellen.

"Sshh—listen," said Martha, spinning the volume dial.

The newscaster's voice filled the gazebo. "—the battered body of the unidentified woman found this morning in the waters of Barton Pond. Raymond Quincy, thirteen, and Paul Quincy, twelve, were fishing near Barton Dam when they saw the body snagged on a log near the edge. The boys called the police."

"Oh, my God!" exclaimed Ellen.

"The victim is five feet two, between forty and forty-five years old. According to police reports, she was hit by a car—"

"Lock the doors!" cried Jessie.

Hastily Martha turned the volume low.

"It's the same news we heard an hour ago," said Mrs. Schautz.

"I didn't hear it," said Ellen.

"The police think she might have been hit by a drunk," said Mrs. Alexander. "They didn't say a student, but I'd bet on it."

"Why, Allison might know him!" exclaimed Martha. "What if it turns out to be someone we know?"

"The milkman," said Jessie.

"Nobody has a milkman anymore," said Mrs. Schautz.

"That was just an example," said Jessie.

"Ann Arbor's not safe like it used to be," said Martha. "Have you looked at the crime map in the paper lately? The dots are creeping toward our neighborhood. I wouldn't even go out after dark to mail a letter."

"I had five proposals," said Jessie. "Two farmers, two foreigners, and your father. And every one of those men turned out well."

At eleven in the morning the air was already humid, and Jessie stood in her front hall and stared at herself in the mirror.

"I'm all dressed up. Is there a party?"

"Allison's wedding is today, Mother."

"Am I invited?"

"Of course you are," said Sam. "We couldn't go to the wedding without you." He had put on one of Henry's old suits, and it hung on him, transforming him on one sartorial stroke into a comic-book gangster.

"Where's Stevie?" asked Jessie.

"He's with Grandma Hanson," said Ellen. "I told you, Mother. Children weren't invited."

"Jessie can ride between us in front," said Sam, and he opened the door on the passenger side.

Ellen stole a glance at her mother and could not find her; Mrs. Alexander's art had turned Jessie into a stranger.

"I'll drop you two off at the church," said Sam, "and park the car."

The two women crossed the vestibule to the door of the sanctuary, and Ellen saw that it was completely filled. Why, we're the last ones, she thought. They're waiting for us.

Two ushers, whom Ellen did not recognize, were hurrying toward them. The taller one asked her if she was a friend of the bride or the groom.

"I'm the bride's aunt," said Ellen, "and this is her grand-mother."

To her alarm, he took Jessie firmly by the arm and led her away, as the second usher laid his hand on Ellen's arm and guided her down the aisle toward the joyful pride of trumpets and the buttery glint of French horns. The fragrance from the gardenia swags at the end of each pew dizzied her.

So this is what it feels like to walk down the aisle, she reflected.

She found herself seated between two young men she'd never met. College friends of Allison's, she thought. Two rows behind her sat her mother, next to Mrs. Trimble. Ellen tried to catch her eye. But Jessie seemed to have forgotten she ever had a daughter.

In the front row Martha, like a profile on a coin, stared straight ahead of her.

Behind the musicians, a woman with a camcorder was balancing herself and her equipment on a scaffolding; the sanctuary appeared to be under construction.

The sacristy door opened, and Elmer stepped out with his best man. Ellen did not recognize him.

I hardly know anybody here, she thought.

Harvey had wanted to come. When she'd told him that only the family and close friends were invited, he'd looked hurt and said, "I guess I'm not as close a friend as I thought."

"I didn't make the guest list," Ellen told him.

The organist struck up "Here Comes the Bride."

Not since Mike's funeral had Ellen felt so alone. She tried once more to get her mother's attention. But Jessie was peering past her, and Ellen turned as Allison, radiant on John's arm, swept past, stepping lightly on her way to meet her partner in the dance.

Just before supper, while Stevie was watching "Family Court" on TV, the telephone rang in the kitchen and Grandma Hanson picked it up.

"Stevie? He's right here."

He listened to Grandma Hanson's sharp heels cross the hall till she appeared in the doorway.

"Stevie, your mother is on the phone. You can take your call upstairs in my bedroom. You'll have more privacy."

It thrilled him when she spoke to him as if he were a grown-up. *You'll have more privacy.* He ran upstairs to her room, picked up the receiver, and settled himself on her chintz flowered bedspread.

"Hi! How are you two getting on?"

They'd been getting on just fine. Why did the sound of her voice make him want to cry?

"Okay," he said. "When are you coming to get me?"

"Day after tomorrow. What did you and Grandma Hanson do all day?"

"We pruned," said Stevie, "and then Harvey came and took us for lunch."

"*Harvey* took you? He never told me he was taking you to lunch. Where did you go?"

Stevie was ashamed to admit he did not know. "We looked at the boats. We sat on a big dock and ate little tiny birds."

"Chicken?"

"They were toy chickens."

"Oh, Cornish hen," his mother said. "I don't believe this. How in the world did Harvey find you?"

"He called up," said Stevie. How could his mother know the sorrow of eating the little birds? They lay on the broad platter, side by side, bare wounded things fenced round with buttered carrots. "Your knife and fork have a purpose, Stevie," Harvey had said, but Grandma Hanson just laughed and told him to use his fingers and watch out for the little bones. The bones had brought tears to his eyes. They were very small, with hardly any meat on them.

"Let me talk to Grandma," said Ellen.

He dozed among the pillows on the love seat and listened to the rise and fall of Grandma's voice in the kitchen. What bored him at home comforted him here. When he came downstairs in the morning Grandma Hanson had set the table in the dining room with toast and marmalade and orange juice and the big yellow box of Cheerios, which she had pared down with her sewing scissors so it would take up less space in the cupboard. The milk she made from powder and served in a glass pitcher. He did not care for the milk, but everything else was so nice he felt it would be ungrateful of him to complain.

After breakfast she let him brush the crumbs from the table into a small silver dustpan and tuck the place mats into the linen drawer and throw the dirty dish towels down the laundry chute. Once she'd thrown them while he stood in the basement and watched them tumble through the hole in the ceiling. He liked the basement very much; it was so cool and empty and peaceful.

Mid-morning she turned on the radio and rolled out the dough for sugar cookies. She turned the dial till she found the weather, which was mostly cloudy and hot, and after the weather she turned to the news, which was mostly people shooting each other. It seemed to Stevie that she liked the news best. After each story she speculated on who might be the guilty party and who the innocent, and the pitiful circumstances of their meeting. Bystanders caught in the crossfire of drug dealers settling their debts on Mack Avenue moved her to a high pitch of indignation which did not prevent her from cutting the dough and arranging on a saucer the little samples she saved especially for him.

"—And a brutal crime has jolted Ann Arbor. According to police reports, the woman was run over by a car and was still alive when her body was thrown into the river. Police working on the case declined to discuss any leads."

The kitchen was very clean. After supper Grandma slipped little hoods over the blender and the toaster, as if she were putting them to sleep. She picked up the *Detroit News*, tied it into a thin bundle, and carried it outside for the trash man.

She had hardly any trash at all.

After supper she took him for a drive to see the Pointes. They drove through all the Pointes: the Shores, the Isle, the Woods, the Farms, and the City.

"I live in the Farms," said Grandma Hanson.

Stevie saw no barns and no cows, only sailboats tossing on the bright water. Grandma said, "The Isle starts here" and "Now we're in the Woods." He could not for the life of him tell where one place ended and another began. Joggers, most of them blond, trotted past the lush lawns and boulevards.

On the other side of the water gleamed the thin rind of Canada.

The drive back made him sleepy. He was glad to sit in the TV room with Grandma and watch one of the nature programs that she specially liked, though on her little black and white set it was hard to tell the desert from the ocean.

After the nature program came the picture of four policemen stomping around Barton Dam. Stevie sat up, interested; his dad had once taken him fishing at the foot of the dam. Grandma said, "All day long it's the same story. I hope they find whoever did it," and she reached over and turned off the set.

At nine-thirty they went up to bed and she drew his attention again to the shelf of books in his room: *Cannery Row. The Human Comedy. The Physician's Handbook.* They had been Grandpa Hanson's books, she told him.

Stevie lay half asleep, listening to the chime of the living room clock. By day it struck so softly he scarcely noticed it. But at night it rang through the whole house. The mynah bird could do chimes like that. The next time he saw Wampus, he would ask for his father's voice. He would offer no bribes. He would just say, "Whenever you want to, Wampus," and hope for the best.

Sometimes he felt as if his father hadn't died but had simply gone on a field trip to the river, and if Stevie whistled for him, his dad would hear him. Over the uproar of cicadas and katydids, wrens and starlings, bullfrogs and loons, he would hear his son calling. And he would smile, wherever he was, and whistle back.

# 13

---

Ellen woke up so suddenly that for an instant she did not recognize her mother, barefoot in her best purple dress, bending over her.

"Help me," she choked, "I can't breathe."

As if she'd grown wings, Ellen leaped out of bed and flew into the hall and yelled up to the third floor, "Sam, come quick! Mother can't breathe!"

"I'll be right there," Sam shouted back. "Call an ambulance."

Jessie brightened. Her breath came back in squeaky huffs. "An ambulance coming here?!" she exclaimed. "Get the vacuum cleaner. The bedroom looks terrible."

"Oh, my God!" cried Ellen, shaking the phone by her mother's bed. "The line is dead."

Sam was pelting down the stairs with his shoes in his hand, as if he were making an escape.

"Never mind the ambulance," he said. "I'll bring the car around."

"Where are we going?" asked Jessie.

"To the hospital, Mother," said Ellen. "Let me help you downstairs."

"Get my overnight bag out of the closet. It has my new nightgown in it."

Ellen pulled a chair over to the closet, climbed up, and saw, on the top shelf, a heating pad, a camera, and a gigantic enema syringe, but no bag. What am I looking for, she said to herself, a real bag or an imaginary one?

A string of wooden beads and half a dozen little hats with veils fluttered to the floor.

"Those are my Camp Fire Girl beads," said Jessie. "I got two beads for making breakfast every morning for a month. My name was A-yi-ki-wa, teller of tales." She picked them up with her big toe. "Did you notice he has wings?"

"Who?" demanded Ellen. "Who has wings?"

"That man," said Jessie.

"You mean Sam?"

Jessie nodded. What, Ellen wondered, had Sam told her about having wings?

"Lean on me, Mother."

The two women staggered downstairs and headed out into the summer night toward Sam's car. The wind was rising. In the distance, garbage cans clanked and clattered. Sam stretched across the seat to open the door.

"Plenty of room in front for both of you," he said.

Jessie sat by the window, clutching her old black purse, and Ellen squeezed herself into the middle. Sam's red hair had escaped its ponytail and was blowing around his shoulders. Ellen stared at his high cheekbones, his brown eyes, his mouth at the edge of a smile, and suddenly he seemed to her as exotic as an ocelot.

"Such a wind," observed Jessie.

"The window's stuck," said Sam, "and the defroster smokes. Do you want my shirt, Mrs. Woolman? It's on the backseat."

Ellen reached behind her and pulled it out, expecting the familiar T-shirt with I AM A MOTHER WHO LOVES TOO WELL across the front. This one, a sweatshirt, showed a skeleton clutching a rose in its teeth, dancing through a tie-dye nebula of greens and yellows. Before she helped her mother put it on, Ellen turned the shirt wrong side out.

"I have a pain here," said Jessie. She put her hand on her heart and groaned.

Sam stepped on the gas. "Mrs. Woolman, would you like a little music?"

"What kind of music?" she asked.

"I don't know. Let's find out." He clicked on the radio and moved the dial across one wall of static after another. "There's a bad storm somewhere."

Suddenly a man's voice filled the car. "This is WPAG, and tonight we have a real treat. Professor Eric Noyer will be demonstrating the gamelan. I wish our listeners could see this wonderful instrument, Professor Noyer."

"You know, some people live their entire lives without ever having the chance to hear a gamelan," said the frail, whiskery voice of Professor Noyer.

A long silence followed, then an unearthly series of deep, lovely notes, falling into each other like basins of water.

"Is something wrong with the car?" asked Jessie.

"It's the gamelan, Mother."

"How do you know?"

"The man on the radio just said so."

"That," said Professor Noyer, "was the female gamelan."

A second silence . . . then a lighter, more ominous linkage of notes, like the call of a distant bird over a new grave.

"I don't know why you don't buy Mike a proper grave marker," said Jessie. "If you don't have a grave marker, people forget where you are."

"That, of course, was the male gamelan," said Professor Noyer. "It's smaller than the female but just as loud."

"We have thirty cemetery lots," she added. "Enough for the whole family. Henry got them for a song."

Sam turned off Washtenaw, and they did not see another car until they reached the University Hospital.

"Emergency Entrance," said Ellen. "See the lights, Mother?"

Her mother gazed at the sign over the door with pleasure.

"Such nice big letters," she observed.

A single green cab, marked THE CHRISTIAN CAB COMPANY, was parked under the streetlight near the entrance. The driver was asleep. Sam parked behind the cab and climbed out and opened Jessie's door, and she reached for his arm.

"I'm glad I don't need a cane," said Jessie. "It makes you look so old."

At this hour the waiting room was deserted, except for the receptionist, tucked safely behind a window.

On the TV screen mounted high over the chairs and magazine tables, a woman was sitting in front of a dozen telephones. "Cleveland here," she said. "Does God exist? We are standing by to take your calls."

"This is my mother," Ellen said to the receptionist. "She can't breathe."

The receptionist glanced at Jessie and handed Ellen a sheaf of papers on a clipboard. "Fill these in and take her to the second room on the right. A doctor will be by to see her."

"I'll take her," said Sam, and handed Ellen his pen.

She sat down in the empty waiting room and ran her eye down the questionnaire.

The image on the screen wobbled and doubled itself, but the woman went on taking calls as if nothing were the matter. "Pennsylvania, speak up."

"God is a feeling," said Pennsylvania. "That's what I think."

"Pennsylvania says God does not exist. We have time for one more. Hello? Fairbanks? Amazing! Come in, Fairbanks."

After "Insurance," Ellen wrote "Blue Cross."

The voice of Fairbanks filled the empty room. "HE EXISTS, LET ME TELL YOU, AND HE HAS PLANS FOR REMODELING."

For "Person to be Contacted in Case of Death," she wrote her own name, crossed it out, and wrote Martha's. Mother is not going to die, she told herself. Not now, not ever.

"LAST WEEK I WENT TO SEE HIM. A VERY SUCCESSFUL JOURNEY. GOD SAYS A NEW WORLD IS COMING, A BIGGER EARTH FOR THE LIVING AND THE DEAD. THE EARTH IS GETTING OLD. THE GRASS AND TREES ARE ALL WORN OUT."

Ellen stopped writing and started listening.

"What's the weather like up there, Fairbanks?"

"TODAY WE GOT SNOW. TOMORROW, MIST. GOD GAVE ME A SONG FOR CONTROLLING THE WEATHER. HE PUT ME IN CHARGE OF THE WEST. GOD SAID, 'THE PRESIDENT WILL TAKE CARE OF THE EAST, AND I WILL LOOK AFTER HEAVEN.'"

"Thank you, Fairbanks, we're running out of time—"

"I WILL KEEP YOU INFORMED. FOR A SMALL STIPEND I CAN FURNISH RAIN WHEN NEEDED—"

With a flick of her finger the receptionist switched channels, and the sound went off. Three men with walkie-talkies were down on their knees in front of Barton Pond. "Terrible," said the receptionist. "Just terrible. This town isn't safe anymore."

Ellen wanted to pity the drowned woman, but she felt numb to everyone's problems except her own. She pushed the clipboard across the counter.

"Your mother is in room 2, straight down that corridor."

In a cubicle separated from the rest of the world by curtains, Jessie was lying on a trolley stretcher with a gray blanket pulled over her. She was still wearing Sam's Grateful Dead sweatshirt, but someone had pushed up one green-and-yellow sleeve and inserted an IV tube. Behind her cataract glasses her eyes looked huge. Ellen could not tell in what way she was attached to the screen behind her, on which an invisible needle scribbled like an angry child the erratic music of her heart. Next to her sat Sam. He was not watching the screen. He was watching Jessie's face.

It seemed to Ellen that whatever sealed her mother's body to her soul had sprung a leak, and life was dripping out of her, slowly, like sap from a tree.

"Mother, it's me, Ellen."

Jessie's eyes flew open. "Thank heaven," she said. "I thought you'd been waylaid. Let's go home."

Ellen wished the room had two stretchers so she could lie down on the other one.

"Not so fast, Mrs. Woolman," said Sam. "They're going to do an EKG on you."

"I want to die," said Jessie. "I want to die in my sleep."

"Mother, don't say that."

"What do I have to live for?" she demanded. "All my old flames are gone. After Henry died, Ira Cuppy asked me for a date, and I said I'd think about it, and two days later his son called to say he was dead."

At that moment Ellen could not think of a single thing her mother could look forward to.

"I thought," said Sam, "we might keep bees."

"Bees!" exclaimed Ellen.

"We could put their hive in the window of the museum," he continued. "Bees are very edifying companions."

Not if Harvey gets it, thought Ellen.

"My father kept bees," said Jessie proudly.

"I know," said Sam.

"How could you know? Did you ever meet my father?"

"Only in your stories."

Footsteps in the corridor silenced them. The intern who entered the cubicle had a round pink face and looked about fourteen.

"I'm Dr. Day," he announced. "Mrs. Woolman, can you hear me?"

"I have excellent hearing," said Jessie.

He glanced at the questionnaire and Ellen's scrawled handwriting. "It says here she has shortness of breath," said the doctor.

"Whose death?" asked Jessie. "Did somebody die?"

"Nobody I know of," said Sam.

"Breath, Mother. He said you have shortness of breath."

"And some pain in her heart," continued the doctor. He turned to Sam. "Are you her son?"

"Spiritually speaking, yes."

Dr. Day did not look pleased with this answer.

"Who's her next of kin?" he asked.

"Me," said Ellen. "I'm her daughter."

"According to this sheet your mother is a code. Is that right?"

"What does that mean?" asked Ellen. She was certain she had not written anything about a code on the questionnaire.

"If her heart stops, all attempts should be made to revive her."

"Of course," said Ellen.

"I have a murmur," said Jessie. "Murmur of the heart. I was not allowed to take gym in college. I was supposed to walk instead."

"Murmurs are nothing to worry about," said the doctor. "Lots of people have them."

"I used to walk through the Forest Hills Cemetery and sit on the tombstones and read. I don't know why Henry bought our lots in a place that doesn't allow tombstones."

The doctor motioned Ellen to one side. "You might want to think about switching to no-code," he said. "The procedures for reviving codes are quite violent—pounding on her chest and so forth. I've heard people say, 'If I'd known we were going to put Mother through all that . . .' "

The end of the sentence hung in the air between them.

"And once the procedure has been set into motion, there's no going back."

"Thank you," said Ellen. "I'll speak to my sister about it."

As if the matter were now settled, the doctor leaned over Jessie and said into her ear, "Mrs. Woolman, the nurse will be coming to take you to your room."

"You look awfully pale, Doctor," said Jessie. "Are you getting enough sleep?"

# 14

---

The room into which the stout nurse wheeled Jessie was delightfully cool, bathed in a fluorescent twilight. A curtain hid the two patients to the left of the door. But the curtain that might have hidden the patient on the right was pulled back. A woman with black hair cropped short was propped up in bed, watching them: tiny as a twelve-year-old child, yet judging by her face she was at least forty. Ellen wondered if she had children at home.

"We'll give you a new nightgown, Mrs. Woolman," said the nurse. "A white one." And she eased Sam's sweatshirt over Jessie's head.

"What a big clock!" said Jessie. "I've slept in some funny places in my time."

"It's a nice room," said the woman. "You can see the river from here."

They all turned to the window.

"I can't," said Jessie. "Can you, Ellen?"

"No," said Ellen.

"That's all right," said the woman. "Just keep looking for it."

Over the dark city rose Burton Tower, its silver hands at ten after two. The nurse was fastening the ties on Jessie's hospital gown while Ellen drew the sheet over her mother's thin legs.

"Nurse!" called a man's voice from the other side of the curtain.

"Now, Mr. Kripps," the nurse called back, "I told you, Stephen King before bedtime is a no-no. What you need is a laxative."

"I'm sure I didn't ask him here," said Jessie. "I never heard of putting a man in a room with two women."

"He won't bother you, Mrs. Woolman. He's ninety-two." To Ellen she said, "Does your mother have an air conditioner at home?"

"No."

"You should get one for her. All our heart patients have them."

After the nurse left, Ellen felt as awkward with her mother as if they were total strangers. She was relieved when the woman in the next bed cracked the silence.

"I'm Monona," said the woman.

"Hello, Monona," said Ellen, and extended her hand.

"The ring finger on my left hand," said Monona. "That's all I can move."

"Oh, I'm sorry," exclaimed Ellen.

How had she failed to notice the stillness in those arms, a doll's arms on a woman's body strapped into the breathing machine that clasped her like a corset? How had she failed to hear its rhythmic wheeze?

On the night table stood a tray set with plates and dishes, all of them heavily armored as if against an attack.

"Here's your dinner," said Sam. He lifted the metal helmet from the plastic plate, and a menu fluttered past him. Gravy had congealed around the pork chop, and the corn on the cob appeared pale and withdrawn.

"I didn't order this," said Jessie.

"The last patient ordered it," said Monona. "And he was so looking forward to corn on the cob. You should check the menu for what you want tomorrow and leave the tray out in the hall."

"I want a chocolate soda," said Jessie.

"It's not listed," said Ellen.

"But you can ask for it," said Monona.

Ellen wrote "CHOCOLATE SODA" at the bottom of the menu and laid it on the tray. She could not put the fate of the last patient out of her mind. Dead? Discharged?

"Mother, is there anything you need?"

"Just you. I want to look at you."

As Ellen leaned over to kiss her mother good night, the nurse bustled in. "Mrs. Woolman, we're going to take you for an EKG."

"Now?" Sam asked. "In the middle of the night?"

"The doctor ordered it," said the nurse. She was easing Jessie back onto the trolley stretcher. "He needs to assess the damage before he prescribes the treatment."

"I hope she can sleep through all this," said Sam.

"EKGs are painless," said the nurse.

The corridors were wide and still, and as they followed Jessie's stretcher Ellen could not keep her eyes from straying into the other rooms. A procession of sunken masks, she thought. The nurse's station was well lit but empty. At the end of the journey lay a small dark room.

Dr. Day was washing his hands. "On the screen in front of you," he said, "you will see the heart in motion."

He arranged cathodes and adjusted wires, as if her mother were an appliance about to be plugged in. The screen lit up, a window full of gray weather undulating in eerie silence; was this a heart, or a mind full of memories? Dark grass blowing on a gray moor, black roots breaking through the gray prairie soil, ash heaps rising and shifting, a field of silver sheaves alive and swaying, dreaming themselves to sleep.

"A little damage here," said Dr. Day, putting his finger on a black spot in the picture. Ellen broke into a sweat. Sam reached over and took her hand.

"Who's that?" said Jessie.

Across the screen a tiny shadow like a pilgrim ant had crawled out of the darkness and was crossing, slowly and patiently, the heart's mountains.

The lone cab was gone, and Sam's car was the only one on the street. Fists clenched, Ellen climbed in beside Sam. She would not cry; no, she would not.

Sam slipped his arm around her shoulder. "Ellen, look at me. Worrying won't help. Your mother is in good hands."

Ellen said nothing, fearing that if she opened her mouth a grieving roar would explode from it, which she would be powerless to stop.

"They're used to seeing people with heart attacks," said Sam.

"I know. I worked in a hospital."

"Taking pictures of newborns in the maternity ward isn't work. People aren't sick."

"True. But I also worked in the morgue."

"The morgue?" That seemed so important she thought he should have told her earlier.

"The summer of my junior year," said Sam.

"What did you do?" asked Ellen.

"Autopsies."

"You cut people up?"

"I didn't do the cutting. I weighed the liver and lights. Everything you take out has to be weighed before it goes back in."

Ellen shuddered. "I could never do that."

"I don't think I could do it now, either," said Sam. "Singing helped. We sang during all the autopsies. It was the only way to get through them."

Perdue chickens in the supermarket. The sheen of wings hugging their sides under the Saran Wrap.

"Sam, do you have wings?"

"Sure."

"You do? Where?"

"Where most people have them," he said, "who have them. Here." And he glanced first over his left shoulder, then over his right.

Ellen reached out and touched one shoulder blade. It didn't feel like a wing. "A wing should have feathers," she said.

"Mine do have feathers." He pulled his T-shirt over his head. By the light of the emergency entrance, she saw his wings, one on each shoulder blade. They were tattooed in exquisite detail, every feather in place.

"They're Egyptian style," he said, "from the god Horus. His wings have all the colors of the rainbow."

At this time, in this place, she could not see the colors. Nevertheless, they seemed beautiful beyond any telling of them.

"Where did you get them?"

"From a guy in Madison. Everybody calls him the Naz. He can do anything in the book—roses, diamonds, anything. There's a whole section on wings. You know, you'd look great in wings."

"I'd never have the nerve to get a tattoo."

"Oh, he's seen a lot of women like you. When they get up the nerve, they all want wings, he told me. Some women ask for just one, on the shoulder. He told me about a girl who wanted a unicorn tattooed over her navel, but her fiancé said no. So the Naz told her that was no problem, and he tattooed it under her pubic hair. A magical creature in the forest."

Sam parked in front of the house. The milky blue sky over the pear trees was flushed with a faint rim of gold. Neither of them made a move to climb out.

"Let's walk over to Island Park," he said suddenly. "We'll have the whole place to ourselves."

The haze in the air told her that by noon the heat would be unbearable. But at this hour, the world was new-minted. They walked hand in hand, past hedges of bridal wreath in blossom and new-mown lawns that smelled of wild onions. A mourning dove behind them called to another far ahead of them.

When they reached the park, the bird darted to the top of the swings. Is he following us, thought Ellen, or are we following him? Sam took one swing, she took the other. At first she kept hers even with his, two pendulums traveling in the same direction. Gradually she found herself gliding backward while he surged forward, his ponytail flying after him.

"There's our friend," he said, "on the merry-go-round."

It was hardly worth calling a merry-go-round, she thought, as she jumped off the swing—just a big wheel with bars for holding. The bird did not fly away until she came close to him. Then he vanished into the trees.

Ellen climbed aboard the wheel and Sam pushed off, and slowly the universe unwound its ancient spool of light and shadow, tying trees to houses, houses to birds, birds to sky. Everything around them was melting, trying to find its way back to the first spinning broth of stars, while the wheel creaked round and round like a chirping planet.

"This is the Master of Confusion speaking," said Sam. "Where would you like to go?"

She did not know. She felt she might throw up. "I've got to get off," she said.

He stopped the wheel with his foot, and she staggered over to the grass, lay down, tipped her face to the sky, and waited for the world to settle. Sam stretched out beside her, leaning on one elbow.

"Next time you come here with Stevie," he said, "I hope you'll think of me."

She thought of Stevie, who never came here anymore because he felt too old for swings and merry-go-rounds.

She thought of Allison's wedding and the video hooked up in front of the altar. She thought of herself hooked up to her job the way her mother was hooked up to a monitor and an IV.

She thought of Toth, who was lost.

She thought of a woman's body floating cold and alone in Barton Pond, and she thought of Monona offering the ring finger of her left hand, saying, "That's all I can move." Not to be loved was bad enough, but not to love was worse. Someday they would be six feet under the sod or six thousand feet under the sea, gazing up out of empty sockets and not seeing the sky while other children played over them, and it would not be a man's hands running over her then but the indifferent snouts of fishes or worms. The long, slow dying into life. She thought of the little shadow crossing the country of her mother's heart and tears started rolling sideways down her face.

"Are you all right?" asked Sam.

"I'm dying."

"Is that all?" he said.

And he leaned over, slipped his arm under her back, and kissed her.

# 15

Ellen said, "Get ready for a shock," and Martha nodded, opened the door, and went in.

With its flimsy curtain partition, the room looked temporary, assembled by nomads. The occupant of the bed nearest the door had vanished, leaving behind an IV, a bottle of Skin So Soft, and a pair of wire-rimmed glasses. The curtain near the window bed was pulled back. Jessie's lids, thin and bluish, looked as if they had not yet opened for the first time, like the eyes of a baby bird. To the left of her bed, the monitor blipped and beeped while across its black face the diagnostic line skipped on, a shining skeletal wave. To the right rose the IV, on which hung the translucent fruit of its fluid.

She's still my mother, thought Martha. She glanced around the room, planning improvements. A Bible. Mother would surely want one. That photograph of her and Henry, taken on their fortieth. Martha felt for the list in her pocket. *Ask Reverend Peele to call on Mother. Buy air conditioner.* In her mind she added: *Bring a bigger nightstand.* Why, you couldn't fit another thing on this one. The lunch tray took up most of the space. The menu had fallen into the cup of broth, and a dish of chocolate ice cream had relaxed into a puddle. Her mother's black purse was flanked by the dish garden from Mrs. Trimble and the ceramic snail Martha had ordered, whose shell held a lavender mum plant. Both plants were eclipsed by a large formal arrangement of red roses and carnations. The card caught in their petals read: "Kindest regards from Harvey Mack."

Surprised, Martha was about to pluck out the card when Jessie's eyes snapped open.

"Mother, are you—awake?"

Jessie knew she'd closed them for only an instant, but it was long enough for Ellen to change into Martha. Or had Martha changed into Ellen?

"Are you Martha or Ellen?"

"I'm Martha. Ellen is in the hall with Sam."

"Tell her to come in."

"She already did, and now it's my turn. There's only one chair."

"What do you mean there's only one chair? We have dozens."

"Mother, this is the University Hospital."

"I'm in the hospital? What for?"

"You had a heart attack."

"Thank heaven. When I woke up and saw so many flowers, I thought I was dead."

Ellen's birth on the sixth floor—no one could take from her the memory of that moment. She was forty-five, the oldest mother on the floor. The doctor had told her she had nice legs. What a funny thing to tell someone at such a time, she thought. And when she'd asked if it was a boy or a girl, the doctor said, "It's a girl, but don't worry. With two daughters you'll have plenty of boys around."

Beyond the curtain that closed off the other end of the room came the rustling of papers and a man's voice.

"I see you've also had trouble with prostate."

Martha found herself leaning forward, staring at the soles of his bare feet and listening to what appeared to be a murmured assent.

"They put a man in this room," said Jessie, "and they never asked me. I think he's a minister. He prays all the time."

"I'll ask for a private room," said Martha.

"Martha," whispered Jessie, "who's paying for this?"

"It's paid for, Mother. Don't worry about it."

"What's my balance?"

"You've got enough. I called the bank yesterday."

"My mother used to call every morning for her balance, it was so tight. How much money do I have in my purse?"

Martha reached for the purse, opened it, and peered in. "Five dollars," she said.

"Is that all? Count it out."

"You have five dollars, a pencil, two checks, and some cough drops."

"I had fifteen dollars when I came. What happened to the rest of it?"

"Ellen took it home. You don't need money here."

"I don't feel right having no money," said her mother.

Something was humming and bumping against the door, and they both turned as a woman with short black hair entered the room in a motorized wheelchair.

"You must be Martha," said the woman, smiling. "I've heard so many nice things about you. I'm Monona."

Why, she hardly looks human, thought Martha. More like a frog than a woman. A glance at her thin arms and rigid posture told Martha that Monona was not only buckled into her stiff black vest but strapped to the chair for support. Without it, she would topple over like a piece of yarn.

Ellen was following her, guiding the chair toward the bed. "I'll call the nurse," Ellen said.

"Thank you, but I think I'll stay up awhile. I want to get today's paper before they sell out downstairs."

"Goodness!" exclaimed Martha. "I'll run down and bring you one."

Monona neither nodded nor shook her head. "Actually, I like the trip downstairs," she said. "The nurse tapes the coins to my armrest. All I have to do is put my finger on the button and I'm off." The steady hum of the motor died. "I had polio. You didn't ask, but I figured you'd be curious."

"You don't run into many people who've had polio these days," said Martha.

"I got it the year before Salk discovered the vaccine," said Monona, without bitterness. "Jessie, didn't you like your lunch?"

"They forgot the chocolate soda," said Jessie.

"No, they didn't," said Monona. "It's the ice cream."

"That's the soda? I thought a soda would come in a big glass," said Jessie. "What's Martha doing?"

"I'm fixing your room," said Martha. From her tote bag, she took out the Rolodex of snapshots and nudged it into place on the nightstand.

"The snow globe would be a great comfort," said Jessie. "Who sent that big bunch of flowers?"

"Harvey Mack," replied Martha.

"You've got to be joking," said Ellen.

"He did," answered Martha. She was taping old Christmas cards to the edge of the nightstand. "Here's a card from your old flame Peter Burke."

"Peter Burke is dead," said Jessie.

"Peter's dead?!" exclaimed Ellen. "I didn't know that. Mother, you always liked Peter."

"I got a note from his daughter about it," said Jessie. "I must have been on the list of people to notify."

Martha pulled down Peter Burke's Christmas card and tucked it into her pocket.

"Don't forget to check the menu," said Monona.

Gazing at Ellen on her left hand and Martha on her right, Jessie was content. The universe was coming to its senses, and the elements were returning to their appointed places.

"You can have peach melba or custard delight," said Ellen, waving the menu.

"Nice names," said Monona. "They want you to like the food."

"John will come to see you tomorrow, Mother," said Martha. "He's at a conference in Chicago today on—well, I don't know the name of it, but it has something to do with money."

"John's coming?" said Jessie. "And Mike?"

"He's dead, Mother," said Ellen.

"Oh, I always liked Mike," said Jessie. She was almost afraid to ask about Stevie for fear he too was dead, and she was thankful when Ellen added, "Stevie's visiting his Grandma Hanson. He'll be here tomorrow too. And Allison."

"How is Allison?" inquired Jessie. "I haven't seen her for ages."

"She got married yesterday," said Martha. "To Elmer."

"And where did they go for their honeymoon?" inquired Monona.

"To Elmer's apartment. They didn't want to take time off from their jobs."

"And where's Sam?" asked Jessie. "I want Sam."

"Sam is in the hall. He's going to stay all night in the hospital with you," said Martha. "The nurse promised to bring him a more comfortable chair."

Jessie smiled. "So many people coming. We'll order a turkey. A big one."

She tried to lift her arm to show Ellen exactly how big, and a long, thin tube tugged at it like a stem.

"Am I attached to this thing?"

"Yes," said Martha. "Don't touch it."

"Don't worry, Jessie," said Monona. "We're all attached to things here."

Such thin ugly legs that woman has, thought Jessie, though she wouldn't have mentioned it to her for the world. I have beautiful legs. Not a varicose vein in either of them.

Behind the curtain that partitioned the room, a man coughed.


Ellen and Martha stepped outside into the late-afternoon light.

"I'm so depressed," said Ellen. "I thought she'd go on forever."

"Let's get a good night's sleep and come back in the morning," suggested Martha.

A fierce hunger seized them both, and they stopped at the Wolverine Den and bought two hamburgers to go and ate them on the way home.

"I can't get over Harvey Mack sending Mother those flowers," said Martha. "He's buttering her up. He's just dying to buy the museum. I think it would be a smart move to sell it. Mother hardly ever visits it anymore."

"Yes, she does. She goes with Sam."

"Mother may need twenty-four-hour nursing care when she gets out. She may need it for the rest of her life." Martha's face remained calm, but her voice trembled. "I hate to mention this, but John and I looked at the books last week, and we're starting to run through her money. If we don't sell the museum, we may have to put her in Hopecrest."

"I can't talk about it now," said Ellen. "I just can't."

When they walked into the empty house, neither of them felt the least bit tired. Martha scoured the oven while Ellen straightened the contents of the freezer and threw out three open half-gallons of chocolate ice cream, furred with a thin sparkle of crystals.

"It's a good time to clean Mother's room," said Ellen.

"Let's do something really major. Let's clean the basement," said Martha. "With Mother out of the house, we can throw a lot of stuff away."

Ellen hesitated, and, sensing her distaste for this project, Martha added, "We won't actually have to throw it away. We can give it to the Goodwill."

They headed for the cellar, Ellen carrying a green garbage bag for the junk and Martha carrying two Mexican shopping bags for Goodwill. For years they had never looked past the washer and dryer and the clothesline strung overhead. Now they poked into corners, lifted lids, pried open cartons, and the cellar gave up its ghosts: torn sheets, purses with broken clasps, a rusty bread box, books on beekeeping, and back issues of *Scientific American* stuck together and smelling of mold.

"Here's your wedding bouquet, Martha."

Ellen held it up. To the dead flowers clung a tiny plastic wheel and a coupon for 9Lives Savory Stew.

"That wheel must go with something," said Martha. "Don't throw it out. Let's start a pile of things we want to save."

They picked up, put down, fitted pieces together, healed the broken, found the lost; and an hour later, both the garbage bag and the Mexican shopping bags were empty.

"We have to throw *something* away," said Ellen. "How about this pillow slip full of panty hose?"

"Mother told me she's saving them for church," Martha answered. "Somebody she knows is making a rag rug."

"She hasn't been to church in years," said Ellen, stuffing the pillow slip behind the box where she'd found it. Martha came over for a closer look.

"What's in all these boxes? I never saw them before."

"Mike's stuff," said Ellen. "Sam helped me move it over here, so I could sort it."

"Mother didn't notice you bringing them in?"

Ellen shook her head.

"What about Aunt Ida's dresses?" asked Martha. "Why, they're still in the paper from Goldberg's. I guess Mother was saving them for when Ida got out of the nursing home."

"Nobody ever comes back from a nursing home," said Ellen. She took the dresses down, one by one, and folded them into the shopping bags.

Martha made a little grieving noise. "Lord, I feel awful giving Aunt Ida's dresses away. Let's just give away one or two."

But Ellen was already rooting around behind the furnace. The single naked bulb cast a sallow light on their father's workbench. His valise, his carpenter's glue and masking tape, his box of pencils, his carving knife, and his watercolors lay at hand, as if he had just stepped away for a minute.

"Remember how good Daddy was at carving birds?" said Martha. "Whatever happened to all those birds?"

"Mike was always loaning him bird books," said Ellen.

"Let's rest a bit," suggested Martha.

They drew up two kitchen chairs with the backs broken off that Henry had never gotten around to fixing.

A glass swan on one of the high shelves caught Ellen's eye. "There's Daddy's barometer," she said. "I used to think the world of that swan. I used to think it was full of cranberry juice." She reached for the swan and brought it down carefully. A dark liquid was rising in the bird's neck.

"Does it still work?" asked Martha.

"I don't think barometers ever stop working," said Ellen. "This one says there's a storm coming."

"Didn't it used to be in the museum?"

"Yes," said Ellen, "but Mother has started moving what she calls her valuables from the museum to the cellar. She says she's keeping away the counterfeits."

"Counterfeits!"

"I don't understand it either."

Martha put her feet up on a large box. One flap sprang open and a jumble of white garments fell out.

"Now, what in the world—" exclaimed Ellen.

"BVDs. Oh, Lord, they're the ones we carried back to the garage. Mother wanted to give them to John. I told her, 'Mother, John wears modern underwear. He doesn't want Daddy's BVDs.'"

Together they gathered and pushed them into the bags for Goodwill. "We've rested enough," said Ellen. "Let's tackle the shelves."

Suddenly out of the darkness rose a low wail that sounded as if it did not belong to this world, and both women jumped.

"It's Sam's cat—she's caught something," said Ellen.

"A mouse," said Martha. "Dead, I hope. I'll get the broom and a paper bag."

The cat stepped forward and dropped at Ellen's feet a small green parcel that stared fearlessly up at her.

"My God, it's a toad," she said. "And the poor thing is missing an arm."

The missing arm did not look like a recent injury, which made them both feel more benign toward the cat. Martha eased the toad onto the dustpan and carried it upstairs. Ellen heard the front door slam.

"I'm putting him outside," called Martha, "under a leaf." And she hurried back to the cellar.

The shelves ran the length of the back wall and were crammed from floor to ceiling with paint cans, broken radios, boxes of snapshots, candles, dishes, a toaster, Easter baskets, and several wire frogs that once held arrangements of flowers.

"Here's Daddy's old map of Ann Arbor," said Ellen. "Mother must have moved it. Remember how he loved that map?"

"Oh, we can't give that away," said Martha.

The sisters were on their knees now, picking carefully through a tray of odds and ends. A pair of eyeglasses. A picture of the Dionne quintuplets clipped from a Karo syrup ad. A paper hand. Martha gave a squeal of delight. "That hand belongs to my old Margaret O'Brien paper doll," she exclaimed.

"Save it," said Ellen. "We may find the rest of her."

They had come to the little pantry at the very back of the cellar. Jessie called it the keeping room and Martha called it the fallout shelter. Above the shelves of Spam and Dinty Moore stood row after row of mason jars in which floated the dark remains of pears, like the shadows of distant harvests. Fifty years earlier, Jessie had gathered the windfall in the front yard after a storm and canned the pears because it seemed such a shame to let all the good fruit go to waste. That was when she discovered Henry loathed pears.

Under the bottom shelf squatted the big crock in which Jessie's mother had made sauerkraut, tamping it down with her bare feet. Now it held cups that had lost their saucers, dinner plates chipped but too pretty to throw away.

Martha ran her gaze along the top shelf. "Lord, whose sandals are those?" she asked. "I recognize Daddy's and Grandpa's shoes, but who do these belong to?"

Ellen lifted them down. The buckles were entangled with their grandfather's stethoscope. "They look like Sam's sandals," said Ellen. "He told me they disappeared right after he moved in, and he had to buy a new pair."

"I thought Mother gave this stethoscope to Stevie," said Martha.

"Guess she took it back. And here's Sam's notebook with his writings. Mother must have hidden it."

"Maybe he gave it to her. We shouldn't read it," said Ellen, and she put it back.

As they tried to untangle the stethoscope, a distant rapping overhead startled them, and Martha said, "Is someone at the door?"

She handed the stethoscope to Ellen and hurried away, and Ellen slipped it around her own neck. The earpieces were gone, and the bare metal chilled her flesh. Adjusting it to her chest, she listened for the beating of her heart and heard instead her sister calling, "Ellen, Ellen, come upstairs! It's the police!"

# 16

If this client's wife were a missing person, thought Elmer, there would simply be no way to describe her except to say "She looks like everybody else." She was moving her lips, reading the diplomas Elmer had framed with such pleasure: B.A., Boston University; J.D., University of Michigan. Between them hung the big watercolor of Kensington Park he'd bought at the Ann Arbor Art Fair.

"We've had the property surveyed," said her husband, "and their deck is two feet over on *our* side. And I happen to know the guy had no building permit. He's jury-rigged it with sand and cement—"

The telephone rang. "Pardon me," said Elmer, picking it up.

For a moment he was certain the weeping party on the other end of the line had the wrong number.

"Jail," she sobbed. "He's in jail."

"Who is this?" demanded Elmer, wiping his ear with his handkerchief. "Ellen?"

Elmer could never remember actually saying "Yes, Sam, I will represent you," as a man may not remember saying "I do" at his wedding but will recall perfectly some odd remark overheard in the receiving line.

Later, when he ran it through his head, he could still not be sure which moment he was looking for. Was it on the telephone he'd consented? Never had a prospective client badgered him so insistently or told him with such certainty that if anyone else took his case, all was lost. *When did I agree?* In the drab waiting room when he'd given his name to the policewoman who checked his papers and waved him into Lieutenant Coles's office? Was it there, among the files and posters of Smokey the Bear, the boxes of latex gloves, the bowling trophies and pictures of missing children? *When did I lose my freedom to say no?*

"Elmer, sit down," said Lieutenant Coles. He was a ruddy, horse-faced man who wore two tie tacks, one embossed with the seal of the United States Marines, the other a pair of miniature sterling handcuffs.

Elmer pulled up a chair, and a set of balances plummeted from the shelf over his head, hit the floor, and exploded into chains, screws, and pans. "Oh, I'm sorry . . ."

He started to gather the pieces, but Lieutenant Coles stopped him. "Forget it. We must have confiscated twenty of these in the last month alone. We even got a digital one. The guy must have paid hundreds of dollars for it." He leaned forward and the jocular note slipped from his voice. "Elmer, do you know this bird we've got down here, this Sam Theopolis?"

"I know Sam," said Elmer. A lie, he thought. I don't know him at all. Nobody knows him.

"Is he a close friend?"

"Not a close friend of mine," answered Elmer. "But he's like one of the family. He was hired as live-in help for Jessie Woolman."

"You know he's been booked on a murder charge. I doubt you'll get bail. Seems like he's done this before."

"What do you mean, he's done this before?"

"He's drowned a woman. The judge feels he's dangerous. It's all in the report."

The lieutenant pushed a handful of papers and photographs across the desk. Elmer picked them up. The top photograph showed Barton Dam, a scenic shot you could hang on the wall except for the back and buttocks rising through the branchy head of a dead willow floating in the water above the dam. Loosestrife and arrowroot lined the shore. Elmer and Allison had once picnicked at the dam and watched turtles sunning themselves on just such a fallen tree.

The second photograph showed only the woman's face, the right side of which was partly eaten away, leaving a pale pulpy mass where the eye had been. The left eye protruded and gave the face an astonished look. An image of Sam's one-eyed cat flitted through Elmer's mind, and he repressed it.

The third photograph was of the body full-length. Four ribs on the left side were crushed, both arms broken. The woman's long black hair lay fanned out on both sides of her head like the plumy tail of an exotic bird.

"The contusions on the left side were made by the tires of a car," continued the lieutenant. "There were traces of rubber embedded in the skin. The skid marks were a good thirty feet from the water. We figure she was hit, then dragged to the pond and thrown in. It was the drowning that killed her. Dr. Blount says she was in the water for the better part of a week before the kids found her."

"It must have been tough on them," said Elmer, shuddering.

"She was wearing Theopolis's T-shirt," said Lieutenant Coles. "The one with 'I am a mother who loves too well. I have fifteen children' written across it."

"Are there any witnesses?"

Lieutenant Coles shrugged. "If you mean to the crime, no. But we have evidence besides the T-shirt that establishes a connection between the victim and the accused."

From the top drawer of his desk, he drew a photograph that had clearly not been made for purposes of establishing the connection. It was a black and white print showing a hillside that sloped down to the river. Elmer recognized Heavenly Rest in the upper left-hand corner.

"A guy who was doing landscapes took the shot. When he enlarged it, he noticed the woman was wearing the shirt."

Lieutenant Coles tossed out another photograph, a detail in soft focus, but Elmer recognized the figures. The woman was picking her way down the weedy hillside, her long dark hair falling around her shoulders. She was wearing jeans and a T-shirt, on the front of which he could just make out the words. Elmer recognized the blurred face of Sam at the top of the picture, looming over the rise.

"Elmer, do you happen to know a Mrs. Pew?"

"No," said Elmer. He saw himself groping in vain for a thread, a word, an idea that would light up causes, reveal connections.

"She's the custodian at Heavenly Rest. That's how we located him. She recognized him from the photograph. He was hanging around the Woolman plot, acting 'funny,' she said. She took down his license number. The car turned out to be registered in Mrs. Woolman's name."

Elmer felt sick. "Have you identified the victim yet?"

The lieutenant shook his head and shuffled the photographs into a neat pile.

"We circulated a restored version of her face among people who work near the river. We think some of Bearheart's relatives know who she was, but nobody we interviewed wanted to tell us. Not even her name. A secretive bunch. There's a graveside service for her this afternoon. I doubt any of them will show up."

"Who's paying for the coffin?"

"Harvey Mack. He can afford it. He also found the minister—a Reverend Lawrence. Methodist, I think."

"Was the water woman Methodist?"

"God knows what she was," said Lieutenant Coles.

"I'd like to talk to Sam," said Elmer, and stood up. "One more thing. Did he think he was obliged to answer your questions?"

"We read him his rights. He said he had nothing to hide. He said the truth would set him free."

"So the case against him is entirely circumstantial."

Lieutenant Coles shrugged. "There's plenty for an indictment," he said, "when you consider the history. He was with a woman who drowned in Wisconsin a couple of years ago. They called it an accident, but there was something funny about it. And we came across this in his room at the Woolman residence. It's got a lot of notes in the margins."

He held up *Invisibility: Mastering the Art of Vanishing.*

"Can I see that?"

"Of course."

As he handed the book to Elmer, he added, "Jack Chu figures there's a pattern."

John Murray realized, as the plane touched down in Detroit, that what he really liked about traveling was coming home, and you couldn't come home unless you left it. When Martha had phoned the night before, he'd managed to calm her down and assure her she hadn't endangered their lives by hiring Sam. All the evidence wasn't in yet, he reminded her. "That's why we have the jury system. Sam is innocent until proven guilty."

But what good were his words? Martha was one of those people who need something to worry about. Mrs. Trimble had offered to help keep an eye on Jessie during the day till the case was settled, if Ellen could cover the night shift.

Everyone around him was standing up, fighting with luggage in the overhead compartments, straddling suitcases and brief-cases in the aisle, all packed into a single organism divided against itself.

"Please remain in your seats until the captain has turned off the seat belt sign," pleaded the flight attendant.

Suddenly the air opened in front of John, and he hurried down the aisle through the door and into the carpeted tunnel that led to the terminal.

Martha was pacing in front of the gate, and she ran forward and kissed him on the cheek. "How was the flight?"

"Fine. Except we were late taking off."

As they jostled for a spot at the baggage carousel, Martha fished in her purse for the photograph of Sam in the *Ann Arbor News*. In it, Sam looked as if he were receiving an award, smiling, his head tilted to catch important instructions from someone offstage.

"We'll need extra papers," said Martha. "Everybody will want one."

"Let's talk about it when we're in the car," said John.

A pair of skis glided by. A duffel bag bumbled after a turquoise garment bag tagged with a red hair ribbon.

"Aren't you going to ask me if I brought any presents?"

"You always bring presents," said Martha, and hugged him.

He could never wait till they got home to give his presents. Now from his briefcase he pulled out a jar on which was printed, in thin gold letters: "PARKINSON'S PREMIUM CHOCOLATE-COVERED BEES. Product of Argentina."

"Good heavens, who gets these?"

"Elmer. Allison tells me he's trying to diversify his palate."

In spite of herself, Martha had to laugh. John slipped the jar back into his briefcase and pulled out two small gift boxes. "One is for Allison," he said. "The other, my dear, is for you. Your present is at least two thousand years old."

He lifted the lid of the box to reveal a gold chain, on which hung half a small stone egg.

"Very nice," said Martha politely.

Suddenly she saw it: in the middle of the stone a fern had fallen asleep and left its shadow, like the spiny footprint of a ghost.

When Ellen came to work an hour late, Mrs. Pickering did not wait for her to apologize.

"I'm so sorry. I know it's been one thing after another. Of course you should take time off when you need it. If there's anything I can do—"

"Thanks. There's nothing anyone can do at this point."

"We have a new patient," said Mrs. Pickering. "I just thought I'd let you know that we're keeping a close watch on him. His name is Tuttle."

"Tuttle?"

"Another one of Bearheart's people. You know they don't like to give us their real names."

She passed the nurse's station on her way to the dayroom. The bright chatter of the TV drifted out over the arrested traffic of wheelchairs. Close to the doorway, Mrs. Kraft was snoring, her head on her chest.

As she entered the dayroom, she noticed a curious figure gathering the tattered issues of the *Reader's Digest* and biting the covers, as if testing their purity. He had so wrapped himself in pillow slips and towels—filched from other patients, she supposed—that it was impossible to guess his age. In spite of herself, she wanted to laugh.

"Do they taste good?" asked Ellen.

The man adjusted the dish towel that hooded him and turned his sleepy black eyes on her. "I'm going to wash them, miss," he said.

She picked up what had once been copies of *Prevention* and *Awake* and *How to Survive on Land and Sea* but were fast turning to papier-mâché.

"Don't worry," he assured her. "Those have already been washed."

"I see you've met our newest patient, Mr. Tuttle," said Mrs. Pickering.

"Mr. Tuttle, you should work in the laundry room," said Ellen.

"Unfortunately, he's not very discriminating. He throws everything he can get his hands on into the river," said Mrs. Pickering.

"The river is a long way off," said Ellen.

"But the pond is very close," whispered Tuttle. "And very deep."

"Tuttle has a throwing arm you wouldn't believe," said Mrs. Pickering. "The Tigers should know about him. Thank God he didn't find the most recent *Prevention*. There's a good article in it about recharging your immunity." And she held up the magazine, handed it to Ellen, and left the room.

Tuttle snatched it from her, bit it in two, and handed both halves back. "Read it to me," he said. "Please, please."

Ellen opened the front half of the magazine and her eye fell on a title she did not remember seeing before, though she had read this very issue in the waiting room at the University Hospital. "Here's one called 'The City Where Women Are Healed and Men Are Mended,'" she said. "Do you want to hear that one?"

"That one," said Tuttle.

"'Walk till you come to the place where a salmon is cooking

itself in a pot. When the salmon says, "Sit down and eat me," you should say, "I'm not hungry. Can you show me the road to the city where women are healed and men are mended?" ' "

Mrs. Kraft woke up. Next to her, Mr. Kessler was blinking, as if he had just stepped into a bright light. This can't be *Prevention,* Ellen thought. She flipped back to the table of contents, but it was gone.

"Read," said Tuttle.

Baffled, Ellen read on. " 'When you arrive at the city, people will ask you why you have come. Tell them you have come to be mended. Tell them you want a new heart. The people will offer you a silver heart and this you should refuse. They will offer you a gold heart and this you should also refuse. Then the people will offer you a heart made of water and send you out to meet the river woman, who is their queen. With only a water heart, you will be afraid. But when you have filled your water heart with stories from the river woman, she will tell her people, "This one has a good heart. Mend her well." ' "

She turned the page, and the magazine disintegrated in her hands.

The afternoon was hot and cloudy, and Martha noted more than one green awning set up over an open grave. Mrs. Pew was running her feet off, keeping at bay two policemen, three photographers, and a man with a camcorder on the bed of a truck.

There were four mourners—Harvey, Elmer, Ellen, and herself. Martha was here because Elmer had urged Ellen to go and keep her eyes open, and Ellen did not want to go with Harvey. You couldn't tell who would show up at the water woman's funeral, Elmer told her. Maybe the person who killed her.

Four mourners—five, if you counted Mrs. Pew. When Mrs.

Pew had taught driver's ed at Pioneer High, her sarcasm reduced
even football players to tears. Needless to say, no teenagers came
to drink and neck in Heavenly Rest. Besides, it was too far from
the center of town for anyone to find it convenient for anything,
including funerals.

"Let us pray," said Reverend Lawrence, and closed his eyes.
"God is our refuge and our strength, a very present help in time
of trouble. Therefore we will not fear, though the earth be
removed and the mountains be carried into the midst of the sea,
though the waters roar and be troubled and the mountains shake
with the swelling. There is a river, the streams whereof shall
make glad the city of God, the holy place of the tabernacles of the
Most High."

Martha stole a glance at Ellen. Must be hard on her, she
thought. The last time we did this was for Mike.

# 17

---

Facing Sam across the table in the little back room at the police station, Elmer was struck by the ease with which he wore his handcuffs, as if he'd chosen them, the ornamental burdens of a Hell's Angel.

"This is Patrick Nolan from my office. He'll be assisting me on your case," said Elmer.

The young man carrying the box of documents nodded. He was tall, muscular, and wore his black hair combed straight back, slicked down and lacquered to a fine gleam. A pity he and Sam couldn't trade looks, thought Elmer, just for the trial. Patrick dropped the box on the table and lifted the lid. Elmer thumbed through the papers in silence till he found the list of the state's witnesses. "The strongest witness is Mrs. Pew. She's the one who took down the license number of Mrs. Woolman's car."

"I know," said Sam.

"We might have been able to discredit that bit of testimony—her office is at least four yards from the road—if she hadn't identified you in the lineup. So that's what we're up against. There's also a Bill Williams, who helped you put a new grille on Mrs. Woolman's car, about an hour after Mrs. Pew saw you."

"I told them somebody must have hit the car while I was in Ellen's apartment."

"According to Williams, you insisted on having the new grille put on right away. In fact, you didn't even want to leave the car in the shop. The state, of course, will claim you wanted to hide the damage to the car."

"I didn't want to hide it, I wanted to fix it. Mrs. Woolman loves that car."

"Where did you happen to find a grille for a 1961 Buick?"

"The woman I met at Heavenly Rest gave it to me. I traded my T-shirt for it. I already told the police."

"Sam, the state's case may be pretty weak, but that story isn't even remotely plausible."

"I can't help it," said Sam. "I'm telling the truth."

Elmer shook his head. "Maybe we can convince the jury nobody would tell such a wild story unless it was true. More likely, though, they'll suspect you've made it up for precisely that reason." He continued turning the pages of the file. "And there's this other drowning on your record. A Molly Flannagan drowned, you said, when your canoe overturned. Jack Chu will try to use that."

Sam was silent.

"And I see that a Dr. Hagopian you worked for at the morgue of the University Hospital in Madison has been called."

"He's coming all the way from Madison?"

"If you knew the prosecutor, you'd know the answer," said Elmer. "Jack Chu is not the most personable man in this business, but he's certainly one of the most thorough. And brightest. Got his undergraduate degree at Harvard and was first in his class at Yale Law School."

"He's a local man," chimed in Patrick. "He was fifteen years ahead of me at Pioneer. He was valedictorian, National Merit scholar, president of the student council, the math club, and the biology club."

"Is he a good friend of yours?" asked Elmer.

Patrick threw him a sheepish smile. "No. I looked him up in the yearbook."

"I see," said Elmer. "More to the point is the case he tried three years ago. A young woman joined a religious community in Ypsilanti—one of those cults you read about, very strange and repressive. When she severed all ties with her family, her parents arranged to have her kidnapped and deprogrammed. She'd signed over everything she owned and a few things she didn't own. Her parents sued the head of the group, and all kinds of things came to light. Child abuse was the least of it."

"Are you saying the prosecutor thinks I'm part of a cult?"

"I'm saying a man like Chu sees you've worked in a morgue and you're reading a book on the art of turning invisible and figures you're into something strange. I gather you have no ties with such groups."

"No," said Sam.

"Good," said Elmer. "I feel like an ass having to tell you this, but Chu has asked that you be sequestered from the Woolman family till the trial starts. He considers you both psychically and physically dangerous."

Sam said nothing for several minutes. He was staring at the box of documents. "Elmer, tell me something. Do they always label boxes this way?"

"What way?" asked Elmer.

"*People of the State of Michigan v. Sam Theopolis.*"

"That's how it's written. You saw the indictment."

"It's me versus all the people in Michigan? People I've never met? People in Grand Rapids and Muskegon and Traverse City, they're all against me?"

"For heaven's sake, I didn't invent the legal form."

"Another thing. Elmer, can I keep The Everpresent Fullness in my cell?"

"No," said Elmer.

"But keeping a cat clears the brain," said Sam. "Some very important ideas only come to you when you're speaking to cats in their own language. There are so many things you can't say in English."

"Sam, I can't tell the guard that."

"It was The Everpresent Fullness who insisted that you represent me. 'The reason may not be obvious at first glance,' she said, 'but trust me—Elmer is the right man.' "

"Be sensible," said Elmer. He did not dare look over at Patrick, who had stopped sifting through the contents of the box and was listening, open-mouthed.

"Here's an inventory of what the investigators took from your room," said Patrick. "They didn't take much." He handed the paper to Elmer, who handed it to Sam.

"There wasn't much to take," said Sam, glancing at it.

Suddenly he craned forward. "My whistle!" he exclaimed. "They took my whistle. What did they take that for?"

"Because it was there."

"They had no right to take my whistle. That was going to be a present for Ellen."

"I'll tell them," said Elmer. "Is there anything else?"

"I had a notebook on my desk. They didn't take that."

"Odd," said Elmer. "It should have been the first thing on the list."

"It's got a story in it I wrote for Ellen," said Sam. "Make sure she gets it, won't you?"


On the back porch, Jessie dozed on the glider while Ellen shelled peas into a bowl and Mrs. Trimble mended one of Jessie's pillow slips.

"I'm not saying it will work, I'm just saying it's worth a try," said Mrs. Trimble. "You never know what the dead can tell you till you call them."

"I've never seen a ghost," said Ellen.

"Not everyone can see them," observed Mrs. Trimble. "My brother never saw a ghost, but he took a picture of one." She opened her purse and held up a snapshot of two little boys playing with a big white dog. Around them danced a white streak like a giant smoke ring.

"Two weeks before this picture was taken, their twelve-year-old daughter died in a car accident. She always loved to rough-house with her brothers and the dog."

"Are you sure it's not a light leak?" asked Ellen.

"Mr. Wissota has seen a lot of pictures," answered Mrs. Trimble with great dignity, "and he was positive it wasn't a light leak." She took from her purse a business card and handed it to Ellen.

### •Wissota & Black Pest Control•

Identification & Removal of Bees, Wasps,
Fleas, Termites, Earwigs, Roaches & Ghosts
CLEAR COMMUNICATION GUARANTEED
24 Hour Emergency Service, 7 Days a Week

"But we don't want to get rid of a ghost," said Ellen. "We want to question one."

"Oh, Mr. Wissota is wonderful with ghosts. So respectful and polite. They'll do anything for him. I know people who won't so much as sign a lease till they've had Mr. Wissota or Mr. Black check the place out. Of course, you can't tell which one Thomas Bearheart will send, but I'd ask for Mr. Wissota."

Lord, thought Ellen. Her talking could drive you crazy.

"I'm going to get a glass of water," she said. "Mother, do you want anything?"

"No use asking her," said Mrs. Trimble. "She's asleep."

Jessie opened her eyes. "A Vernors for me," she said.

"I'll get it," said Ellen, and fled to the kitchen with Mrs. Trimble right behind her.

"When my grandfather was buried, the grave digger broke ground and found a whole congregation of skeletons sitting up in their graves. That's how the Pawquachas buried their dead. Facing the firepot."

"My God," said Ellen. "How bizarre."

She opened the icebox and poked around for a ginger ale. There was one can of Vernors left.

"When I was growing up, people used to go out behind the golf course looking for the firepot," said Mrs. Trimble. "It's supposed to be made of black stone carved with snakes. The fire never goes out, on account of it was sent by the gods so the dead could find the river to heaven. Boy oh boy, when I had to walk four miles along the river to school in winter, I sure wanted to find that firepot and maybe sit and warm myself. Dad thought it was under the fifth hole. But nobody knows for sure. He never would go hunting around there. You'd think you shot a deer and it turns out you hit one of those old Pawquachas. Or maybe one of their great-great-grandchildren."

In spite of herself, Ellen found herself listening. It was the kind of story Sam would love.

"A man who has been a deer or a loon is bound to be one again, sure as a snake sheds its skin, and there ain't a thing in the world he can do to keep it from happening. Those changes are in the blood."

.    .    .

Ellen said, "I think Mother should go to the trial," and Martha exploded.

"Are you crazy? She won't understand what's happening. She won't even remember what she's heard."

"She might remember a little. She keeps asking about Sam. We could say, 'Remember the trial? Remember Sam sitting up there?' "

Martha reached down and lowered the flame in the fireplace. "Ellen, the trial will only confuse her."

In the end, they compromised. They would take her to court for the opening statements. Mrs. Trimble could sit with her. If trouble arose, Mrs. Trimble could take her out.

When they left the dingy corridors and the little flock of newsmen, Ellen was glad to slip into her seat in the front row. Jessie folded her hands and put on her church face: perfectly content, waiting for the sermon.

Familiarity had made the courtroom less depressing. In the last two days Ellen had heard both Elmer and Jack Chu question the prospective jurors, and she'd heard the judge remind them, over and over: Sam is innocent till proven guilty. She wondered if outside this courtroom she could recognize the judge, stripped of her robe and gavel. Small, mousy, brown plastic glasses— Judge O'Brien would look dowdy and forgettable, like someone's aunt at a wedding.

Though Ellen did not know the judge personally, at least she was no stranger. Her views were a matter of public record. But Jack Chu, the prosecutor, seemed as distant to Ellen as if she'd never laid eyes on him, though Stevie had been best friends with Joseph, his youngest son, all during second grade, and Ellen had often called at the house.

From outside, the Chu place looked like the other expensive homes in Huron Hills: a large, well-landscaped yard, a swimming pool, a greenhouse. But inside it resembled no other house Ellen had ever seen. A faint spicy fragrance pervaded the air, as if a ghost were opening invisible tins of cinnamon and jasmine. On the long silk scrolls in the dining room glowed peonies so finely rendered they seemed breathed rather than brushed onto the cloth. A black lacquer screen inlaid with ivory divided the living room, and two porcelain urns painted with butterflies flanked the early American fireplace. When Ellen called for Stevie, the only sound in the house was Joseph's older sister practicing the violin. She was a prodigy, Joseph explained; he himself practiced two hours a day on the piano.

From Stevie she heard about the blind grandmother who kept a jar of candied ginger by her bed, which she rationed out in unequal portions to her grandchildren: a small chunk for Joseph, a big chunk for his sister. "And Joseph is scared to take any more," said Stevie, "because her left eye sees ghosts, and even though she's blind she can see him with that one."

Standing in the hallway, Ellen had once heard Jack Chu shouting at his mother through her closed bedroom door: *You want ghosts, Mama? Okay! Okay! You get yourself some American ghosts!*

After the grandmother died, the urns and screens were replaced by a sofa covered in leather, a glass-topped coffee table, and two Lucite chairs. Joseph and his sister were sent to a private school.

The Jack Chu who was making his opening statement bore no resemblance to the angry young man who shouted to his mother through a closed door. That young man wore threadbare trousers; this one dressed smartly in a blue summer suit, with a red paisley ascot and a dark gray shirt.

"The evidence places Mr. Theopolis in the Heavenly Rest Cemetery at one o'clock in the afternoon. He was seen standing before the grave of Mike Hanson, apparently speaking to the deceased, and later to the victim. We are asked to believe that the victim admired Mr. Theopolis's shirt and inquired of him what he would take in trade, and that Mr. Theopolis replied he needed a grille for a '61 Buick. We are further asked to believe that the victim disappeared in the direction of the river and returned with the grille requested and that Mr. Theopolis traded his T-shirt for it, a shirt distinctive for its inscription: 'I am a mother who loves too well. I have fifteen children.' Ladies and gentlemen of the jury, a grille for a '61 Buick is not an easy item to locate, and if you are fortunate enough to find one, you can expect to pay several hundred dollars for it."

Sam was listening, fascinated, as if these events had happened many years ago and had nothing to do with him.

"The moon was full on the night the victim disappeared. I do not pretend to know the significance of the full moon to those involved in the occult sciences, nor the role that death and sacrifice play in the ceremonies of those who live by the teachings of these sciences. But the evidence shows us that Mr. Theopolis is no stranger to the occult, and I will ask the jury to keep this in mind when weighing the possible motives for the murder of a stranger."

Ellen was so absorbed in watching Sam that she hardly heard the conclusion of Jack Chu's opening statement. When Elmer jumped to his feet she started as from a dream in time to hear Judge O'Brien suggest a recess, which Elmer declined. With an air of great calm, he addressed the jury.

"Ladies and gentlemen of the jury, I urge you to consider only the evidence. Possible motives are not evidence. You cannot send a man to prison for offering his shirt to a woman on the eve of the full moon. The moon has been waxing and waning for millions of years, and it will wax and wane for a million more, regardless of how the prosecutor wishes to interpret it. A man is known not only by his beliefs but by his deeds."

He described Sam's kindness to animals, to the elderly in general and Mrs. Woolman in particular. He read from the letter Sam sent when he applied for the job of watching over Mrs. Woolman, and Ellen saw herself sitting on the glider beside Martha reading it and saying, "This has got to be a joke." The joke was on me, she thought. She wanted to weep.

" 'At the age of thirteen I cared for a dozen sled dogs left to my father by an old friend. In college I worked at Calling All Strays Small Animal Clinic. I had responsibility for birds and amphibians under two pounds. I am presently caring for a wounded cat whose paw was crushed in a trap and who was brought in to be "put down." The veterinarian from whose lethal injection I saved her says she is probably twelve years old. In cat years that amounts to 72 years. So I've had some experience in caring for the elderly.

" 'As Black Elk says, This life is holy and good to tell, and the two-leggeds share it with the four-leggeds and the wings of the air and all green things. . . . I hope someday to start my own clinic for healing both four-leggeds and two-leggeds.' "

Outside, the sun dipped under a cloud and the light faded from the courtroom, as if something that lived on light had just drawn its last breath.

# 18

---

Ellen and Martha stood at the kitchen sink, scraping and rinsing the dinner dishes.

"Do you think they'll put Mother on the stand?" asked Ellen.

"Good Lord!" exclaimed Martha. "I can't imagine why Elmer would call Mother."

"He's calling you and me. He's calling John. He's calling the cook from the Buddha Uproar. There's nobody else left."

"Except Sam," Martha reminded her. "Did he ever talk to you about Molly?"

"I never asked him about her," said Ellen. "I never dreamed Chu would be allowed to use that against him."

Martha turned off the hot water and pointed out the window. A white pickup truck was backing into their driveway. On the door was written, in weatherbeaten script, WISSOTA & BLACK. ASK THE PROFESSIONALS. The man who climbed out was small, white-haired, and wiry. He wore a white shirt and a Hoot 'n Scoot cap, and he carried a tackle box.

"Why, he looks as if he's coming to fix the furnace," said Martha, with a twinge of disappointment.

"Mother, the exterminator is here," called Ellen.

Mrs. Trimble helped Jessie rise from the sofa, as Allison and

Stevie and John and Elmer hurried to the front door for a good view.

"Is that Wissota or Black?" Allison asked Mrs. Trimble.

"That's Mr. Wissota. Mr. Black moved up to Mackinac Island."

"Elmer said he was kooky. He doesn't look kooky," said Stevie, and Mrs. Trimble snapped, "Of course he's not kooky."

"If he can make the dead woman tell her story, I'll never say another word against him," said Elmer.

Mr. Wissota paused on the front steps, and Martha rushed out to meet him. "Did you have trouble finding us?"

He gave her a broad smile. "Nope. That's my profession. But I sure will be glad to step in out of the heat."

Ellen showed him into the living room, and he surveyed it quickly, as if he were appraising it.

"What a nice fireplace," he observed. "A fire in August is an unusual sight."

"It's natural gas," said Martha.

"And a grinding wheel," exclaimed Mr. Wissota, pointing to the little wheel in Stevie's hand. "You don't see those in many houses anymore."

"Grandma gave it to me," said Stevie. "See, I can stick it on things."

And he clamped the wheel to the coffee table. Mr. Wissota did not seem interested.

"I need a straight chair," he said. "Bad back."

John brought him a chair from the dining room.

After everyone had found places around him, Mr. Wissota opened his tackle box and took out a clipboard. "Yes, indeed," he said. "Natural gas. Now I have a little questionnaire that will help me to serve you better. We can go over it real fast. Voices?"

"What?" asked Ellen.

"Have you heard voices?"

"Just our own," said Elmer.

"Flying objects?"

"No," said Ellen.

"Lights going on at odd times and places?"

Jessie narrowed her eyes at Mr. Wissota. "Do you have a Ph.D.?" she asked.

"I have ten years of experience in this business," replied Mr. Wissota. "And let me tell you something, Mrs. Woolman. A Ph.D. doesn't impress *them*. Nothing impresses them."

An uneasy silence followed this statement.

"But there's nothing to fear," he added. "If you see or hear one of them, remember to be polite. Simply address it as another human being."

"Mr. Wissota, we're mainly interested in questioning the ghost of the murder victim," Elmer reminded him.

Mr. Wissota nodded and pushed the clipboard back into the tackle box and pulled out a tape recorder. "Some people use a Geiger counter, but they're expensive. You do have to check your batteries, though."

"How long will this take?" asked John.

"Depends on what we find," answered Mr. Wissota. "Last week I was at the house of a nurse who was caring for an older woman, and the ghost of the woman's husband followed her home. He tried to attack her—" a delicate pause—"sexually."

"Did you nab him?" demanded Mrs. Trimble.

"We got rid of that one, but not the others," answered Mr. Wissota. "This woman had a lot of problems. I mean, we're talking about an infestation."

"Are you the exterminator?" asked Jessie. "We don't need you. The carpenter ants left on their own."

"I don't do much in the insect extermination line these days,

Mrs. Woolman. Once in a while I get a call to clean out a nest of bees or carpenter ants. A gentleman in Barton Hills asked me to help him get rid of an invasion of toads." He chuckled. "Ghost hunting is pretty much a full-time job. The truth is, the dead are all around us, trying to find their way back. Sometimes they use mirrors or cracks in the ceiling or stains on the wallpaper. Sometimes radios or the TV."

"TV?" exclaimed Stevie.

"Wherever the living remember the dead, a doorway opens to let them into our lives. If you'll excuse me, I'm going to switch on the tape recorder."

"Can a ghost come through the tape recorder?" asked Stevie.

"Only their voices," answered Mr. Wissota. "The difference between using a tape recorder and a mirror or a candle is the difference between a telephone call and an unannounced visit. With a telephone call, you can hang up. I hope nobody will mind if we turn off the lights."

"No, of course not," said Martha. "Shall I turn off the lights in the kitchen and the dining room as well?"

"All of them, please."

The others stayed in their chairs, listening to the click of lights being switched off in the kitchen, the dining room, the hall, and the living room. With each click a new shovelful of darkness dropped over them.

"Now, there's a little problem about the fireplace," said Mr. Wissota.

Ellen waited till Martha found her seat, then reached down and turned off the fire. Moonlight touched their faces, draining them of color.

"It's awfully dark, isn't it?" said Jessie.

"I'll get a candle," said John, rising, but Mr. Wissota reached out and stopped him.

"I wouldn't do that. You might attract something you don't want. I use a flashlight myself."

A searing light in the window followed by a clap of thunder made them all jump.

"Big storm a-comin'," said Mrs. Trimble. "I heard about it on the news."

"I don't want to see a ghost," said Stevie in a small voice. Suddenly the universe felt unfriendly to him, as if it did not want these eight people meddling with it, prying open the door that kept the living from the dead.

"Don't worry," said Mr. Wissota. "We might not see it. We might smell it."

"What would it smell like?" asked Stevie.

"Cigars. Perfume. Dead fish. I met one ghost that smelled like dead fish."

*Click. Click.*

"Now, what's that noise?" asked Mrs. Trimble.

"The lights don't work," said Jessie.

"Must be the storm," said John.

"Or it might come as an animal," continued Mr. Wissota in pleasant tones. "Or a group of ghosts. I knew a woman who had to put up with a family of ghosts. They had their get-together once a year, just after New Year's Eve. They'd turn the thermostat up to ninety."

"The light bulbs are in the kitchen," said Jessie, "unless Ellen used them all up."

"How can you call up the victim's ghost if you don't know her name?" asked Ellen.

"We're not going to call her up. We'll just make room for her," said Mr. Wissota. "Has anyone died in this house recently? I mean, within the last ten or twenty years?"

"Where did Henry die?" asked Jessie.

"In the ambulance, Mother," said Martha. "Not in the house."

"Henry was her husband?" asked Mr. Wissota.

Ellen nodded and realized that in the darkness no one could see her.

"I smell Life Savers!" exclaimed Mrs. Trimble.

"It's only me," said Elmer. "I popped one in my mouth."

"You could offer them to the rest of us," said Mrs. Trimble.

"That was the last one."

Something terrible was happening, Jessie felt sure. When the lights came back on, she would find that all of them, including herself, had been replaced with substitutes. Was Mr. Wissota at the heart of the conspiracy?

"There's nothing to fear," said Mr. Wissota. "Each of us is protected by the white light."

"I don't see any white light," said Stevie.

"You can't see it," said Mr. Wissota, "but *they* can. It's like a big cocoon that folds around you when you say, 'I am protected by the white light of God. No evil force can harm me.' My sister throws one around her car when she goes shopping to protect it from drunk drivers. Let's say it together, folks."

Their voices shuffled along behind his: "I am protected by the white light of God. No evil force can harm me."

The light chatter of rain followed. A peaceful sound. Elmer closed his eyes. No difference now whether they're open or closed. Got to remember to tell Ellen about that notebook of Sam's.

He shifted his weight and heard a tinkle of loose change slip out of his pocket. In the darkness he knelt and stroked the rug, searching, fingertips nosing the nap, pausing to identify a penny, a piece of—was it cottage cheese? The next instant he felt it hop away, and his fingers were crushed by a paralyzing pain which entirely eclipsed his promise to Sam.

"A mouse touched me," said Mrs. Trimble, "but I stomped on him. Thank God I've never been afraid of mice."

Elmer's fingers flew to his mouth; he sucked them as if the pain were a venom he could draw out. Tentatively he tried to move them, then put his hand, still throbbing, into his pocket for safekeeping.

"There are no mice in this house," said Jessie. "Sam's cat has eaten every last one of them." She heard the little grinding wheel on the coffee table spinning and spinning, like a cog in the axle of a universe that does not know it is dying.

"The rain has stopped!" exclaimed Mr. Wissota. "But God knows when we'll get power again."

"I'll turn up the fire," said Allison. "Elmer, you look as though you've seen a ghost."

"Not me," he assured her.

"I can run my recorder off the battery," said Mr. Wissota. "Let's see if we picked up anything."

They listened to the screech of the tape winding itself back. A thin roar as of wind rising, a crackle, and then voices that sounded as if the speakers were under water:

*I hope nobody will mind if we turn off the lights. . . . It's awfully dark. . . . I'll get a candle. . . . I wouldn't do that. You might attract something you don't want. . . . Big storm a-comin'. I heard about it on the news.*

"Do I really sound like that?!" exclaimed Mrs. Trimble. "Oh, tell me I don't."

"You sound nice, Grandma," said Allison.

"I had elocution lessons," said Jessie.

"Why, Mother," exclaimed Ellen, "you never told me that!"

"I only had three of them. They were too expensive."

"Hush," said Mr. Wissota. "Listen, now."

For a few minutes nothing was heard except the shifting and creaking of chairs.

"I don't hear anything but ourselves," said Ellen.

"They can't do a clear human voice," said Mr. Wissota. "What we're trying to get is their energy. Sometimes you hear things on the tape you didn't hear at the time. Listen hard, folks. See if anyone can make out a few words."

Elmer strained to make sense of the crackles and clicks and heard nothing but the beating of his own heart.

On the tape, thunder was muttering. John hunched forward, his head dropped nearly to his chest, and tried to shut it out: the VC mortars, the choppers coming in with ammo, the rain lightening to a drizzle through the vaulted canopy of palms, the banana trees waving their fringed flags, the elephant grass twisting around his knees, the boot with a sheared-off foot in it floating across the rice paddy, the steaming heat, the smell of fungus and flesh and everything coming apart or peeling away in this godawful place, the deafening silence, the whole village gone.

Suddenly the crackle gave way to a violent static.

*Along State Street my name is no longer spoken. When I was alive, I could make things happen. I want you to save Sam in my honor.*

Mr. Wissota stopped the tape. "Let me play that bit again. We might have caught something."

Ellen's throat felt as parched as if she'd hiked across the desert. The static twittered into a broken tune, the singsong speech of a madman.

"I heard something," said Mr. Wissota. "I heard a voice say, 'Turn up the heat.'"

"I thought it sounded like 'Two left feet,'" said Martha.

"Did anyone hear 'What awful meat?'" asked Mrs. Trimble.

"I didn't hear that," said Allison. "Grandma, did you hear anything?"

"No," said Jessie. She would never tell them what she'd heard, clear as the rinsed sky: Henry's voice crossing the universe, creaky with living and dying, rising and setting, singing and silence, to give her the words by which she would know him anywhere: *Oh, for a shredded wheat.*

*Sam, I love you,* whispered Ellen to the darkness.

Something small and warm dropped into her hand. It was Sam's wooden whistle.

# 19

Ellen had come to the conclusion that Harvey was mad. Though she'd grown up among gatherers and savers, Harvey's appetite for collecting the details of Sam's case reached beyond anything she could imagine. Day after day he hung around the prosecutor's office. He'd told Jack Chu's secretary he was writing a book on the case. Could he speak to Mr. Chu in private?

"I can assure you that Mr. Chu will not reveal anything to you he does not intend to reveal in the courtroom," said the young woman behind the desk.

He went to the courtroom sessions every day as if he were going to school. The selection of the jury—six men and six women—interested him enormously. Two of the women were housewives; the third owned the Thief of Baghdad clothing store; the fourth was a bank teller, the fifth a waitress, the sixth a carpenter. The men included a pediatrician, a contractor, a plumber, a commercial photographer, a man who had managed Kresge's before it closed and was now collecting unemployment, and a groundskeeper at the Michigan League who was a distant relative of Thomas Bearheart.

He bought a bicycle and gave up drinking. Not even a glass

of wine with dinner, he told Mrs. Trimble. He also gave up driving; every evening he bicycled down to the river and chatted with the fishermen and the salvage divers, who scoured the river for whatever had fallen in and fallen out of use—fenders, grilles, oars, oil drums, a safe. When he broke ground for Pawquacha Plaza, he said, they would all have real jobs. They would share in the good times ahead; they would be the builders of the new world.

Rich man, poor man, beggar man, thief, sang the children who lived along the river. They skipped flat stones across the water and called out the skips by name: doctor, lawyer, Indian chief. When Harvey realized they were describing the jury, he took it as a sign that a power greater than Judge O'Brien was orchestrating these events. He began to buy fortune cookies at the Buddha Uproar, first one box a day, then two boxes, then four and five, sharing them with Mrs. Trimble when she came to cook his supper, insisting they sit down at the kitchen table and open them and urging her to take some for herself.

"And take one for Ellen and one for Stevie."

As Mrs. Trimble wrapped up the fortune cookies in a napkin, Harvey stopped her. "Open Ellen's here," he said.

"I can't open somebody else's fortune."

"Yes, you can. Open it."

The fortune lurked under the thin, dry lip of the cookie like a hermit crab. Mrs. Trimble shook her head, cracked the cookie in two, pulled out the little paper, and read:

" 'Something spectacular will happen to you. Watch for omens and pack your bags.' "

"Now I'll open mine," said Harvey. He bit the cookie in two. No little paper fluttered out.

"Did you swallow it?" said Mrs. Trimble.

"Of course I didn't swallow it."

"What did you get?"

"Nothing," said Harvey. "Absolutely nothing. I'll return it tomorrow."

"You can't return a fortune cookie."

"You can if it's not what you ordered."

He took out his handkerchief and wrapped the shards of his cookie as carefully as if he intended to mend it.


When Jessie asked what place this was, Ellen said, "It's the courthouse, Mother. And this is the courtroom."

"It's incredible," whispered Martha. "She really doesn't remember. All the times she's been here—and she still has to ask."

Call it what you like, thought Jessie. She knew very well they were on campus, in the old auditorium of Haven Hall, though it had been redone since she took classes there. Why her daughters should want to keep this information from her was beyond her, unless they were afraid the exam would make her nervous.

But they weren't examining her. She already had her B.A.

The fat woman on the witness stand didn't look too bright, and Jessie wondered what degree she was trying for. Probably she would fail. Elmer and Sam were waiting patiently for their turns. Jessie smiled at Sam to encourage him and took a seat between Ellen and Martha and wondered about the weather.

Nothing beats an outdoor graduation, she said to herself. The potted palms and flowers on the platform, the procession of faculty in full plumage, the students cheering and tossing their caps under the bright sky. She hoped the marching band would be on hand to lead them in "The Victors."

*Hail to the Victors Valiant,*
*Hail to the Conquering Heroes,*

*Hail, hail to Michigan,*
*The leaders and best!*

The examiner stepped forward. He looked like her professor in Botany 1, the one she'd had such a crush on. What was his name?

"That's the prosecutor, Jessie," whispered John. "Jack Chu."

Mr. Chu was speaking, and Jessie hushed to hear him.

"State your name and occupation, please."

"Janet Pew. I'm in charge of the front office at Heavenly Rest."

"How long have you worked at Heavenly Rest?"

"Five years."

"And before that, what was your occupation?"

"I taught driver's ed at Pioneer High till my husband retired. He worked at Duncan's Sporting Goods. Used to be on Main Street near the old post office."

Is that a right answer or a wrong answer? Jessie asked herself. The questions were very tricky. They sounded simple, the kind of question you might ask someone you'd just met at a church supper. The trickery was, nothing in this place was as simple as it sounded.

"Mrs. Pew, exactly what does your job involve?"

"I handle orders for burial plots and arrangements for grave-side services and perpetual care. I work from nine till four, five days a week."

"Now, Mrs. Pew, will you tell the jury the location of your office?"

"It's in front, on the left side of the building. It has one glass wall that faces the cemetery."

"Are there any trees between you and the grave of Mike Hanson that might obscure your vision?"

"No, sir, I have a clear view of the Hanson grave."

Jack Chu smiled. "Will you tell the jury when you first saw the defendant?"

Mrs. Pew seemed to consider the problem, and Jessie's heart went out to her. A story problem. Those were the worst kind.

"On the day he killed the wom—"

"Objection!" shouted Elmer.

"Objection sustained."

Jessie had almost forgotten the presence of Judge O'Brien, who now turned sharply on Mrs. Pew. Mrs. Pew's face darkened.

Jack Chu did not give her time to lose her temper. "Please tell the jury when, to the best of your knowledge, you first saw the defendant."

"It was on July fifteenth."

"At what time of day did he come?"

"At three-thirty. I was getting ready to leave."

"Will you please tell the jury exactly what the defendant was doing when you saw him?"

"He was standing in front of the Hanson grave and talking."

"Was there anyone with him?"

"No."

"Then who was he talking to?"

"It looked like he was talking to Mr. Hanson."

"Are you suggesting that the defendant was holding a conversation with a dead man?"

Mrs. Pew hesitated. "Well, I don't know if you could call it a conversation."

A ripple of laughter animated the jury. Jack Chu appeared not to hear it. "Were you close enough to hear what the defendant was saying to Mr. Hanson?"

"No," said Mrs. Pew. "No, I wasn't."

"Mrs. Pew, do you recognize this shirt?" Jack Chu pointed to Sam's T-shirt on the table of exhibits.

"It looks like the one he was wearing."

"Do you recall how many cars were in the cemetery at the time, other than your own?" he asked. His voice was steady and pleasant, as if they were reminiscing about a holiday they'd taken together.

"Only one. A '61 Buick, blue."

"Where was the car in relation to your office?"

"It was parked at the bend. I could see the back of it."

"Did you notice any damage on the car at that time?"

"Not as far as I could see."

"Will you tell the jury what you did next?"

"I took down the license. Then I closed up the office. By the time I got outside, the car was gone."

"Mrs. Pew, do you recognize the man in this photograph?" Jack Chu held up a photograph. The enlargement showed a woman with long dark hair walking down the weedy hillside toward the river. At the top of the photograph a man's head was visible above the sumac and saplings.

"Oh, yes," said Mrs. Pew. "That's him."

Nonsense, thought Jessie. Even God couldn't recognize him in that picture. It's too fuzzy.

"If you see him in this courtroom, please point to him," said Jack Chu.

Mrs. Pew raised her arm as if she were taking an oath and pointed straight at Sam.


When Dr. Hagopian took the stand, it seemed to Sam that a whole chapter torn out of the book of his life was assembling itself before him. God, how he'd hated that job. Shepherding the corpses. He'd learned to stop up orifices, close eyes for good, unbend limbs knotting toward rigor mortis. If he ran into Dr. Hagopian by day, the doctor's narrow face with its sharp nose and hollow cheeks looked no more dangerous than a cup of weak tea. But at night you could think yourself in the underworld of Osiris, sentenced to weigh the human soul, pitting it against a feather dropped from the wing of the god. Every organ had to be weighed before it was put back, as if the touch of the living added a thin film of grief.

"Dr. Hagopian, in what capacity did you work with the defendant?"

"He was my assistant in the morgue at the University Hospital in Madison, Wisconsin."

"Will you tell the jury exactly when he worked for you?"

"It was the summer of '86."

"Before his graduation."

"Yes. He was a junior."

"And what was the nature of his work?"

"He helped me with the autopsies."

"Did his behavior strike you in any way as unlike the behavior of those who have worked with you in this capacity before?"

"There were a few things," answered Dr. Hagopian. "He read aloud to the corpses. A bedtime story, he called it."

"Do you recall what he read to them?"

"I do, because I found it fascinating. I'd never heard anything like it. He read to them from the *Tibetan Book of the Dead.* Sometimes he came early to work so he'd have time to give them a whole chapter."

"Was there anything else you recall as inappropriate about his behavior at that time?"

"Well, he sang during the autopsies. He has a great voice."

The courtroom was very still. Turned to stone, all of them, thought Sam, except Mrs. Woolman, who was nodding at him, and Ellen, who was rocking in her seat.

"What did he sing?"

"Different things. 'You Are My Sunshine,' 'Hark the Herald.' We sang 'Hark the Herald' a lot."

Ellen caught the switch from "Sam sang" to "we sang"; Elmer was writing—noting it, she hoped, for the cross-examination. The members of the jury shifted in their seats. A few were smiling.

"Was there an inventory kept of the body parts in the morgue?"

A puzzled expression settled on the doctor's face. "Well, we had to note the weight and condition of everything we took out before we put it back."

"Dr. Hagopian, would the defendant have had free access to the cadavers?"

"Well, sure."

"Could he have taken parts from these cadavers for use in occult ceremonies?"

Both Elmer and Patrick leaped to their feet as Judge O'Brien's gavel pounded the table hard.

# 20

Something was wrong, Ellen felt sure, and she crawled out of bed and peeked into Stevie's room to check on him. He was sitting in front of the aquarium, staring at the angelfish. The Everpresent Fullness was curled next to him, but the cat was watching Stevie, not the fish.

"What are you doing up?" demanded Ellen. "It's way past your bedtime."

"The moon platy died," he said.

She knelt down and searched water. Through spindly strands of seaweed she spied the tiny blue body of the fish, bobbing in the bubbles from the air filter like a sleeper restrained by a chain of pearls.

"Honey, I'm so sorry. Get the dipper and we'll take him out."

Stevie pulled the dipper from under the bookcase and handed it to her. As she scooped up the fish, she saw it was already decomposing, and by the time she'd rushed it into the bathroom and flipped it into the toilet, nothing remained of its brief life but a shining gel. Knowing that Stevie was listening, she gritted her teeth and flushed.

"Burial at sea," she said, and laid the dipper across the top of the aquarium.

"Sam isn't coming back, is he?" said Stevie.

"Nobody knows when Sam is coming back," said Ellen. "Not till after the trial."

The aquarium gurgled its steady stream of bright syllables.

"Do you want a Vernors?" asked Ellen, who wanted one herself and did not wish to drink it alone.

"Sure," said Stevie.

Jessie's door was closed; Ellen could hear her snoring as she tiptoed downstairs to the kitchen. Without bothering to turn on the light she opened the icebox. As she plucked two cans of ginger ale from the rack inside the door, she spied something gleaming behind half an apple pie on the center shelf. Ellen leaned closer. Hidden under the wax paper Jessie used for covering leftovers were Sam's singing bowls.

Two of them held vegetables in a brown sauce rotted beyond recognition; the third, a crusty chunk of macaroni and cheese. Hastily Ellen put the two ginger ales on the counter and carried the bowls to the sink. She dumped the leftovers into the garbage, squeezed the bottle of liquid soap into the bottoms, rinsed the bowls, and dried them. It was while she was drying the rims that suddenly, like a choir of conch shells, the bowls loosed into the dark kitchen a sonorous hum, then a second, higher one, then a third one, higher still. As they blended into a single moonlit chord, she heard yet another voice, hidden under the others like a fish in deep water.

*I want you to travel to the places where you fell in love with him. I want you to stop at each one and leave daisies. The museum, the Buddha Uproar, the Wolverine Den, the emergency room, the merry-go-round in the park. I want you to visit places you don't even know exist, places you won't know until you find them.*

She stacked the bowls, gathered up the two cans of ginger ale, and bounded up the stairs. When she reached Stevie's room, she was breathless. She popped open the cans and arranged the bowls on the floor and sat on the edge of his bed. The cat leaped into her lap.

"Close your eyes," she said. "We're going to take a walk. We're going to look for Sam. Keep your eyes closed. Do you see Sam?"

"Yes," said Stevie.

"What's he doing?"

"I'm getting ready to take him swimming. Now we're swimming."

"Where are you swimming?"

"At Fuller Park."

"I see both of you," said Ellen. "You're having a good time."

"I can hear him thinking," said Stevie.

"You can? What's he thinking about?"

Stevie listened hard. "Me. You."


As Sam handed over the pieces of his story to Jack Chu in the cross-examination, the sense of danger filled Ellen with panic. Why had Elmer let him take the stand?

"According to a report from the Madison Police Department dated June 25, 1987, you took a young woman named Molly Flannagan canoeing on Scroon Lake."

"That's correct," said Sam.

"You paddled out to the deepest part of the lake. The moon was full and the water was calm. Did you know when you took this woman out that she couldn't swim?"

"Yes," said Sam.

"Miss Flannagan was not wearing a life jacket, though the proprietor of the canoe livery offered to furnish one. Did you suggest to Miss Flannagan that she wear a life jacket?"

"No. She hated life jackets. She called them straitjackets. She'd never wear one."

"Did you take Miss Flannagan canoeing often?"

Sam hesitated.

"I think we went two or three times."

"And you never urged her to wear a life jacket."

"If you knew Molly . . ."

Ellen shivered. She could not bear to think of him with this spirited girl who wouldn't wear a life jacket. First love. There's nothing like it.

"Please answer the question."

"I never urged her."

Why didn't we ask him things? thought Ellen. Why didn't we find out who he was before we invited him into our lives?

"In the middle of the lake, on a calm night, the canoe overturned. Please describe what took place in the canoe before it overturned."

"We had an argument."

"Were you arguing where others could hear you?"

"No. There was nobody else around."

"What did you argue about?"

"Molly had just found out she'd gotten a Marshall fellowship to study in England, and I said she should take it."

"And she didn't want to leave Madison?"

"No, she didn't."

"But you wanted her to leave."

"I didn't want her to leave. I just didn't want to stand in her way."

Ellen couldn't stop trembling. Martha took off her blue cardigan and handed it to her.

"Will you tell the jury what happened next?"

"She got upset and stood up." Sam's voice was barely audible. "I tried to make her sit down. She tipped us over."

"You knew Miss Flannagan couldn't swim. Why didn't you save her?"

He looked down at his hands and did not seem to understand the question.

"Why didn't you save her?"

"She wouldn't let me. She was hanging onto me, pulling me down."

"Mr. Theopolis, can you swim?"

"Not very well."

"But when the canoe overturned, you swam a mile back to shore."

"I was a good swimmer then," whispered Sam. "After the accident, I couldn't swim at all. I had to start over again."

"When Miss Flannagan's body was recovered, there were bruises on her face and chest. These are clearly visible in the photographs taken by the police."

The photograph Jack Chu held up showed the puffy face of a girl with short blond hair who must have been pretty before the water blurred her features. Jack Chu pointed to a dark bruise across her chin.

"Did Miss Flannagan put up a struggle?"

"No— Yes," said Sam. He avoided looking at the photograph. "I fought her off in the water. She wanted to drown us both."

The members of the jury stirred uneasily. Ellen hid her face in her hands.


She was standing behind Harvey in line at the post office on Saturday morning when he turned and asked her to marry him. He asked the question so casually that she thought he was asking her if she could change a ten, and she said, "I don't know."

"I hope you'll give it your serious consideration," he said.

She replayed his voice in her mind and thought, It sounded as if he asked me to—Oh, God, I run into him at the post office and he asks me to marry him.

"Next," called the clerk, and while Harvey was paying for a dozen business-size envelopes, Ellen fled.

# 21

Saturday night a knock on the apartment door woke him; Elmer turned over in bed, his muscles tensed. Allison, curled into a ball, had pulled the sheet around her and was snoring. By the light of the moon on the nightstand, he could just make out the time: three o'clock.

Careful not to wake her, Elmer climbed out of bed, snatched his bathrobe from the bedpost, wrapped it around himself, and hurried through the living room to the front door. Through the peephole he saw, in the enchanted eye of his electronic beholder, two strangers. One man was so much shorter than the other that at first glance Elmer thought he was looking at a deformed child.

"Who is it?" he called.

"We have important information about the Theopolis case," answered a muffled voice from the other side of the door. The tone was friendly but strained, as if the speaker had a bad cold or wanted to disguise his voice.

"Who are you?"

"I'm Toth," said the short one, "and my friend here is Tuttle."

Elmer opened the door as far as the chain would permit; a stink like old cat food almost made him retch.

"What's your information?"

"Can we come in?"

Against his better judgment he lifted the chain, and immediately he regretted it. By the light of the vestibule he understood their condition at a glance: street people. Homeless. But as far as he could tell, not armed. No doubt they would promise him information for the chance to step inside, where they would try to con him into giving them money. If Allison woke and found them, she would call the police. Well, he would offer them nothing until he heard their story.

He pulled up three wooden chairs in the kitchen. God only knew what strange forms of life were crawling off his visitors, ready to take up residence in the plush upholstery of the sofa.

Drenched in moonlight from the kitchen window, the three sat down and faced each other. The short man, Toth, was not nearly as old as he'd looked in the corridor. He wore fatigues splotched with camouflage and a khaki jacket, one sleeve of which hung empty. A veteran? The man didn't look old enough for Vietnam. Probably one of those Rambo freaks. Yet he carried no weapon, nor did he look strong enough to wield anything bigger than a jackknife. In spite of his slender frame, there was a fleshiness about him that suggested inactivity.

But next to the taller man, Toth was the picture of health. Lean or plump—who could tell? Tuttle was swathed in dickeys and collars, turtleneck sweaters and shawls, all piecemeal and patchwork, so that he seemed encased in a quilted shell, from which his face emerged, wrinkled and tan. His eyes were bright and black as nuggets of jet.

"Okay, shoot," said Elmer.

They both started at this.

Tuttle recovered first. "I was swimming at Barton Pond," he said. "The only human being in sight was my cousin. She was walking away from the bridge."

"Your *cousin*? Wait a minute. What time did this take place?"

Toth looked blank. "Time?"

"Yes—what time? Was it day or night?"

"Night. It was dark."

"And did she see you?"

"Oh, no. I was in the cattails, watching her. A car came speeding toward the bridge and hit her. She never saw the car. It did not kill her but she was badly hurt. When the driver got out of the car, he saw she was alive. That was when she cursed him."

A chill passed over Elmer. "Do you mean she swore at him?"

"With the strength of water she cursed him, with the secrecy of air she cursed him, with the darkness of earth she cursed him," said Tuttle. "He dragged her over to the pond and held her head under the water."

"Great God!" cried Elmer. "Why didn't you come forward earlier?"

"My situation was such that—I couldn't," faltered the man.

"I see," said Elmer. Probably the guy was on the lam himself. As if he guessed Elmer's suspicions, Tuttle added, "When I'm not diving, I'm a plumber."

Elmer let it pass. "Did you see the man's face?"

"No. But I can tell you he was bigger and heavier than Theopolis. Also, he was bald."

"But you didn't see him close."

"No."

"I did," said Toth. "I saw him close."

"What did he look like?"

"He had two eyes facing front like yours and a nose here and ears here, on both sides of his head like yours."

"For heaven's sake!" exclaimed Elmer. "I mean, how did he look different from other people?"

"He didn't. But he looked different from Theopolis. He was bald."

"And where were you?" demanded Elmer. They were mocking him, he felt sure, but he would follow the joke to the end. "Taking a midnight dip as well?"

"No, I was sleeping. The splash of the body woke me."

"Do you usually sleep outside?"

"Only in the summer, when I dive for salvage. In the winter I put up TV antennas."

It would be awfully risky—God knows what they'd say to the police or the prosecutor. But things couldn't get much worse than they already were. He should never have let Sam take the stand.

"Have you ever given testimony under oath before?"

Toth grinned. No doubt he was an old hand at talking his way out of a tight spot. Best to drop that topic.

"I want you both at the courthouse by nine o'clock," said Elmer. He hesitated, not wishing to offend them. "Does either of you own a watch?"

They shook their heads.

"You can borrow mine," said Elmer. "I have a spare."

This suggestion seemed to distress them. Rummaging through a drawer full of screws and paper clips and batteries, he pulled out the cheap digital he'd bought in Logan Airport long ago, when he'd forgotten to wear his expensive gold one. He felt their commitment waning at the sight of the watch. "Keep the watch," he said, pressing it into Tuttle's damp palm. "You don't have to give it back."

"Time is such a burden," said Tuttle. "Always to be feeling the weight of it on your hand."

"Do you need a ride to the courthouse?"

"We'll hang around the vicinity," said Toth. "Nine o'clock tomorrow. We'll be there."

"You mean nine o'clock on Monday," Elmer corrected him. "The court's not in session till Monday. And we'll need depositions from you."

Both men looked uneasy.

"Is there a reason you can't be in court on Monday?" demanded Elmer.

"I might be sick," said Tuttle.

"You *might* be sick? But you aren't sick now?"

Tuttle waved his hands helplessly. "It's sort of—it comes and goes. You feel all right and suddenly it hits."

"Sometimes you can feel it coming a few days before," said Toth. "Everything you love has an aura around it."

"That's how it is for me too," said Tuttle.

Sounds like epilepsy, thought Elmer. The weight of their uncertainty was settling like a stone in his stomach.

"Would you rather meet me at the police station tomorrow? We could make it around four."

They shook their heads vigorously.

"Monday, then? You name the time."

"In the morning. Three o'clock in the morning," said Toth.

"Look, be reasonable. Come at nine, and I'll have a doctor on hand."

Still they hesitated.

"Trust me. If anything goes wrong, I'll cover the cost of the treatment. I know a very fine doctor."

Tuttle stood up, as if the matter were now settled. "We should go," he said.

"Don't go," said Elmer. "Are you hungry? Have you eaten anything recently?"

"What do you have?" asked Toth.

"Leftover cold ham and succotash, macaroni and cheese, and apple pie."

Without waiting for their reply, Elmer opened a package of

paper plates and plastic spoons. As their gaze roamed from him to the cans and jars in the pantry, he saw with awful clarity the stages of his own life, moving through offices and courts, settling into marriage, growing old. Talking, from time to time, about his toughest case. Running it through his head at night, savoring it.

"What's in that one?" asked Toth suddenly, and he pointed.

Elmer gave a snort of contempt. "Chocolate-covered bees," he said.

Tuttle picked up the jar, unscrewed the top, and crammed a fistful of bees into his mouth. Then he passed the jar to Toth, who poured himself a dark handful and licked them up from his palm.

*Crunch, crunch.* It was the most nauseating noise Elmer had ever heard.

After they left, he discovered that between them Toth and Tuttle had finished the whole jar.

In the morning Elmer could not call Sam before eight, and when he asked the guard to fetch him, it seemed an eternity before Sam came to the phone.

"Sam, I've got good news. Two witnesses have come forward."

"Who are they?"

"Two divers. They got a good look at the killer, good enough to know it's not you. The family's going to celebrate over dinner today at Liberty Hall."

"Liberty Hall." Sam chuckled. "Set a place for me. Did Ellen find my notebook with the story?"

"Sam, I'm sorry. I forgot all about it. I'll call her right away."

The notebook was exactly where Martha and Ellen had noticed it the night they tried to clean the cellar, and Ellen carried it upstairs and sat down on the back porch and opened it. The last entry was called "The Whistle," and Sam had written her name across the top of the first page.

# 22

## "The Whistle"

Anybody who has lived in Drowning Bear can tell you what the Dog Star Man looks like. They've seen him in the snow globes, which you can buy in Woolworth's for five dollars (six if you get the musical version, which plays "White Christmas"). He's standing on the back runners of his dogsled, crossing the universe in a tiny blizzard, as if eternity were no more than a snowy field.

When I was growing up, you could not find anybody in Drowning Bear who had actually seen him. And if it hadn't been for my father's music store, I might not have seen him, either.

I was twelve years old when my father, who rarely touched anything stronger than 7Up, got mildly drunk with a man named Olaf Starr who kept dogs. My father, Carl Theopolis, owned the Treble and Bass Music Store there. The store carried accordions, drums, trumpets, harmonicas, guitars, pitch pipes, tambourines, and sheet music. Five free lessons came with all the instruments, except the harmonica, and my father built a tiny soundproof practice room in the back. Saturday mornings a boy from Drowning Bear High School came to give the free lessons to languid young girls, who emerged from the practice room sweaty and bright-eyed, all of them promising to practice. My father also repaired instruments. By the time I was in high school, he'd sold the business and was doing repairs full time and making lutes, dulcimers, and Irish harps on commission.

He kept shelves of exotic woods, rosewood and purple heart, teak and lignum vitae. One man ordered a guitar made of lignum vitae for his son, who played in a rock band and smashed his instrument every night, but by God, he wouldn't be smashing this one. Mainly my father stocked the commoner varieties, basswood and oak and black cherry and ash, which he used for the curved bodies of the lutes and the harps. He also had a few odd pieces of golden chinquapin and water tupelo, hornbeam and hackberry, for which there wasn't much demand except when he did inlay work on the sound holes of the lutes. You never knew, he said, what a customer would ask for. He wouldn't work with ivory, out of respect for the elephants, though he loved Chinese ivory carvings, especially those that keep the shape of the tusk. I believe there's not a book on Asian art in the Drowning Bear Public Library that my father hadn't checked out.

Olaf Starr lived outside Drowning Bear on land which he claimed to have inherited from his Pawquacha grandmother. His grandfather Starr was part owner of Pawquacha Watermarks, the only printing company in town. Today the building is gone. His father had farmed the land; all the Starr cheese in Wisconsin was made there, and it was a big business in the thirties and forties. That ended when Olaf took it over. Forty years later, when I was growing up, the house was gone and the barn that stood on the north acre was in ruins; snow had caved in the roof, leaving a confusion of broken timber in its wake that made me feel I was peering into the stomach of a vast beast. The windows of the stable were broken, and stars winked through the holes left by shingles that had blown or rotted off. Over the stalls you could still read the names of horses: Beauty, Misty, Athena. Behind the stable Olaf parked his pickup truck.

On the south acre Olaf had built himself a log cabin and a dog yard, with seven small cabins low to the ground for his dogs. He was a big man, with white hair, who carried a knapsack and wore the same Levi's, suspenders, and down jacket and boots day after day, shedding the jacket in summer, resurrecting it at the first snowfall.

People said that Olaf's wife had left him long ago for a more comfortable life, so during the one evening I spent at the cabin I never looked for any evidence of her. I was in sixth grade and trying to write a report on cheese as part of a unit on agriculture. I did not like agriculture, which was a vast general thing. You could not put anything in the report about how cows look, standing in a rolling field, though that is so important it should come first. From far away, they look like ciphers that someone has written with a thick brown pen, and I wished I could write my whole report using the ponderous alphabet of cows. You could not put in anything about the hiss of milk in the pail, or the salt licks that rise in the fields like ancient shrines, and you could not put in the peculiar appetite of goats for wind-dried bedsheets on the line and children's sunsuits and anything scented with human use.

So I asked the teacher, Mrs. Olsen, if I could write a story about cheese, and she said yes, but it could not be a fairy tale. The cheese must not talk or sing or dance or have adventures. The story must be about how cheese is made. I could write that story.

I did not know the first thing about how cheese is made. My father told me to go to the library and find a book that would tell me. But my mother said, "Go and watch somebody make it. That's better than a book." My father agreed and suggested I call the Wisconsin Wilderness processing plant to see if they gave tours.

Suddenly my parents had the same thought at the same time and said almost in unison, "Olaf Starr makes cheese. He'd be glad to show you."

Olaf Starr had no phone, so on Saturday afternoon my father and I drove out to the farm. Ten inches of snow had fallen the week before, and the cold had kept it on the ground, though the main roads were clear. My father turned off the highway and took the road less traveled. Sled tracks cut a deep ribbon across the white fields on either side of us, and where the road ended at the broken barn and we got out of the car, the tracks disappeared into a pine woods.

You could hear Olaf's dogs yapping and yelping. A hundred seemed a modest estimate.

"We should've brought our skis," said my father.

That would have been far easier than walking in, which took us twice as long. I'd seen the outside of Olaf's house in summer but not in winter, and I'd never seen the inside.

In the dog yard, seven huskies sat on the roofs of their houses and barked at us, and the hair on my neck prickled in a primitive response to danger.

"They're tied," said my father.

Only when I saw that they could not spring far from the stakes to which they were leashed did I begin to savor the adventure of doing something entirely new. I thought of our yard, so small and neat that when my mother bought two metal lawn chairs and a patio umbrella, my father complained of the clutter. Olaf's yard was a sprawl of empty cable spools, old oil drums, ropes, ski poles, harnesses and a dogsled, which hung from a row of pegs on the wall.

Hearing the racket, Olaf opened the door. He knew my father as a man who ordered firewood from him; he was surprised to see both of us on his doorstep. His face remained perfectly impassive as my father explained our errand while I stared at him with the greatest interest, as if I were examining a hawk or an otter, some wild creature always seen in motion and from a distance.

A brief silence marked the end of my father's speech, and when Olaf was quite certain it *was* the end, he nodded and motioned us into his house. It was not so much a house as a lair, a den that an animal might make and stock with all that instinct told him would carry him through the winter. Firewood was stacked solid against one wall. Against the opposite wall stood five fifty-gallon drums of water, a shelf of dishes and crocks and large cooking pots, a treadle sewing machine, and a dozen huge bags of dog food.

From under the four burners on the surface of the wood stove shone a thin rim of fire. The flame in the oil lamp on the table danced in its glass chimney with such shifting brilliance that the air in the cabin seemed to be alive and breathing, steadily and quietly.

My father and I drew two stools up to the table.

Olaf took down a large crock and set it on the table between us.

"The secret of cheese is patience," he said. "Cheese has taught me everything I know about life."

He set three spoons and three brass bowls of different sizes on the table.

"I traded a year's supply of firewood to a professor at Madison for these. And when I got them home, I made a discovery. Listen."

He struck the rim of the largest with a spoon and a deep hum filled the room. He struck the smallest and a higher hum, a fifth above the first, spun out of it. He struck the last bowl, and it sent forth a note that completed the triad. But if I say the bowls hummed, I do not tell you *how* they hummed. Not like a cat or a spinning wheel, but like a planet whirling down the dark aisles of the galaxy.

"The best way to make cheese is to put it in singing bowls," said Olaf. "This is also the best way to eat it."

He dipped his spoon into the crock and began to ladle cottage cheese from the crock into the bowls.

"Also," he said, "the voice of the bowls quiets the dogs."

My father, astonished into silence by all these marvels, finally found his own voice.

"But these are singing bowls from Tibet!" he exclaimed. "I'm sure they're worth a good deal of money. If you ever want to sell them, come to me with a price."

"But I won't sell them," said Olaf. "I'll trade them for something I need."

"What do you need?" asked my father.

"Nothing now," he said, "but next week, dog food. I buy dog food by the ton. Ground barley is good," he mused, "and fish meal."

He kept on spooning cottage cheese into the bowls.

"When I was at the University, I didn't study at all."

"You went to the University?" exclaimed my father.

"For one year, in 1927. And when my father asked me what I was majoring in I told him I wanted to major in philosophy. Philosophy! He didn't understand about philosophy. I told him that philosophers consider problems of time and what is the true good. I told him it was like majoring in cheese; something solid emerges from what is thin and without definition."

The whole of our visit, he talked and talked—and not one word about how to make cheese. The next day my mother took me to the public library where the *Encyclopædia Britannica* revealed to me the secret of making cheese. In my report, I mentioned rennet and casein. I did not mention singing bowls, and I did not write a story. I got my report back with praise from Mrs. Olsen written across the top: *Good work, Sam! You put in a lot of information and you stuck to your subject.*

.   .   .

The next afternoon Olaf appeared in my father's music store. He admired the guitars, the accordions, the new shipment of tambourines, and asked my father if he could make a whistle that his dogs could hear from a great distance.

"How great a distance?" asked my father.

Olaf opened his pack, drew out a map of the United States, and spread it out on the counter.

"Here," he said. "I'm planning to visit my sister, and I want my dogs to know I'm thinking of them."

And he put his thumb down on the whole state of Florida.

To humor him, my father agreed. In three days he had finished the whistle, and Olaf drew from his pack the largest singing bowl and gave it to him. It was as if an honored guest had moved in with us. My father made a little house for the bowl to sit in, a replica of a Tibetan spirit-house, he said. This he put on top of the china cabinet. Once a day the bowl was played. Sometimes my mother played it, sometimes I played it, and sometimes he played it himself. Often I dreamed of whales singing, a music I did not yet know existed.

The next day Olaf returned and said he wanted to exchange the whistle that called dogs for one that called birds. So many of the birds he loved had gone south. He wanted to let them know he'd welcome them back any time, if the warm countries weren't to their liking.

"Why did you tell me to make a whistle that calls dogs if you wanted one that calls birds?" asked my father.

Olaf was interested in more practical questions.

"Can you fix it so it will call both?"

My father laughed and said he would try. He added a section of wingwood with a dovetail joint that was nearly invisible, and Olaf was very pleased and said it was exactly what he wanted. He reached into his knapsack and pulled out the middle-sized singing bowl. My father closed the shop and carried it home at once and nested it in the other bowl, in the little spirit-house.

The bowls were not beautiful but they were immensely present, and when we ate in the dining room we were always aware of them, and we did not complain about the cold weather or who should have taken out the garbage the night before. No, we were pleasant to one another, in the way that people are pleasant before a guest or stranger to whom they wish to show their best side.

A postcard arrived from Paradise, Florida, showing the roseate spoonbill in glorious flight. Olaf's message was brief: "It works!"

Three days before Christmas, Olaf appeared again, holding the whistle.

"This whistle," he said. "I wonder if you could fix it."

"In what way is it broken?" asked my father.

"It's not broken," Olaf assured him. "I just wonder if you could improve it."

"Improve it?"

"I was wondering," said Olaf, "if you could fix it to call the moon."

"The moon!"

"I thought I'd get me in some ice fishing. The fish do like a full moon best."

My father took the whistle back. The section he added this time was purely ornamental. He cut it from coral, which has no resonating properties, and he vowed to go Olaf one better. He added a link of hornbeam, on which young stags love to rub their budding antlers, and a link of alder, which beavers prefer above all other trees for building dams, and a link of mulberry, whose small dark fruit the woodmouse loves. He did not cut these links into simple rings but joined them in interlocking shapes, pieced with bits of shell and horn, bone and silver.

On a Saturday morning, when I was helping my father put new price stickers on the sheet music, Olaf arrived, and my father gave him the improved whistle and waited for some sign of praise, a whistle of admiration perhaps.

But Olaf said nothing about my father's exquisite workmanship. He tucked the whistle into his breast pocket and reached into his knapsack and took out the smallest singing bowl and set it on the counter.

Then he looked at me and said, "Do you like books?"

"Sure," I said. I never say no to a book.

Out of his knapsack he pulled a volume bound in leather softer than the chamois my father used to polish the violins. When he put it into my hands, I felt he had just given me a small animal seldom seen and beautiful to the blind who see with their fingers.

I opened it to the title page: *Invisibility: Mastering the Art of Vanishing.*

"Merry Christmas," he said.

I flipped through the book. There were short chapters on alchemy and ectoplasm and a long chapter called "Forming the Cloud," and I hadn't the faintest idea what any of it meant. Still, I was the kind of kid who would read anything, and I knew I would have a go at *Invisibility: Mastering the Art of Vanishing.* But I could not say it gladdened my heart.

"Thank you," I said.

My father had the habit of carrying the spirit-house, with its nested singing bowls, from room to room, to keep them near him. On Christmas Eve he put them on the mantel to watch over the tree. Of course I didn't believe in Santa Claus, but I played the game and so did my mother and father. Growing up is watching faith descend to the level of a beloved ritual.

At nine o'clock I put my two presents under the tree: a Sheaffer pen, which I had bought at the drugstore, and a pillow with the name Jerry Garcia embroidered on it, which I had made in school after the principal went to a conference on new trends in education and became convinced that boys should take home ec for one semester while the girls took shop. I was not convinced. I would never make one of those sleek, useful projects the teacher recommended. I would not even make a pattern. The pillow turned out to be the size of an overgrown pincushion, nothing you'd choose to sit on, unless you had hemorrhoids. I knew Mother would love it, because it looked handmade.

The card said, "For Mother and Father," as the pen and pillow were suitable for both.

At ten o'clock, when I announced I was going up to bed so as not to displease Santa, my mother looked relieved. She had all the presents to wrap yet. I hung my stocking under the singing bowls and was halfway up the stairs when the doorbell rang and the door, which was unlocked, burst open.

Olaf Starr filled the front hall with his enthusiasm. He'd spent the day ice fishing on Scroon Lake. He'd pulled from the still, chill bottom of the lake three bass, two trout, a sunfish, and a pike, and he was the first person in the county to catch a two-point buck with a fishhook. He'd brought in enough meat to feed himself the rest of the winter.

He pulled out a bottle of schnapps and presented it to my father and lingered, waiting for him to open it.

I could not possibly go to bed now. I might miss something.

My father and Olaf sat down at the dining room table and drank. That is to say, Olaf drank a lot and my father nursed a single shot-glass, which was nevertheless enough to skew his judgment. He had left his singing bowls on the mantel by the tree.

"All I own of value in this world is my sled and my dogs," said Olaf, "and when I am gone, no man is worthier to have them than yourself. Give me pen and paper, and I will write my will."

Every shred of scrap paper, which usually cluttered the area around the telephone, had vanished from sight, and my father could find nothing better than a circular for a grand sale at Happy Jack's—"Everything must go, to the bare walls." Olaf turned it over, and on the blank side wrote his will, making my father heir to seven dogs. He ended by writing out the names of the dogs.

*Swing dogs: Eleanor Roosevelt and John Kennedy*
*Team dogs: Lou Gehrig and Babe Ruth*
*Wheel dogs: Finn McCool and Melville*
*Lead dog: Hermes*

"What an odd list," said my father. "Swing, team, wheel."

"Those are their ranks in harness," said Olaf. At that moment it dawned on me these were sled dogs.

Olaf turned to me and my mother. "I've left space for you to sign. Two witnesses."

To humor him, my mother signed. I signed because I'd never been asked to witness anything before and I did not want to pass up this opportunity. Without reading it over, Olaf pocketed his will, shook hands with each of us, and took his unsteady leave, and my father and mother thought no more on the matter.

At midnight on Christmas Eve, the snow started falling, and it did not stop until the next afternoon. And then, quite unexpectedly, it turned warm.

The day before New Year's Eve Olaf Starr disappeared. A skier, hearing the howling and baying of the ravenous dogs, called the police. Because the snow around the dog yard was deep and undisturbed by human tracks, the police broke into Olaf's cabin. The presence of the will on the kitchen table suggested suicide, but the circumstances convinced them otherwise. At the lake they found his pickup truck. On the ice they found the shelter he'd built. The current ran strong under the thin ice where the shore curved toward the jagged hole, through which they concluded he had fallen. They did not find the man himself. It is hard to grieve for a man who has disappeared and might return someday. I think my father and I expected to receive another postcard from him. We did not really believe he was dead until the sheriff stopped by our house and asked my father to come and fetch his dogs.

Seven dogs at a stroke! Neither my father nor my mother knew the first thing about caring for dogs. Days of lawn chairs and umbrellas, farewell! My father bought a book called *Your Dogs and How to Care for Them* and hired a man to put in seven tethering stakes and help him move the sled and the doghouses into the backyard. Then he phoned a veterinarian, Dr. James Herrgott, and told him what had befallen us, and I felt we were saved. There was no one I admired more than Dr. Herrgott, whose skill at nursing sick animals was almost miraculous.

Dr. Herrgott made a house call and examined the dogs. From the kitchen window we watched him, a tall lean figure in a wool cap and down jacket and boots and Levi's with holes in the knees. He knelt before each dog, examined its fur, its eyes, the lining of its mouth.

Wrapped in an aura of arctic air, he sat down at our kitchen table and told us what we owned. Finn McCool and John Kennedy and Melville and Eleanor Roosevelt and Babe Ruth and Lou Gehrig were young dogs, between two and three years old, all mixed-breed huskies. Hermes was at least five years old and part Siberian malamute.

My father looked terrified. For the first time, I perceived a weakness in him and a superior strength in myself, and I took on

the job of feeding the dogs in the morning. This meant rising at
six instead of seven; ten minutes of snoozing and I'd miss the
school bus. The front door slamming shut in the milky light
before dawn would wake them, and by the time I'd hauled the big
canister of dog food into the yard, they would be yapping and
tugging at their chains and stretching, their tails switching and
waving like flags. The smell of their food—a thin yellow gruel
of ground barley and fish meal and fat, which I ladled into deep
tin bowls—made my father nauseous.

After school I fed them again and fetched a shovel and cleaned
the dog yard.

My mother assigned herself the task of putting fresh hay in
the doghouses. That was a fragrant and pleasant occupation; the
dogs would crawl into the hay and turn round and round, hol-
lowing it into a nest.

Sometimes my father ran the dogs and sometimes I did it, but
soon he relinquished that job too, because I enjoyed doing it and
he did not. The intricate maneuvers of running dogs in harness
daunted him. He could never remember who hated whom and
what dogs got on well together.

After school I slipped their harnesses on and hitched them to
the sled and we headed for the golf course behind the house. I
never saw snow so deep that Hermes could not break a trail in
it. When we crossed the frozen stream at the back of the course,
the clicking of their toenails on the ice always startled them. I
loved the crossing; the shadow we cast made a grand sight.

On February 1st the temperature fell to thirty-five below and
stayed there. My mother could not bear to leave any animal
outside in that weather. My father reminded her that we had no
basement, no garage, no shed of any kind.

"We have a big living room," she said. "We could partition it.
Half for the dogs and half for us."

She kept after him till he put a chain-link fence down the middle of the living room, while my mother took out the rug and the furniture. From then on, the dogs slept indoors. A maze of smaller fences separated them from each other. The gates on these fences were never locked. When I stayed up to watch the Saturday night movie in the living room with my parents, the loping and breathing and snuffling and growling did not bother my mother or me, but it drove my father wild. I think he could have gotten used to this, but something happened to me that changed everything for all of us.

I got the flu, the kind that keeps you in bed for two weeks. I felt as if someone had sucked all the strength out of me and left me on the small white shore of my bed to find my way back to health. My father took over my tasks and did them, in his own way.

He exercised the dogs, but he did not take out the sled. He walked them singly. Of course, as he pointed out to me, he could not walk seven dogs every day. My mother walked them when she had time, but she reminded him that Olaf had willed the dogs to him, not to us.

My father fed the dogs, but he refused to handle the fish meal and fat, and he bought canned meat and dehydrated chicken kibbles in hundred-pound bags that scarcely lasted a week. Soon the dogs were demanding four meals a day and howling at night. My mother found that if she opened the gate in the living room fence, the dogs grew quiet. After everyone was in bed, they would leave their quarters and gather in my room.

It is not easy sleeping with seven dogs, even when you love them. In the safety of my bedroom they went on dreaming their old fears, just as I went on dreaming mine. Roused by a remembered injury, Lou Gehrig would leap out of sleep and sink his teeth into John Kennedy's neck, and I would fly out of bed to part them. When sled dogs fight, generations of jackals and wolves snarl in their blood. All night part of my mind stayed awake, listening for the low growl that signaled the beginning of a quarrel. When morning came, I never felt rested.

And Melville got sick. His fur fell out in patches, though my mother washed him with castile soap and sponged his legs, chest, face, and tail with a special foam that Dr. Herrgott recommended for shedding animals.

A thaw surprised us at the end of February, and my mother agreed to let the dogs sleep in the yard again. But they had caught the scent of being human and could not get enough of it. From darkness till dawn they howled. I was back in school but not strong enough to take over caring for the dogs, and I suppose it was the howling and complaints from the neighbors that finally drove my father to make what he warned me was an important announcement.

"I'm going to sell Olaf's dogs. I can't afford to keep them."

We had just sat down to dinner, and he looked at me to see how I would take his words. I said nothing.

"We'll only sell them to someone who can really take care of them," said my mother.

That night I fell asleep to the howling of the dogs. What woke me was a silence so sinister that I jumped out of bed and hurried to the window, certain they'd been poisoned. My heart nearly thudded through my chest when I saw someone was indeed in the yard. He was unchaining them. First John Kennedy, then Babe Ruth, then Hermes.

I never thought of calling my father. No, I pulled on my clothes, snatched my jacket from the bedpost, and marched out into the yard. When the thief turned his face toward me, I was speechless with fright.

"I've come for my dogs," said Olaf. "They miss me, and I miss them."

"You're dead," I whispered. My teeth were chattering. "You fell through the ice and drowned."

"That's true," said Olaf. And he went on unchaining them. They were lining up, letting him slip the harnesses over them, taking their old places. Hermes first, then Finn McCool and Melville in the second spot, then Lou Gehrig and Babe Ruth, and in the last position, Eleanor Roosevelt and John Kennedy.

"If you're dead, how are you going to take your dogs?"

"Easy," said the Dog Star Man. "They can cross over. Didn't you know that? Didn't they teach you *anything*?"

The dogsled was leaning against the back of the house, and he pulled it down and took his place on the back runners. I knew I would never see him this close again. But maybe on mornings when I went out cross-country skiing on the golf course behind our house, I would catch a glimpse of him on the horizon, his dogs strung out in a thin line like Christmas lights.

The Dog Star Man beckoned me closer.

"For you," he said. "I don't need this where I'm going."

And he dropped the whistle my father had made into my hand.

# 23

When Ellen saw Harvey climb out of a cab and stride up the front walk carrying a huge casserole dish, she called Martha out of the kitchen. "Who invited Harvey Mack?"

"I thought you did," said Martha. "He called this morning and said he was bringing his special lemon chicken."

"I mentioned Sunday dinner," murmured Mrs. Trimble.

"So what did you tell him?" asked Ellen.

"I told him we'd be eating at two, indoors, because it looked like rain."

"For Christ's sake, did you ever hear of such nerve?"

"Never mind. He's already here," said Martha, and she flurried out to meet him.

"Just bring it to the kitchen door," she called. "Goodness, what a lot of food for nine people." She led him around the side of the house, past the garbage cans and the overgrown honeysuckle.

"Better too much than too little," said Harvey.

The kitchen table and all the counters were crammed. Radishes and celery lay like sleepy passengers in a cut-glass relish dish; the brown-and-serve rolls on the cookie sheet waited to be given their proper crust; the fruit salad glowed like a ruby hubcap on a silver platter, next to a carton of KFC Golden Drumsticks.

Harvey stared at the drumsticks. "Who brought these?"

"Elmer," said Martha.

"I'll put the carton on the table and then we can eat," announced Ellen. "Mother and Stevie are starving."

"What about my lemon chicken? I have to heat it."

"You already cooked it once, didn't you? We can eat it cold."

"At least let me put it on a platter. And I'll need some wine glasses."

"Wine glasses? You brought wine? Nobody in the house drinks it."

Stevie was setting the table, awarding the souvenir plates. Niagara Falls went to Jessie, the lobster pots of Maine to Allison. Mrs. Trimble got Idaho, and Harvey Mack got Montana, which was chipped. To his Aunt Martha went Hyde Park, and to his mother, the Kentucky Derby. He gave Washington, D.C., to John. Elmer got the Michigan Law Quad.

At Sam's place he put the plate Sam had always asked for when he was still among them: the pilgrim plate from Plymouth.

Beyond the plates, the empty wine glasses sparkled.

"Can we eat now, Mom?"

Ellen poked her head out of the kitchen. "Looks good. You can call people to the table."

"I'll call them," said Harvey.

Allison and Elmer and John and Mrs. Trimble shuffled away from the TV into the dining room.

"Stevie will show you your places," said Martha.

"I'll pour the wine," said Harvey, and he filled Elmer's glass. "I haven't had a drink in weeks."

"I think everybody else would like cranberry juice," said Martha.

Next to the drumsticks gleaming in their coat of golden crumbs, Harvey's chicken looked naked, a sacrifice rather than a meal.

"A toast before we sit," said Elmer, raising his wine glass. "I propose a toast to the two witnesses."

"And to Sam," said Ellen.

"And to Mother," said Martha. "A toast to Mother."

"Freedom and justice," said John.

"Freedom and justice!" they shouted, and held their glasses high and drank.

There was a scraping of chairs as they took their places.

"I'll carve the lemon chicken," said Harvey. He stood at the head of the table and raised his knife as if he meant to conduct Jessie on his left and Mrs. Trimble on his right. Slowly and methodically he tried to pare away the wings, pausing long enough to refill Elmer's glass before he shifted his attention to carving the breast.

"It's real nice eating in the dining room with family," remarked Mrs. Trimble. "When I was growing up and we had company, my daddy ate in the dining room and Mamma and me and Grandma had to eat in the kitchen."

"He made his own wife eat in the kitchen?!" exclaimed Allison.

"Always, when we had company," said Mrs. Trimble. "We used to laugh and carry on out there, and the guests would hear us, and Daddy would say, 'The vimens are in the kitchen.'"

"'The vimens'?" asked Stevie, puzzled.

"That's how he said it," said Mrs. Trimble. "'Vimens.'"

"Harvey, you've been sawing away on that chicken for half an hour," said Ellen, and the first slice fell away and Harvey speared it.

"All hungry people, pass your plates forward," said Harvey.

"I've got Hyde Park and the Roosevelt mansion," said Martha. "What do you have, Mrs. Trimble?"

"Idaho," said Mrs. Trimble. "I can't read the fine print without my glasses, but the pictures are nice."

Harvey leaned over her plate and adjusted his own glasses.

" 'Silver City and Orograndas, Ghost Town, U.S.A.,' " he said. "That's what yours says."

Mrs. Trimble turned to him. "Do you believe in ghosts?"

"No," said Harvey. "Now here's a nice bit of white meat for you, Mrs. Woolman, if you'll pass me your plate."

Jessie tapped Stevie on the shoulder and whispered, "Where are my teeth?"

"I'll look for them," exclaimed Stevie, jumping up from the table.

He seized a breaded drumstick from the carton and went away gnawing it. Everyone in the dining room could hear him bounding down the basement stairs, two at a time.

"I used to run downstairs like that," said Jessie, and she passed her plate to Harvey. "Now, where's Sam?"

"Mother, we *told* you," said Martha. "He's in jail."

"Sam, in jail? Why, what did he do?"

"Nothing," said Ellen. "It's all a terrible mistake."

"When is he coming home?" asked Jessie.

"Soon, we hope," said John.

"I'm seventy-five," whispered Jessie. "I've lived long enough. I want to die." She was poking her chicken with a fork, peering underneath. "It doesn't look like white meat."

"What plate does Sam have?" asked Ellen.

"Plymouth Rock," said Allison.

"It's all raw," said Jessie. "Look."

She pried the slice apart with her knife, exposing the translucent bloody surface inside, but no one seemed interested. The traffic of plates held their attention, as Harvey laid a slice of chicken on each one.

"I found them, Grandma!" Stevie burst into the dining room, breathless, waving a set of false teeth.

Jessie glanced at them. "Those aren't mine."

"For heaven's sake!" exclaimed Martha. "Whose would they be?"

"They're bigger than mine," said Jessie.

Ellen reached for the teeth and examined them. "Stevie, where did you find them?"

"In that old cigar box on Grandpa's worktable."

"Is Henry dead?" asked Jessie.

"Now, you know he is, Mother," said Martha. "You rode with him in the ambulance."

"Henry was a gentleman of the old school," said Jessie. "He would never have left his teeth lying around the house."

"You could try them," suggested Mrs. Trimble. "They might fit you. You can't chew without teeth, and that's a fact."

"I'll heat up one of those Stouffer's macaroni dinners for you, Grandma," said Allison. "You hardly have to chew those at all. It will only take me a minute."

"Heat up an extra," said Martha, "in case anybody else wants one."

"Does anybody else want one?" asked Allison. Not even Mrs. Trimble had touched her chicken; she had only cut a seam in the side.

"Me," said Stevie. "I do."

"I believe I'll have one of those breaded drumsticks," said John.

"Me too," said Ellen.

"Ellen," said Harvey, "you love my lemon chicken."

"Harvey, it looks sort of raw," said Ellen.

"Oh, Lord," said Martha, "we should have gone to the Wolverine Den."

Harvey helped himself to a large slice of chicken, cut off a bite, popped it into his mouth, and chewed vigorously.

"It looks raw," he said, "but in fact it's lightly cooked. Lightly cooked chicken is considered a great delicacy in Japan."

"The Everpresent Fullness would like a piece," said Stevie, and he offered Harvey an empty plate. Harvey did not fill it.

"Whose plate is this?" he asked.

"Sam's."

Harvey picked a breaded drumstick out of the carton. "I hear you've found some witnesses. Two salvage divers."

Elmer nodded, his mouth full, and Harvey added, "I'm sure we'd all like to hear what they've got to say."

"You'll have to wait till they've given their evidence," said Elmer. "But I can tell you they saw enough to know Sam wasn't the killer. The killer was bald."

"Can they identify him?" asked Harvey.

Elmer shrugged. "I doubt it. How did you hear about them?"

"Mrs. Trimble mentioned them," answered Harvey, "when she invited me to dinner."

"I didn't think it was a secret," said Mrs. Trimble, turning to Elmer. "You told me they were Bearheart's people."

"Bearheart's people?" said John. "If I were you, I'd never have let them out of my sight."

"They loved your chocolate-covered bees," said Elmer. "They ate every last one of them."

"Would you believe that I saw chocolate-covered bees for sale in the gourmet section at Kroger's?" said Allison. "The clerk told me there was an article in some health magazine that claimed eating bees cures arthritis."

"When are you meeting them?" asked Harvey.

"Nine o'clock tomorrow morning at the courthouse."

"I have some words stuck in my head," interrupted Jessie.

" 'This above all, to thine own self be true. Thou canst then not be false to any man.' It's enough to drive me crazy."

The sun stepped down slowly, winding up the warmth of the day. Through the trees, the last light dissolved everything in Harvey Mack's yard. Even the white wrought-iron chairs were weightless receptacles of light. He sat down on one of them and closed his eyes. Suddenly the air felt as dangerous as if he had stolen it.

I have to drive the car tomorrow, he reminded himself. No one else can do it for me.

He reached into his pocket and pulled out the keys. Whether it was the shaking of his hand or his body's refusal to take part in his resolve he could not be sure, only that the keys flipped from his hand into the bed of red impatiens that edged the side of the garage.

He clapped twice and his keys answered him, *beep! beep!*, and he scooped them up in an instant. Ah, it would be lovely if he could put sonic devices on everything in his life. When he rose in the morning, he would be welcomed by the joyous hum of the toaster; and when he came home at night, by the nasal purr of the electric carving knife and the modest buzz of the martini mixer. The small appliances would blend their voices with the hum and sizzle of the icebox and the stove. And Ellen's heart, set with a sonic receiver no bigger than a ring, would trill when he came into view.

Through the privet hedge, he saw Mrs. Trimble's shadow and heard the *click click* of her shoes on the flagstone and hastened into the house to greet her. They drank coffee together in the kitchen like an old married couple, she telling him of her triumph: because she had bought the last Video Fireplace in the store, she got two dollars off the reduced price of nine ninety-nine.

"The man said it's better than a real one," she said. "Listen: 'Video Fireplace. Sixty flame-filled minutes. A fire for all seasons: loving, dining, reading, entertaining, quiet moments, meditation. No logs to haul! No ashes to clean! Relax in the flickering glow of a crackling fire.' I offered to get one for Jessie, but Ellen said her mom would never give up her real fire. And they don't have a VCR. I don't have a VCR. But I might someday."

"You should check it out right away," said Harvey. "If it's defective, you should return it."

Mrs. Trimble rose from the table.

"I told Ellen you have one VCR for upstairs and another for downstairs, and she was amazed."

"What did she say?"

"She said, 'How amazing.' Can you reach me the can of filberts on that high shelf?"

Harvey followed her gaze to the small jar with the golden label beside the Grey Poupon mustard. "Those aren't filberts," he said.

"They're not?" She squinted up at the jar. "Why, they're chocolate-covered bees!"

"I've heard they're very good," he said. "Would you like to try one?"

"No, thank you. Save them for my night off."

Now Mrs. Trimble was standing in front of him, the Video Fireplace in her outstretched hand. He slipped it into the VCR and she sat down beside him on the sofa. Gray glowed rose, like a dawn breaking. Suddenly a fireplace, in which crackled a modest fire, filled the screen.

"Nice fireplace," said Mrs. Trimble. "It's got andirons and all."

The fire burned.

And burned.

And burned.

"Doesn't this kind of thing usually have music?" asked Harvey.

From the left side of the screen a hand clutching a poker reached in and adjusted the logs, turning the flames a faint lime green.

"I don't know," said Mrs. Trimble. "Do you want to borrow it?"

Suddenly there flashed across his heart a longing for the pleasant heaviness that came over him as a child when he sat in front of his grandparents' fireplace, watching the flames and listening to the grown-ups chatter. "Yes," he said.

He was glad to see her go. He trudged upstairs, kicked off his shoes and slid the Video Fireplace into the VCR at the foot of his bed. The room felt chilly. He could not bear the thought of slipping off his clothes. He stretched out and turned on the machine and fell asleep.

Even with the overhead light on in his bedroom—for he could never fall asleep in a dark room—the Video Fireplace flickered and glowed.

Was it the hum of the TV that woke him? The fire was finished now, the screen a uniform gray. He reached for the remote control dial and switched it off, and the gray dissolved into a single pinpoint of light, an eye that did not close but glared at him. Like a camera shutter, it watched him. He could not take his gaze from it.

Downstairs, two clocks struck twelve, but not in unison.

After the last stroke the stillness was intolerable. And the room was so hot—he could not even look at a fire.

He climbed out of bed, dragged his overnight case out of the closet, opened it, and ran his hand over the inside, checking for toads before he packed a change of clothes, carefully folding the clean T-shirt, the clean Jockey shorts, the clean black socks.

He pulled his pillow and two blankets off the bed and dragged them downstairs.

He marched back upstairs, unplugged the TV, and locked the door of his bedroom.

From the linen closet he took clean sheets and made up a bed on the living room sofa. On the sofa he felt safe and delightfully cool. Rain ticked, faster and faster, against the windowpane. He would have a science store in Pawquacha Plaza. He would call it the Rain Forest. Everybody was interested in the environment these days. He could almost hear his father saying, "That's where the money is. You have to be on the alert for what people want and be there when they want it."

A car passed, and its headlights gleamed on the wet glass and showed him her eyes. The maple leaves parted the darkness and showed him her mouth.

What's happening to me?

Trees had never bothered him with their secrets before. Live and let live. But give them an inch and they'll take a mile.

"I have nothing against trees," he announced to the air.

At five he telephoned Mrs. Trimble. "There's a bird in the house." His voice exploded into a shriek. "It flew down the chimney."

"I'll be over," she promised in a sleepy voice.

He found it easy to believe his own lie. In such a large house, a bird might have flown in without his knowledge. He opened the front door and the living room windows, and when Mrs. Trimble arrived, he met her on the driveway. With a scarf pulled over her uncombed hair and a raincoat wrapped around her nightgown, she looked as if she'd just been rescued from a fire.

"I think it flew out," he said. "I couldn't find it anywhere."

"What kind of bird was it?" she asked.

What kind? What kind? He uttered the first name that came into his head. "An owl. It was an owl."

She frowned. "That's bad luck."

Oh, it wasn't a real owl, he told himself. No harm could come to him from an imaginary owl. But he had the terrible feeling that in naming the owl he had summoned it, and somewhere in the universe an owl felt called upon to wish him ill.

At nine o'clock two men, one short and missing an arm, the other tall and swathed in sweaters and rags, appeared at the Amtrak ticket window in Toledo. They said they'd been picked up near Hoot 'n Scoot just outside Ann Arbor and dropped off in front of the Toledo art museum by a man wearing a straw hat who told them he was taking them to meet Elmer. They had supposed he was taking them to the courthouse; they confessed to having been lured into the car with a jar of chocolate-covered bees. The ticket seller was baffled. "The train to Ann Arbor won't be through here for three hours."

"We'll wait," said the one-armed man.

But by twelve o'clock, when the ticket seller called the train, he found they had left the station. Shortly thereafter he heard a commotion on the platform, and a little girl rushed in shouting, "There's a turtle and a toad on the tracks! Get a box!"

They were looking for water; everyone was sure of that as the toad hopped and the turtle scrabbled over the tracks. By the time the ticket seller brought a box, they'd made it to the other side.

The train to Chicago roared into the station and a throng of passengers crowded around it.

In the exhausted silence that drifted across the platform after the train pulled out, the ticket seller walked up and down, looking for signs of a toad or a turtle.

He found none.

## 24

Monday morning at a quarter of nine, Elmer was standing in front of the courthouse, mopping his face with his handkerchief. The sky behind him was knotted into dark clouds.

John was right, he said to himself. I should never have let those two out of my sight.

So many people were chronically late to everything, and though Toth and Tuttle had kept the gift of his watch, neither seemed to have a very strong grasp on the notion of time. The time they had chosen to visit him, for example. Why hadn't he found it odd then? He had admitted them as if it were the most normal thing in the world to call on a stranger in the middle of the night.

At ten minutes of nine, Patrick strode toward him with Ellen at his heels.

"They got the lights back on in the courtroom," he said. "And the air conditioning."

"I didn't know they were off," said Elmer.

"Oh, it was a real mess," said Patrick. "An upstairs pipe burst early this morning. You should see the ceiling."

"Where are the witnesses?" asked Ellen.

"They're not here," said Elmer. "Toth and Tuttle aren't here."

"Maybe they got the time mixed up," suggested Ellen.

"The session's about to start," said Elmer. "I can't wait any longer."

Ellen watched the two men disappear into the courthouse as a warm rain started to fall. Then she stepped into the little park behind the building. The benches were empty. She sat down and put Sam's whistle to her lips and blew.

No dogs barked, no angels shouted, no footfall of a miracle startled her into joy. The cicadas went on with their brassy humming.

*Your greatest obstacle is fear of the unknown. Remember that many men, and women too, have faced the unknown and come through. What they did, you too can do.*

The words filled her head; who had spoken them? She stood up. Pear trees and honeysuckle, recent additions to the land, paled and departed like a watercolor bleached by the sun to empty space. The land was dreaming its way back to a time out of time, long before any of her people lived on this land, maybe even before the Pawquachas lived on it.

*There is a river, the streams whereof shall make glad the city.*

The river that appears before her is much larger than the Huron. Animals she has never seen except in dreams are gathered on the banks to drink. The water is shallow but swift, and the great throng of the dead walk upstream in silence. They walk backward, slowly, their eyes on the living. So many jagged corners of life still snag them, tug at them, slow them down. The sound of a child drumming on the piano. The color of Jessie's eyes. The smell of thyme.

One girl is calling for a life jacket, but the words sound confused, as if she were singing under water.

*They are going to the city where women are healed and men are mended.*

Her father walks with his head up; he is looking for the bend in the river whose waters he fished in as a child and marveled at on a tea-green map and treated as an honored guest in his museum and admired in all seasons, by moonrise and sunset and starlight—how could he have known the stars had died long ago and it was their light traveling toward him he'd taken for the truth, as light over dark water looks like an easy road to the sky? He had told both Martha and Ellen, "We came from the water. Before you were born, you had gills. And you lost them." Martha wouldn't believe him; Ellen was not so sure.

Beside her father trots a deer, and sometimes Ellen sees the deer and sometimes she sees her father, and sometimes she sees them both at once, the deer's face imprinting itself small and soft on her father's arm, as if her father had joined the river and his body could reflect the whole world.

Behind him walks Mike, his hand on her father's shoulder like a blind man, stumbling, for this is like no riverbed he has ever known, and Ellen's heart cries out to him; he hardly knows where to put down his feet and does not see that a great blue heron is striding beside him, keeping him safe in her gaze.

"I'm here!" calls Ellen. "I haven't forgotten you. Stevie hasn't forgotten you," but her voice blows off into the silence of still water. Only the animals shepherding the dead prick up their ears and take notice of her.

"Don't forget us!" she shouts after them. "Don't forget us—"

Badger, otter, wolverine, bear, butterfly, trout.

*He hasn't forgotten you. He is looking for you in the world of the living.*

Seven dogs are trotting beside her. Though she cannot see their master, she's certain now that it's Olaf Starr who is speaking to her.

*The only person who can save Sam is the water woman herself. But it's not easy and she won't do it for nothing.*

She's here?

Ellen peers all around. Only one creature flies out of the procession, an owl who circles her, as if she were a mouse to be hunted.

I don't see her, says Ellen.

*That doesn't matter. Give her my whistle. It's time to pass it on.*

Ellen slips the whistle from her neck and holds it out. The owl does not snatch it, only circles and circles the hand that offers it.

*She wants to ask you a question. She died before she could find the answer, and nobody on this side can help her.*

Oh, God, what is it?

*What did the Buddhist say to the hot-dog vendor?*

Ellen's heart lifts.

Make me one with everything.

The even light of the stream darkens to twilight and the mottled shadows of branch and leaf dance on the grass. The cicadas blow a long note on their shrill horns. Falling silently and invisibly on all of them, dust rests on field and tree, on the sick and the well, the quick and the dead, and in another part of the city Jessie decides not to get out of bed that morning and Mrs. Trimble empties the dust bag from the old Hoover, scattering the molecules that once were lovers, of whom this day nothing is known, not even the names of the rivers that sent them.


Before Harvey could grab the seat next to Ellen, Allison had slipped into it. The family presented to the judge a united front, except for Stevie and Jessie, who were home, and Mrs. Trimble, who was with them. A deputy walked up and down closing windows; a smell of mildew from the damp ceiling permeated the room.

Something had flown into the room during Jack Chu's closing statement; Harvey was sure of it. Yet as he gazed around, he saw nothing that had not been there before except the water stain on the ceiling, which looked now like an island, now like a house, now like a face. Quickly he glanced away. In moments of confusion, the safe evidence of numbers comforted him. He began to count heads, starting with the members of the jury: rich man, poor man, beggar man, thief—

Jack Chu.

Patrick Nolan.

Sam.

Elmer beside Sam at the defense table.

Sam was watching Ellen so intently that Harvey wondered if she was sending him a secret signal.

The air was charged when Elmer rose for his closing statement.

"You are asked to believe," said Elmer, "that a man with no previous criminal record, whose interest in spiritual matters inclines him to nonviolence—you are asked to believe that this man was suddenly transformed into a hit-and-run killer who covered his tracks by drowning his victim."

A deepening silence greeted these words, broken by the distant rumble of thunder.

"The evidence that has delivered Sam Theopolis to this court is purely circumstantial. Only two people know the truth, the killer and the dead woman herself. Let us imagine for a moment that the dead woman stands among us, and we can call on her to give her version of the events that have brought us here."

The lights flickered and dimmed but did not go out, and panic filled Harvey. Some presence hostile to himself and just beyond the range of his sight was filling Elmer, fanning him with its great wings, and his words gathered strength like the morning brightening. Rain drummed against the windows. Overhead, the stain rested like a veil on her features; she was staring at him with great hollow eyes.

Elmer raised his voice. "Let us assume that the woman, walking home at night, had just crossed the Barton Pond bridge when the car hit her. Perhaps the driver was guilty of nothing more than a moment's inattention. He glances down to adjust his tape deck, he feels a thud, perhaps he hears a cry. He slams on the brakes, thinking he's hit a raccoon or a possum. Imagine his feelings when he sees a woman lying on the road. He jumps out of his car and bends over her. She is badly hurt but she is still alive.

"In that instant the driver sees his freedom in jeopardy. Perhaps he has been drinking. How easy to finish what an accident started, to drag his victim to the pond and hold her under the water. Members of the jury, I can produce no witnesses to this crime, but neither can the state. How easy it would be for that man to go back to his old life and let another man take the punishment."

In his chest Harvey felt a tightening, as if he were drowning. A flame of pain spurted along his arms. He pitched forward, gulping for air. The scream that rushed out of him brought Judge O'Brien to her feet.

The crash of a window opening and slamming shut in the storm woke Jessie. Overhead, Mrs. Trimble bustled about in Sam's room and locked the window.

Too late.

The angel at the foot of her bed was as magnificent as he had been at her first sight of him when she lay hidden in the cellar of the house where she was born. His hawk's head did not frighten her; she knew it hid his true face, and she remembered the glass of water left at her bedside during that other storm.

"I leave to children exclusively," whispered the angel in a

voice of infinite sweetness, "but only for the life of their childhood, the dandelions of the fields and the daisies thereof, with the
right to play among them freely, according to the custom of
children, warning them at the same time against the thistles."

"Why, I know those words!" exclaimed Jessie.

"Appropriate, don't you think?" murmured the angel. "We try
to make the departures a little special."

He offered her his shining sleeve, and, leaving her old body to
fend for itself, she accepted. At the bend in the river she heard the
heavenly choir singing "Just As the Tide Was Flowing." Leaves,
roots, Niagara Falls on porcelain, Sam's shoes in the cellar, The
Everpresent Fullness purring at the foot of her bed—everything
was letting her go.

". . . all the distant places which may be visited, together with
the adventures there found," said Jessie, to show the angel she
had not forgotten. "I leave to children the long, long days to be
merry in, in a thousand ways, and the Night and the Moon and
the train of the Milky Way to wonder at; and I give to each child
the right to choose a star that shall be his, and I direct that the
child's father shall tell him the name of it, in order that the child
shall always remember the name of that star after he has learned
and forgotten astronomy."

They were walking on the ten thousand faces of the water, like
a map coming alive under her feet. On every bridge children were
entering the traffic of the known world.

"Wait," said Jessie. "Sam told me if you see the Angel of Death
before your time comes, he's bound to grant you one wish."

The angel looked divinely uncomfortable. "It's true we've met
before. But there are restrictions. The gifts of angels are invisible
to those who receive them."

As they soared past the courthouse, Jessie saw through the
window that the jury box was empty. The members of the jury

were surging past the witness stand toward Sam. She could not see his face, only that he had one arm around Ellen and the other around Elmer, and Ellen was jumping for joy.

With a hawk's far sight, Jessie counted heads to make sure no one was lost in the shuffle: Sam and Ellen and Martha and John and Allison and Elmer.

"Where's that odd friend of Ellen's?"

"Harvey?" The angel smiled. "He has a bad heart. I'll be stopping by for him soon."

"My daughter Ellen—I want you to give her a gift."

"What gift?" asked the angel.

Jessie drank in the sight of them, one last deep draft of the water of life.

"Wings."

# Permissions Acknowledgments

Imaginary passages from the magazine *Prevention* were
suggested by the Hausa story "The City Where Men Are
Mended," in *African Folktales*, selected and edited by Paul Radin
(Princeton University Press, 1970).
The text of the eye chart in the first chapter was taken from
"A Last Will" by Williston Fish, originally published in 1898
in *Harper's Weekly*.
Special thanks to Stan Brakhage for his 1964 film *The Dog Star
Man*, and to John Tagliabue for his collection of poems *The
Buddha Uproar*. Both titles appear in different contexts in these
pages.

Grateful acknowledgment is made to the following for
permission to reprint previously published material:
*Doubleday*: Chapter 22 of *Sister Water* is based on the story
"Dog Star Man" by Nancy Willard, copyright © 1991 by
Nancy Willard, from *Full Spectrum 3* edited by Lou Aronica,
Amy Stout, and Betsy Mitchell. Reprinted by permission of
Doubleday, a division of Bantam, Doubleday, Dell Publishing
Group, Inc.
*Ice Nine Publishing Co., Inc.*: Excerpt from "Uncle John's Band,"
music by Jerry Garcia, words by Robert Hunter, copyright ©
1970 by Ice Nine Publishing Co., Inc. Reprinted by permission.
*The Video Naturals Company*: Excerpts on page 244 from
slipcase of "Video Fireplace," copyright © 1982 by S. Steven
Siporin. Reprinted by permission of The Video Naturals
Company, 600 E. Vista Chino Road, Palm Springs, CA 92262
(800/950-5545).

# A Note About the Author

Nancy Willard grew up in Ann Arbor, Michigan, and was educated at the University of Michigan and Stanford. In addition to to her novels, *Things Invisible to See* and *Sister Water*, she is the author of three books of short stories and essays and nine books of poetry, most recently *Water Walker*, which was nominated for the National Book Critics Circle Award. Her collection of poems for children, *A Visit to William Blake's Inn: Poems for Innocent and Experienced Travelers*, won the Newbery Medal. A teacher at Vassar College, she is married, has one son, and lives in Poughkeepsie, New York.

# A Note on the Type

The text of this book was set in a typeface called Bell. The original punches for this face were cut in 1788 by the engraver Richard Austin for the typefoundry of John Bell (1745–1831), the most outstanding typographer of his day, and they are the earliest English "modern" type design. Though the design of this face was influenced by the work of the members of the Fournier and Didot families, the Bell face has a distinct identity of its own.

Composed by ComCom, a division of Haddon Craftsmen, Allentown, Pennsylvania

Printed and bound by Arcata Graphics/Fairfield, Fairfield, Pennsylvania

Designed by Robert C. Olsson